-1-

DEAD END

Leslie J. Hall

ISBN-13: 978-1-63821-805-0
ISBN-10: 1-63-821805-6

Cover design by: Plethora Creative
Library of Congress Control Number: 2018675309
Printed in the United States of America

This book is dedicated my support system,
all the people who championed my dream for many, many years:
my family, my friends, my critique group members,
and my writing colleagues.

FORWARD

This is a work of fiction. Names, characters, places, and incidents are products of the author's imagination or are used fictitiously and are not to be construed as real. Any resemblance to actual events, locales, organizations, or person, living or dead, is entirely coincidental and not intended by the author.

In addition, the author has taken a few liberties around the exact events and weather of the locale in the time period. She's also changed a few things around code enforcement work for the sake of the story.

Wally is a unique and fictional animal. No cats were harmed in the making of this book.

CHAPTER 1

Friday, September 15, 2017

Bright red blood oozed from a wound in his head while more blood spurted from the gaping hole on his left calf.

"Sir! Sir!" John Tsai said in a tight, tense voice, as he bent his long legs into a crouch. "Are you okay?"

No response.

"He's unconscious. Check to see if he's breathing," I ordered.

John lowered his head so his face was next to the victim's mouth. "Nothing."

I pressed two fingers against the rubbery skin on the victim's neck. No pulse. I shook my head.

"Let's start CPR," John said, kneeling down on the pavement beside the body.

I turned to the huddle of impatient faces gathered around us. "Make sure someone's called 911 and go find the AED." As I spoke, I pointed toward City Hall where, inside the main door, a defibrillator was attached to a wall.

"And one of you put pressure on that wound." The spurting blood from the calf hit the long sleeve of my white t-shirt and spread into a dark red stain. Shit!

I swiped the back of my gloved hand across my brow, pushing renegade strands of long blond hair out of my face. Next time I went to an emergency, I'd bring a hair band. And a clean shirt.

Our Public Works receptionist, Cheryl Erickson, crouched next to us. Huge pink peace signs dangled from her ears. She slapped a gauze pad over the spurting blood. "Eeeeew!" she squealed. She looked a little green but held firm.

John leaned over the body, readying his arms and hands for chest compressions.

Dreary dark clouds swirled overhead like a washing machine filled with dirt. Great. Any moment it would start to rain. "I am not doing the breaths. No way."

"You've got a mask! Use it." John sounded a little panicked.

"No. I did it last time. Move over. I'm doing the compressions."

John didn't move. "You suck at compressions. I'm a guy. I'm bigger. I'll do it."

I glared back. John often hogged the spotlight, trying to one-up everyone, and I was sick of it.

"Team one, your patient is dying." Jeff, our barrel-chested firefighter first-aid instructor tapped his watch. "Over 30 seconds without breathing."

Frowning at John, I knelt over the resuscitation dummy and slapped a plastic mouth guard over its face.

John pushed down the chest with the heel of his hand. A rhythmic popping noise accompanied his counting, "One and two and three and…"

I jabbed my fingers under the dummy's head and cranked its chin back. When John said, "twenty nine and thirty," I stuck my mouth on the plastic and blew. Nothing. The dummy's chest didn't move.

"Pinch the nose," Jeff, Mr. Patience, suggested.

"Oh, yeah." I pinched the nose while holding the chin. I felt like an idiot. My knees ached from kneeling on concrete. Leaning over in an awkward and painful position and giving the whole class a view of my butt, I blew into the dummy's mouth twice. Its rubber chest rose and John started in again.

"Okay. That's good," Jeff said.

John and I scrambled to our feet. I brushed the debris off the knees of my jeans and shook my sleeve trying to dislodge the fake blood. No luck. I was marked. The rest of the class of city employees stepped back and gathered around Jeff.

"They did pretty well," Jeff said. "What did you notice?"

Grant Russell eagerly raised his hand and spoke, "Kaitlyn killed the guy while she complained about not wanting to do the breathing, then did it wrong."

Thanks for pointing that out, Nimrod. I glared at Grant, an overweight nerd who worked in Public Works doing data entry and other computer stuff but fancied himself a field worker. Usually I made a point of getting along with my co-workers, but today I found it a challenge. My mood was as sour as the expired milk in my fridge.

The Mayor of the City of Cedar Grove had decided all city employees needed to re-certify in first aid. The Mayor based his wise decision on direction from the real power, the City Manager, Mitcham Iles. So down came the mandate--get trained or find a new job.

I had no problem listening to the presentation, looking at gory pictures, and discussing scenarios, but I found the hands-on practice--in the Cedar Grove City Hall parking lot--corny and humiliating.

"Team One did very well. Always make sure the wound is taken care of before you start compressions. It's a lot of work if you're just pushing blood out his leg," Jeff said. "However, if Seattle has the 8.5 earthquake that's been predicted for years, you could have several people with multiple injuries from fallen debris. You'll have to make choices on who to handle first—or at all."

"What would you do if the victim has big boobs?" asked Marcus Trask, another co-worker, as he ogled me like he wanted to open up my shirt and start compressing my chest.

"Push 'em out of the way," Jeff said, not taking the bait.

I reflexively crossed my arms over my D-times-three-sized chest (in reality there is a G in my bra size). Suddenly self-conscious, my face grew hot. I glared back at Marcus. *You wish, creep.*

"Who can remind us what triage means?" Jeff said.

And on it went. Thankfully, we ran out of time before Team One had to run another scenario. No more mouth-to-mouth on dummies today. And I wouldn't have to put my butt or anything else on display, something I avoided. I threw away my gloves and packed up my things. I knew this was important training, and I prayed I'd never have to do it on a live person.

I enjoy my job working for the City of Cedar Grove, a medium sized city north of the metropolis that is Seattle. I spend my days driving around in a city truck talking to citizens. I'm a CEO--Code Enforcement Officer. Being youngish (37 and holding), a woman, and a well-endowed blond isn't what most people picture when they think of code enforcement. Most of the time, I like the work. I put up with the riff raff like Marcus and Grant. (The allure of government benefits, I guess. If I was in HR, I'd be more discerning in who I hired).

Sharon Stone patted my shoulder as we walked past City Hall, a long two-story former strip mall, toward the Public Works building. "Ignore them guys, Kaitlyn," she said. "That's the only way to survive." Sharon is no relation to the actress and no resemblance either. She's a large black woman with a deep voice who sang perfect alto. Rows and rows of beautiful rust-colored braids covered her head.

I picked at the stain on my shirt, uncomfortable being on

display. And that stain would be a bitch to get out no matter what Jeff said. *Grouchy-pants!* I was just uncomfortable with being on display.

"And don't worry about that either. I'm sure fake blood comes out in a cold rinse."

"Thanks, Sharon. Sorry I'm in a crabby mood."

"It wasn't so bad."

Sharon is about the kindest person I know; the one I go to when I feel beat up because she puts a smile on my face on the worst day. She's the one you wanted with you on a job when an angry homeowner decided they didn't like your last posted notice. She was big and tough and didn't take crap from anyone. Probably came from having ten siblings and five kids of her own.

"You weren't the one with your butt up in the air," I said.

"Nobody's wantin' to see my ass," she replied. "I just had to whack that little rubber baby on the back. Shit, in my old neighborhood that was called child abuse."

"It still is if the kid isn't choking."

She chuckled.

* * *

We left the parking lot and headed into City Hall. I needed to pick up my messages and make sure there weren't any code enforcement emergencies before going home. Usually about half of the little pink slips Cheryl left me contained abbreviated swear words. She'd come up with a very creative shorthand for our messages. For example: AH w/ rst-v wts U. Some others in the office (Grant) didn't get it, but I did. An asshole with a rusted vehicle in his yard wasn't happy about his citation and request to move the car.

When I started in Code Enforcement, I thought I would be helping my community, cleaning up the streets. But lately it seemed more like a game. I tag something, not an official ticket but a notice. The homeowner is "it." They ignore. I go back. And back and forth we go. A bureaucratic pain-in-the-ass game. Once in a while, residents are angry and want to take it out on the messenger--me. Other than that I like my job. I work with good people and help keep our city nuisance free.

I never got the notice.

What's wrong with my fence?

I don't see any trash in my yard.

You tryin' to tell me how to run my own home?

When we entered, Cheryl was back at her desk, a rounded counter inside the main lobby of the Public Works division of Cedar Grove City Hall. Marcus, the creep, was just exiting into the office area. Cheryl perked up and waved a form as Sharon and I entered. "I got a live one for you, Sharon."

Sharon looked at her watch. It was almost four o'clock. "Why didn't you give it to Marcus?"

"He said he's got a doctor appointment."

"Sure he does. Can I put it off until tomorrow, honey? I've got two kids home sick with the flu, one with a school project due, and two I need to track down and drag out of whatever trouble they's in."

"Guy sounded pretty pissed off and wanted action now," Cheryl said. "You're up in the rotation, Shar."

I glanced at Sharon. I saw the struggle between work and home in her face.

"I'm supposed to swing by the Tolefson's on my way home," I said.

"Fudge. I gots to get home to the kids." Sharon sighed. "And if the complainant's that riled, it may not be a short call."

Cheryl, a 25-year-old brunette, looked like a quiet, shy wall flower. Looks can be deceiving. Her phone started to ring. She waved the piece of paper across the counter. "Sharon, take the frickin' complaint and go! I got shit to do here."

Crap. I felt exhausted and had planned to have dinner with my brother, Kale. "I'll take it," I said.

Sharon paused as if I might change my mind.

8

Usually my evening plans were limited and included take-out Italian and a movie with my feet up on the couch. I had wanted to meet my brother, but we could catch up another time. Sharon's face brightened. "Really? You sure?"

I nodded. "I can change my dinner plans." I reached over Sharon to grab the slip. "Yes, I'll take it. Sounds simple enough, shouldn't take long."

She looked visibly relieved so I knew I'd made the right decision.

"Don't look so shocked."

Cheryl hummed, "We get by with a little help from our friends."

"Cheryl, log me out to that address," I said. "I'll take the truck, then go straight home. Tomorrow I'll stop back by the Tolefson's on the way in and look at their dying Alder tree."

The Tolefsons were personal friends of our Mayor and were quick to call him if we didn't respond to their complaints immediately. The huge Alder tree in question really was on their property and, therefore, their responsibility to remove. But they continued to argue it was on City property and we should pay for the removal.

I took the paper. Cheryl grabbed the phone, looking like she was about to scream at someone. Instead, she smashed the receiver against her ear and in an ultra-calm, sweet voice purred, "Cedar Grove Public Works, how may I help you?" She paused and stuck her tongue out at me. "Absolutely, sir. Hold just a moment; I'll transfer you." She mouthed "go."

"I'm going," I mouthed back. "See ya round, Sharon."

"Thanks again, Kaitlyn. Ciao."

I headed for my portable office--a white Ford pick-up--and my stash of Gummi Bears and Diet Sprite. As good as that sounded, I was ready to go home. After the day I'd had, I could use an attitude adjustment and some creamy mac and cheese, extra cheese. And maybe bacon.

Situated on the west side of town, the address on the complaint form I'd wrestled from Sharon was about a mile from city hall. The neighborhood sat a few blocks from the main drag, close enough to be re-zoned when the city grew. Just a few blocks away, I saw a small law office, a quilt shop, and an insurance agent in what looked like converted homes. True suburbia.

Caring homeowners and obvious improvements made the street shine. Newer sidewalks clear of debris and cracks. Houses, some with two stories and fresh paint, all blues, grays, and white, looking like they belonged in another city, different from the rest of Cedar Grove where small, one-story cinder block homes were prevalent, including the one I owned. Here, lawns were green even though we were just finishing summer. That meant irrigation systems, not common in the Northwest. If our city had an upscale area, this was it. These homes were primed for the city's upcoming redevelopment. They'd be walkable to the new downtown or torn down to make way for mixed use buildings. Either way, the owners would get a pretty penny for them.

The homes were large, I'd guess about 2,000 square feet and most obviously built by the same builder. Even though they had different paint, different shutters, some with one-car and some with two-car garages, the basic design was the same: three to four bedrooms, two or three baths. Not mansions, but certainly bigger than my 900-square-foot bungalow.

But for all the niceness, the street gave me the creeps. Too clean, too upscale. Something off, something going on under all the freshness, like sticky glue under glitter. *Ugh.* Now I was pawning my sour mood off on a street!

I pulled my work truck in front of the address on the form and killed the engine. The blue sky we'd enjoyed the past few days had been overpowered, as if someone painted it gray. September had arrived and summer was over. Sometimes the Northwest got another month of summer, but today it didn't look promising. Although, at four-thirty, it was still a comfortable 63 degrees with just a nip in the air as the day sank toward its end.

I took a few moments to peruse the complaint before I got out to investigate. A "concerned neighbor," who'd asked to be left anonymous, complained of strange noises and a noxious smell coming from the backyard of house number 23525.

The house in question looked less kept up than its neighbors. Its faded dark gray paint had seen better days. A sizeable Douglas fir filled the corner of the front yard towering over a patch of grass lined by bark-covered flower beds. Scattered weeds poked through the bark. It appeared the backyard of the house pushed up against what could be called a greenbelt, but was really just a gully that ran through this part of town and part of the city's official watershed area.

Not a lot recorded on the complaint form. A smell? That didn't seem like a CE issue unless they were storing garbage or unmanaged compost. Or toxic waste. I mostly enforced rules about how a property looks and how that look reflects on the neighborhood and the city. Abandoned cars, RVs and inoperable vehicles parked on non-approved surfaces, disputes about trees bordering city property or blocking sidewalks, unsightly falling down fences, trash in yards, tall weeds, that kind of thing. Even in our suburban city, the code enforcement team of four stayed very, very busy.

I thought about how to approach the house and potentially the homeowner. Most CE complaints stem from the street-side of a property, but here nothing out of the ordinary was visible from the front of the house. I saw no cars in the cracked driveway so it was a safe bet the owners were not at home, unless they actually put their car in the garage instead of filling it with junk.

I slipped on my official City of Cedar Grove orange vest. It didn't come close to covering my chest. I'd tried the men's XXL size, but it hung almost to my knees and the arm holes were huge. Cheryl teased me that they just didn't make vests in a full-busted size. She'd sent one to a tailor for me, but it wasn't back yet. The ugly vest looked official and that was the point. I grabbed my clipboard and climbed out of my truck.

A slight breeze slid down the street, blowing the first fallen leaves of the season into the storm drain. I assumed the neighborhood housed mostly working adults or older folks still making their way home from Seattle in rush-hour traffic that could last almost two hours.

I walked slowly up the driveway. The house was definitely run down. A crooked gutter dangled precariously away from the roof and one down spout hung loose away from the main gutter. The front windows didn't appear to be double-paned. That's an expensive heating bill. Drapes swathed the large front windows, keeping out prying eyes.

I knocked on the door. No reply. I spotted a doorbell button off to the left, half hidden by an overgrown Rhododendron. I pressed it. A chime rang through the quiet house. No dogs barked. No cats jumped onto the windowsill and pushed aside the drapes to see who was calling. I walked to the north side of the house and tried the gate that presumably led to the backyard. Locked. I sniffed and caught a whiff of an odd odor. Filth? Rancid? Did they just leave their garbage in the backyard? That would be easy pickings for the raccoons that inhabited the gully.

Being the trained observer I was, I sniffed again. And listened. I could hear the dull sound of traffic from the I-5 freeway. In the distance, I heard the echo of a ferry horn bouncing up from the waterfront five miles away.

Suddenly the hair on the back of my neck stood at attention. A weird tingle crept over me and, for some reason, my heart began to pound. I heard another noise. A whine. Then a moan.

Scanning the length of the house, I guessed there might be a gate at the other end. I jogged across the front yard and followed a stone path around the corner of the property toward the back. Another gate stood open. One gate locked, one open. Odd.

I should have returned to my truck, picked up the radio, and called someone. I really wasn't supposed to enter the backyard without permission.

But what if someone was injured? I should help, right? Never mind that I'd just learned you should always call 911 first in an emergency, but I didn't know what I was dealing with yet. Should I investigate? I was on a first-name basis with many of the local cops so I could call non-emergency, but I didn't want to humiliate myself by reporting a cat in a tree. Suddenly a horrid smell fluttered on the breeze and enveloped me.

So I stepped into the backyard. I sure wish I hadn't.

***

Behind the house, a rectangular backyard stretched the length of the long, thin lot. Tall evergreens at the back of the property formed a green wall separating the yard from the gully. An enormous cherry tree leaned into this yard from the next-door-neighbor's property, dropping its deep burgundy leaves on the ground where they mixed with yellow and orange maple leaves. Other than a small walkway, wire cages of all shapes and sizes, many stacked on top of each other, covered the brick patio.

Cages filled with animals.

As I stepped farther in, the stench overwhelmed me. Feces, wet animal hair, and something else. Something worse. All I could do was stand and stare. I think my mouth dropped open in shock, but I had to close it right away because the nauseating odor rushed in. I gagged and put my arm over my mouth. Some of the animals noticed me and jostled in their cages trying to get my attention. Some never moved. Sleeping? Doubtful. My stomach clenched and my chest felt tight.

I took a few tentative steps forward. One small gray dog in a cage to my right let out a feeble bark. The cat in the cage to my left hissed. The animals that weren't sleeping looked at me through milky eyes. They all had thin coats and skin covered in mange. A few more steps and I saw a caged ferret, then a gigantic raccoon that was very much alive. His beady eyes followed me as I moved, his striped tail swishing menacingly. I'm not a pet lover, but this sight made me want to cry.

No, no, no! This wasn't right! It was by far the worst thing I had ever seen, and I'd seen some gross things on this job. How could someone keep animals in this condition? How could this cruelty be happening right in my city? How had no one known? What would possess someone to do this?

What to do? Should I open the cages and let them out? Wait, maybe they needed water or food! I looked around for a hose or dish--something I could do to help.

A movement on the ground caught my attention and the creepy prickly sensation on my neck surged back. Something alive was not in a cage! *Oh, shit. I need to get out of here!* I took a step back and bumped into a cage. I grabbed at the wire frame to keep it from tipping. Inside, a thin gray cat howled. I steadied it then quickly let go and wiped my hands on my jeans.

I darted my gaze around the yard looking for a way to escape when something on the ground by the racoon cage caught my eye. It was a boot. Poking out from behind a cage. I twisted to see around the corner. Yep, a boot. Attached to a human leg. *Damn.*

CHAPTER 2

Fighting the overwhelming urge to run away, I took a step forward, breathing shallowly through my mouth to avoid inhaling the revolting smell. I moved around a five-foot high, double-decker cage that held two small coffee-colored dogs, both lethargic. The one on top tried to raise its head as I passed. The corners of its eyes were filled with yellow goo. It tried to look at me but seemed to decide I wasn't worth the effort.

"I'm so sorry," I said to the little dog. "I can't stay, I can't help. This isn't my job!" I sounded and felt hysterical. The dog turned his head slightly and looked at me with beseeching eyes.

I didn't want to look at the leg, but something pushed me on. I peered around the end of the cage, my heart banging against my ribs. A man was attached to the boot, sprawled on his back; his left arm flung sideways, his right bent under his body. He had a red stain on his shirt and a lot of brownish red on the ground around him. An acrid metallic scent drifted my way, mixed with bad bathroom smells that made me gag. I pulled the flap of my vest over my nose. The training from earlier in the day kicked in. "Sir?" Pause. "Sir, are you okay?"

No response. My heart flipped cartwheels inside my chest. If I had a heart attack, would someone have to come and do CPR on me? My stomach tightened as I squatted beside the body. The man appeared to be Hispanic, with a thin mustache and dark hair that fell over his ears. His skin looked pale and gray, his face frozen in a ghastly grimace, like something from a haunted house. I started to reach out and touch his neck when a white ball streaked past me. I was so startled I fell backward onto my butt. "Shit!"

One of the animals was loose! I scrambled to my feet and looked around. No movement. Nothing. I thought it had been a cat, but I wasn't sure. If the thing was starving, would it try to bite me? Fear skittered up my spine and zapped my heart into action.

"I'm sorry. I've got to get out of here," I said to the guy who was obviously past the need for first aid. I hurried around the cages of dead or dying animals and ran for my truck. I hadn't quite made it when my guts revolted and I up-chucked into a flower bed.

My throat hurt and the aftertaste was horrid, like battery acid with a backwash of curdled milk. I wiped my mouth on my sleeve, the sleeve already covered with a red stain from the fake blood earlier in the day. This shirt was toast.

I finished the walk to my truck on shaky legs. When I pulled the door open, I saw my package of Gummi Bears on the passenger seat and just about lost my cookies again. I yanked the seat forward and grabbed a water bottle from my little cooler. I took a long swig and spit it out. Then I reached for my radio and contacted City dispatch, asking them to send the police—and animal control.

***

Just over five minutes later, I sat sideways in my truck, hunched over, legs dangling out the open door, with my head between my knees. I desperately tried to keep my stomach acid in my stomach. Two Cedar Grove squad cars skidded around the corner and pulled up in front of the house, lights flashing but no sirens. I raised my head slowly and who did I see climb out of the driver's seat of the first car? My own personal stalker.

Okay, that may be a bit harsh. Joshua Caperelli is like a puppy that follows you around and decides he'd like to live with you. You're allergic so you leave him outside and tell him to go home, but he keeps coming back. Joshua'd been coming back since we were in the fifth grade.

He rushed over. "Katie, are you all right?"

"Damn it, Joshua. How many millions of times have I asked you to call me Kaitlyn?" Obviously my bad mood had not improved.

Joshua stepped back, a hurt expression on his pudgy face. "You look awful pale. Do you need water?"

I raised my hand that held the water bottle.

He shrugged, his face creased with concern. "I worry you don't get out enough, I never see you. We could have dinner some time."

I just sighed.

Joshua's military short hair was swiftly receding to the back of his head, leaving a wide triangle of hair on top. This gave him a pointy-headed look like the Kewpie dolls my grandmother used to collect. With brown eyes and hair and a small nose, his face was unremarkable. He had an irritating habit of running his tongue along the inside of his cheek when he was concentrating, as if there was something there. It made him constantly look like he had a lump in the side of his face.

The other policeman, who'd walked up behind Joshua, cleared his throat. "Wasn't there something about a dead body?" Officer Brad McKenzie looked good in his navy-blue uniform. Joshua tended toward softness, cheeks, arms, gut. Brad had the look of a personal trainer who had a personal trainer. His dark skin gleamed and he had one of those patches of hair on his chin that looked like he missed a spot shaving or had spit up a hairball.

Joshua frowned at Brad. "It's not going anywhere, is it?"

"Give it up, Caperelli. Let's go have a look."

"It's not just the body. There are animals," I whispered. "Lots of sad little animals."

"Some kitty cats scare you, Kaitlyn?"

"Very funny." I've known Brad since we both went to Shoreline Community College together. Not as long as Joshua, but quite a while.

The two officers started toward the locked gate on the north side.

"The other side!" I hollered.

They turned and looked at me, then wandered the other direction. They paused by the flower bed. "This puke yours?" Brad called back.

I nodded and returned my head to my knees.

Brad and Joshua returned shortly. They both looked pale and a little green. They jogged straight to their cruisers, I'm sure to call for reinforcements. I stood and stretched. I felt better, stomach-wise, but I couldn't shake the image of all those animals seared on my brain; and a dead man.

Not long after, the area moved from a photo shoot to a full-scale movie production. Police cruisers lined the street, along with a two CG fire trucks, an aid car, and the County's Medical Examiner van. A couple of Animal Control vehicles as well. Another city truck joined the party. Everyone lingered in the street waiting for the detective to arrive. Joshua and Brad strung up yellow tape and secured the scene. Joshua stood to the side of the house near the gate, logging in everyone who entered the backyard.

I leaned against the tailgate of my truck reading through the complaint for the hundredth time when something brushed my leg. I almost screamed but slapped a hand over my mouth before I embarrassed myself. I tried taking shallow breaths to relax but that didn't seem to calm me. One more deep inhale and I looked down. I saw a giant blob of white fur coiled around my foot. "Jesus!" As I jumped away, the ball uncurled. It had a cat-like head but was larger—fatter—than any cat I had ever seen except those funny pictures on Facebook. The thing must have weighed 40 pounds! Its fur spread out all around its tiny feet. In a fight with the big ugly raccoon, this cat would win hands down.

"Meow!"

"What do you want?" I hissed. "Go away. Shoo."

It plopped its huge rear end on the ground and stared at me. Dirty white fur just about obscured its small green eyes and little pink nose.

What was an obviously overfed animal doing among all the starving and dying ones? I realized this creature must have been what scared me in the backyard. "What are you doing here?"

"Talking to yourself, Willis?" My co-worker, Marcus, had slipped up behind me. No orange vest for him. He wore a black City of Cedar Grove jacket. His dark hair swept back perfectly on his square head. He was younger than I was, but not by much.

"No, I'm talking to..." When I looked down, the fat cat was gone.

"So you saw the dead body?" he asked eagerly.

I nodded.

"And..."

"Dead. And smelly."

He waited, as if I would add more detail, then gave up. "Police and county Sheriffs are pretty tapped out since there's an accident on Highway 99 and a domestic disturbance at the QFC. We're supposed to help canvas the neighborhood. See what they know about the residents of that house and confirm who made the complaint." He smiled a Cheshire Cat smile.

Marcus was secretly a cop-wannabe, code enforcement being his second choice. "Have the owners been located?" I asked.

Marcus hitched up his dark pants. "Nah. They're MIA."

I needed something to do, some task to keep my mind busy. "I'll head north," I said. "Why don't you do the other side of the street heading south. Ping me if you find the complainant." Taking charge made me feel better.

"Sure." He shrugged and ogled my chest. "Whatever. Nice vest. You'll probably get everyone to confess."

I gave him a *"you are an evil troll"* look. He sauntered away. I scanned the ground again for the fat cat, but it was gone. Maybe it lived at one of the other homes on the block. Hell, maybe it was feral. But that wouldn't explain its size, unless all the homeowners on the street fed him. Maybe it played the field and had them all hoodwinked into thinking he was a stray.

***

A haze of evening settled over the neighborhood and the breeze had picked up speed as if a fan clicked on and pointed down the street. A small piece of white paper, a wayward grocery receipt, fluttered past my feet.

At my car, I stripped off the vest and replaced it with my own City of Cedar Grove jacket. Boring and it wouldn't zip, but it covered more and dusk was falling, along with the temperature. I walked to the large brownish-beige two-level across the street from the crime scene. Its yard was simple, not much adornment, a short fence, neat grass, no extra planters. A white metal mailbox on a post that stood at the top of the driveway had numbers but no name. I knocked. There was a light on somewhere in the house. I knocked again. No answer.

I moved on. Next house had a dark green SUV in the driveway--someone might actually be home. Hopefully, it wasn't a person who worked nights. I'd woken up a guy once who was on the night shift at Boeing. He'd come to the door wearing dirty, baggy Hooters boxers and a beer gut that rivaled any eight-months' pregnant woman. He had not been happy. In fact he had been very, very angry. A lot of yelling and some running ensued.

Sporting the same layout as the other houses on the block, this house had an added extra room above the garage, which looked like a giant zit jutting out of the otherwise aesthetically pleasing rambler. Light blue trim hovered above gray siding. The manicured yard was right out of a landscaper's brochure. I thought it looked too perfect--boring. But my yard was usually a mess so who was I to judge?

I followed the curved sidewalk toward the house. A basket overflowing with a healthy pink fuchsia hung to the left. A brass lion's-head knocker perched in the upper center of the front door. The beast looked at me suspiciously. I knocked with my knuckles.

No response. Knocked again. Nothing.

I lifted my hand to knock one last time but pulled it back when the door swung open.

"Yes?" A woman, tall and slim with a stretched and bony neck, peered out at me. She looked a well-aged 50-something, but the tightness I saw in her face spoke of plastic surgery or Botox. She wore snug-fitting black leggings under a blood-red tunic and black slippers with Asian symbols embroidered in gold. Her out-of-a-bottle dark auburn hair was swept off her face into a low bun.

"Ma'am. I'm Kaitlyn Willis with Cedar Grove Code Enforcement. I..."

"What has Randall done now? Is our fence wrong? Our driveway too short?"

"Nothing like that. Who is Randall?"

"Randall," she said with exasperation, "is my husband."

"I'm sure you've noticed the commotion--"

"What commotion? I've been working. I work from home. I've been very 'involved' in my work." She made a snorting sound. "I'm a consultant."

"As you can see..." I stepped to one side so she had a full view of the melee on her street.

"Oh, shit!" she exclaimed with a squeak. "Where did all that come from?" Before I could answer she continued. "Oh, at the Maddens' of course." She relaxed and put her hands on her hips, her professionally manicured dark crimson nails pointing forward.

"That's the Maddens' house?" I got out my pad and pen.

"The neighbors from hell." She looked at me closely, staring directly at my chest before meeting my eyes. "You said code enforcement, right? A little late, aren't you? We complained and complained. God, my husband the actuary has a spreadsheet! What brought you out--finally?"

"Were you the one who reported a smell today?"

She shrugged and leaned on the door frame. "Not this time. Probably Stanley, but it doesn't matter. We all hate them."

"Stanley?"

She flicked a hand carelessly. "A neighbor."

What an odd one. I couldn't get a fix on her and what she wanted. On the surface, she seemed not to care about anything. Underneath, she simmered with rage.

The Wymans' house smelled of nothing or maybe it smelled of wealth because it was so clean. No dishes in the sink smell, no stale garbage or overused air freshener. Nothing antiseptic or alcohol—nothing. Seemed strange. How could there be no smell?

"Why did you dislike the Maddens?"

"Honey, you got some set of boobs. Real?"

"Ah, yes," I muttered uncomfortably.

She eyed me. "You ever get back pain?"

"Sometimes. Now, about the house..."

"I could hook you up with a good surgeon. Give you a reduction. A new sense of freedom."

"Ah, no thanks." I paused, uncomfortable, and tried to regroup. "Could I ask your name?"

"Mary Wyman."

"Do you think I could come in and chat with you some

more, Mrs. Wyman? About the Maddens?" There must be something she could tell me to shed light on what happened across the street.

She rolled her perfectly made-up eyes and sort of frowned. Must be Botox; the frown was incomplete. Her over-plucked eyebrows didn't make her look younger, just meaner.

She glanced up and down the street, looking for something. She must have decided it wasn't there because she gestured me in. "Come in, I guess. I'm supposed to be working." She rolled her eyes again like it was a big joke. "Telecommuting."

"Don't get much work done?"

"Oh, I get lots of work done. I can finish everything in half the time. But what to do with the rest of the day?" She paused. "You want a drink?"

I shook my head. "I'm working."

"Of course. The loyal city employee." Another eye roll. Maybe that's why she needed Botox.

New-looking modern furniture dotted the room: lots of black and white and leather and square corners. A display of crystal spheres lined the mantel over a fireplace that looked like it had never seen a fire. She slouched onto the arm of a sofa that was long enough for an NBA player. Even with her height, at least three or four inches taller than me, she was dwarfed by the size of it. She didn't offer me a chair. "So you gonna tell me what's going on out there?"

"Not sure it's my place to say. I'm just trying to find out more about the complaint and what you knew about the Maddens."

She shrugged and looked at her over-done nails, holding them out in front of her. "Time for a touch up, don't you think?" She paused. "Anyway, the Maddens are a pain in the ass. They don't keep up their yard. They aren't very friendly; in fact the Missus is downright weird."

"How so?" I said.

"I dunno. Just a little mental. I mean we've all lived here for ages, except the brown house and the one down on the end." Eye roll. "Some foreigners moved in there."

I began to think this woman was "a little weird" herself. "What exactly did the Maddens do to cause you to dislike them?"

"Do? They didn't do anything. Didn't fix up their yard or their gutters. They don't leave their garbage at the curb on Tuesday nights. They don't come to neighborhood parties or participate in the neighborhood garage sale except the time they put ten boxes of outdated yogurt in their driveway. They are just bizarre, coming and going at all hours. I think they really needed to clean out over there."

"Why?" I nodded and did my best to smile congenially and not think about the dead body and the smells.

"Rhonda has a shopping compulsion or something. She's always carrying boxes and bags into the place."

"Rhonda?" I could look up the owners of record back at the office but getting info from Mary was definitely faster.

"Rhonda Madden." Mary stood up looking nervous. "You know, my husband is going to be back any time. I should really work on dinner or something. He flips out if he comes home to nothing."

"Did you ever see the Maddens with any animals?"

She pulled her chin back and eyed me down her long nose. "Animals?"

"You know. A dog. A cat...."

"Nah. Never saw them with any animals."

"Really? What about a big white cat? You ever see one hanging around the neighborhood?"

"Nope." She looked away. Distracted? Bored? Or nervous?

I stood and handed her one of my cards. "If you think of anything else about the Maddens you'd like to share, give me a call."

I glanced out the front window. Dusk had descended on the street. I couldn't believe it had been less than an hour since I'd found the body. It already felt like days—starting to feel unreal,

24

as if I'd made it up or dreamt it, but then the faces of the animals would appear.

I noticed a large white SUV pulling into the driveway. A man climbed out and surveyed the gaggle of vehicles on his street. He reminded me of my high school history teacher: late 50s, receding hair, plump waist. This guy looked tallish, with reddish-brown hair with significant gray at the temples styled straight back, held in place with some kind of shiny gel.

The man strode toward the front door like he owned the place, and I guess he did. He moved with confidence as if inside he still believed he was a viral 25-year-old who was loved by the ladies and worshiped by the men. If that had ever been the case, I'd be surprised. Thinking no one could see him, he held his face in a frown, the lines around his mouth and eyes etched as deep as a crevasse in a mountain, stern. Or pissed off. He moved as if his joints pained him or he had an old injury. A man gone to seed, a shell of his former self, former glory. Must be the husband she's worried about.

"So what'd the Maddens do?" Mary said. "It must have been something big for all the police cars."

"We haven't located either Madden. After we have, you'll find out more. Right now—"

A rattling at the front door caused Mary to shrink back, then the mask of indifference spread over her face again, hiding whatever she'd been fearful of. She leaned back against the overstuffed chair, crossed, and uncrossed her legs, then jumped up. "I'll be right back." And she disappeared into the back of the house, leaving me alone in the living room.

***

The front door banged open and the man strode in. He'd shrugged out of his jacket and tossed it on the back of the sofa before he noticed me. His mottled and very weathered face scowled at me, serious frown lines appeared between his bushy eyebrows. "Mary!" he hollered.

Mary scurried back into the room. "Who's this?" he said in a deep, commanding voice that reminded me of my high school principal.

Mary flicked a hand toward me. "She's with the city. Dealing with the Maddens—finally."

The man frowned some more and stood up straight, strong and muscular but with a middle-aged spare tire around the waist. "What's going on over there? I could barely get down my own damn street."

I went up to this man that I assumed was Mary's husband. He was taller than me and intimidating. I felt more in control if I began with a formal intro. "Kaitlyn Willis." I extended my hand.

He shook it reluctantly, his grip firm. "Randall Wyman." He resisted but then his eyes went right to my chest. Sigh.

"There's been an incident at your neighbor's house."

His eyes popped back up. "Well, no shit. I saw all the vehicles. Street looks like a god damn parking lot."

"Lighten up, Randall," Mary said examining her fingernails again. "At least they're finally doing something."

Randall looked like he wanted to move out of the foyer but wasn't sure where to go. He rocked back and forth on his feet, and then stuffed his hands in his pants pockets. "Our property values will plummet if this is perceived as a bad neighborhood."

Mary turned back to me. "We've been complaining for—ever about those people."

"They aren't that bad," Randall said as he stepped into the room. "My wife tends to exaggerate."

"I do not!" Mary stood up suddenly.

It struck me what an odd pair these two were. She had the look of a woman who was fighting her age tooth and nail. She dressed well and was in decent shape. She seemed fanatical about her appearance. Randall, on the other hand, wore a nice suit, but it looked ill-fitting, like he was gaining weight instead of keeping trim. His face looked his age and he'd taken no action to cover the gray.

Randall turned toward me, ignoring his wife. "What did our neighbors do? Not something that will permanently damage this community, I hope."

I ignored the *do*. "At this point we haven't located the Maddens. You wouldn't know where they are, would you?"

"Try the local casino," Mary snorted.

I sat up a little straighter and made a note

Randall threw his wife a sharp look. "No. I've no idea where they might be." He cleared his throat. "What have they done?"

"As I told your wife, we share details until after the homeowners are notified. The police will... "

"What? They bury dead bodies in their backyard? That'd be a hoot!" Mary laughed a witch's cackle. I wondered why no one ever said a man laughed like a warlock.

Randall didn't laugh, only scowled.

I took it as my cue and left.

Mary Wyman didn't know how close to the truth she was.

CHAPTER 3

I continued up the block and across the street heading back toward the crime scene but found no one else home. People had started to gather on the street—there was too much activity in the neighborhood not to notice. By now, several media vans had joined the party. They sure got here fast. If I wanted to go to Seattle, it usually took me over an hour because of traffic.

As I walked back to my truck, a black Lexus turned the corner, moving cautiously around the parked cars, and pulled into a driveway across the street and one over from the Maddens' house. A man jumped out looking alarmed. I guess I'd be alarmed too if I can home and my neighborhood looked like a war zone.

The man was probably late 50s, a little older than Randall and a lot shorter. He wore a wind-breaker type jacket over a polo shirt and dark slacks. The jacket didn't hide a gut that looked like he'd swallowed a basketball. His thinning and receding hair, once black but now mostly gray, swept over his head, thin strips of stringy hair creating a really bad comb-over. What makes a man ever think that looks good?

He hurried to the sidewalk as I approached. "What the hell is going on here?" When he got close to me, his jacket flapped open I noticed a small embroidered green lizard climbed up the chest of his polo shirt.

"Hello. I'm Kaitlyn Willis with the Cedar Grove Code Enforcement. We responded to a complaint and found," I paused. "… some issues with your neighbor's home."

The man's gaze darted around and landed on the house across the street.

I jumped right in. "What can you tell me about your neighbors, the Maddens?"

"For Christ sake, took you guys long enough. Those damn people been ruining this neighborhood for years and no one gave a crap." His face reddened as he spoke. He reached up to run his hand through his hair but stopped himself just shy of messing up the comb-over.

"Did you make this most recent complaint?"

"You bet I did. Not that I expected you lazy government people to do anything," he said. "You didn't on the last three."

"What was the problem?"

"The problem? The problem was that place smells like a garage dump." His face reddened as he spoke. "Some days you wouldn't notice it, but others days… damn. This summer, on some of them hot days, you'd thought they had bodies buried back there."

Interesting. That's the second neighbor who had mentioned bodies. I swallowed hard to push the vision of the dead man from my mind. "So you've complained before?"

"Course I have. Those people were weird. Dave not so much. But the wife. Geez. What a piece of work. Nut job." He seemed to have gotten his fill of looking at the house and the vehicles lining the street. He turned his attention to me and did a doubletake, his eyes popping out of his pale squishy face. "Wow. Nice rack. You want to come in for a drink?"

"Ah, no. thanks. Anyway, about the Maddens…"

"Girl, God give you a set like that, you ought to be dancing. You ever been to Sugars? It's closed now. But I could fix you up with a guy who runs a club up north."

"No." I took a deep breath, holding my anger in check. I was used to comments about my chest, but I <u>hated</u> being called "girl".

I inhaled deeply, trying not to puff up my chest in the process, and tugged my coat tighter around my front. *Exhale. Stay calm.* "What's your name, sir?"

"Stanley. Stanley Pitowski. Here." He dug a business card out of his jacket inside pocket and handed it to me.

It read: Stanley Pitowski. Sales Manager. Northwest Office Automation.

He gestured to the Maddens' house. "So what's going on over there?"

"The police will fill you in when they are done investigating. Do you have any idea where the Maddens are?"

"Who knows? They're gone a lot. At least Dave is."

"Who lives in that other house, the brown one?" I said gesturing to the first house I'd tried.

"That's Ralph. He don't come out much. Rarely see the guy."

Dark settled on the block and the orangish-yellow streetlights winked on in long parallel rows. Someone jogged toward me. It was Marcus. "Willis! Richter wants a report!"

Richard Richter, Public Works Director and our boss. "Thanks for your help, Mr. Pitowski."

"Any time, little lady." He leered. "You call me."

I felt like smacking the guy, but I was on duty and he was a customer. Way to make me feel like crap. *You control your reaction, K. Breathe.*

I walked back toward my truck and Marcus followed. Brad leaned against his police car, writing in a notepad. I headed in his direction. "So what's the word on the dead guy?" I asked Brad, trying to sound calm and in control, but this whole experience was starting to seriously raise my blood pressure.

Brad shrugged. "No ID on the body."

"How long has he been dead?"

"No idea." He kept writing.

"Not the homeowner?" I said. It was a possibility.

"Don't think so. We haven't located them yet." He consulted a note pad. "Dave and Rhonda Madden. You get anything from the neighbors?"

"Everyone hated their guts," Marcus said.

Brad looked at me.

"Consensus, they were...not well liked. If that animal thing has been going on awhile..."

Brad said, "I can't tell you much, you know that. But man, I ain't never seen or smelled anything like that."

I shivered, then turned and looked at the house. From the front, it looked so... normal. I knew the sight of those cages would with stay with me a long time. "What did Animal Control have to say?" I asked. "Will they be able to save many?"

Brad crossed his thick, muscular arms over his chest, trying for tough guy look, but I could tell the sight had upset him too. "Doesn't look good. They had to send for reinforcements from the County trying to get the animals out of the crime scene."

"What a mess," I said.

Suddenly a loud wail—an excruciating howl of pain and fear--split the air causing everyone around to wince. Even Marcus shivered.

"What the hell was that?" Brad said.

Shouts came from the backyard and one of the animal control guys came running around the side of the house.

"Sounds like that raccoon didn't want to go willingly," I said.

"Raccoon?" Marcus asked.

Brad and I ignored him.

The animal control officer gathered some equipment from a truck, including something that looked like a giant tranquilizer gun. Then he hurried back toward the house.

I left Marcus and Brad and jogged toward him. "Hey, did you find a big white cat?"

The guy was young, maybe late 20s. He stared at me like I was nuts. "We found lots of cats. Big, small, black, white." He kept walking.

Had I dreamed up the fat cat? Stress hallucination? "What will happen to them?" I asked, not really wanting to hear the answer.

"By the looks of it, I think most of them are beyond help." The guy rounded the corner of the house and disappeared into the backyard.

I walked back to join Marcus. "Richter's waiting," he said. "We'd better report."

We headed over to a parked city truck running with its lights off. Richard Richter mostly worked as a hands-off kind of boss. A long-time government employee, at 61 he was counting the years and months until retirement. This was the kind of incident he abhorred—overtime and lots of scrutiny. He rolled down the window of the driver's side as we approached.

In the growing dark, it was hard to see his square jaw, thick gray hair and skin tanned from summer golfing. I was surprised to see that one of our councilmen was in the truck with him. Theodore Newman had been on the Cedar Grove City Council for years. Usually quiet, but the rumor was that he wielded a lot of power and tended to sway other council members to his point of view. I had no idea what he was doing here. Maybe he just wanted to know what's going on before anyone else. I wondered what his relationship was with our boss.

Marcus and I quickly gave our reports. Marcus had talked to a few more people than I had, still we had little information to provide. "Get what you need but stay out of the way," Richter said, and took a sip from a steaming Starbucks cup. "I'm taking off." He paused and seemed to be making a decision. "Marcus, you stay here until it is clear we are not needed. Willis, you go home. I don't want any extra overtime today. I'm sure you'll have to put in extra time to wrap up this complaint." He sighed. "And no one talks to the media."

"Thank you, sir," I said knowing I sounded like a suck up. I couldn't help it. I really did want to go home. My stomach had somewhat relaxed and told me it was past dinner time. "What will happen to the animals?" I asked.

Newman jumped in. "Not our concern. Animal Control will do their own accounting."

Richard frowned. "First thing tomorrow, I'll expect a full written report on the complaint so far. The City Manager will want to be briefed."

I hesitated. "Tomorrow is Saturday, sir."

In the dim light, I saw his tanned brow furrow, weighing the overtime and missing his regular Saturday tee time.

Newman opened his mouth, but Richard continued. "First thing Monday will be acceptable."

I sighed. I'd have to work overtime, no getting around it.

As if reading my thoughts he said, "Do your follow-up work tomorrow so the preliminary report is ready for my 3 p.m. Monday meeting."

I nodded and turned away before he changed his mind.

***

As I pulled into my driveway, I sighed with relief. Home is a tiny two-bedroom, one-bath house, almost a cottage if it was nestled by the sea instead of on a residential road in Cedar Grove. It's not much, but it's perfect for me. It has a long driveway with a carport but no garage, so I don't bring the city truck home very often. Today was an exception. No way was I going back to City Hall to get my old blue Toyota RAV4 after what I'd just experienced. I dragged myself out of the truck, grabbing my backpack and cooler before shutting the door. I almost fell as I stepped on a wayward rock. My tired body didn't seem to want to hold me up.

Dark blanketed the city, the sun hidden behind the hills to the west. My neighbors across the street were quiet, for once. They preferred Mariachi music at very high volumes, often parked their truck on the street and left it running with the radio cranked to ten, base thumping. Today the quiet felt a bit unsettling.

Before I headed inside, I turned back to make sure I hadn't left anything in the bed of the truck. If I lost city-owned tools, I'd have to pay to have them replaced.

I leaned over the side of the bed of the truck. A giant white ball of fur launched itself at me. I shrieked and stumbled back as the fat white cat landed on all fours on the ground and dove behind the back tire. "Holy shit!" My empty stomach felt like it had jumped to my throat. "What in the hell are you doing here?" I screeched.

The cat peered out at me, its green eyes glowing in the shadows like an evil zombie in a B-grade horror movie. I took a step away, and the cat hissed.

"You scared the freakin' bejeezus out of me!"

It glared at me, not blinking.

"You can't be here." What was I going to do with this thing? I couldn't let it in the house. I don't have a litter box! It could have fleas! I was not a cat person, not a pet person at all. I had a fish tank once as a kid, but that was it. The fish ate each other.

Should I just leave the thing here? The cat didn't look like it was starving. It could fend for itself. I thought of calling Animal Control but knew they wouldn't/couldn't respond anytime soon since it was after hours and they were dealing with the huge mess I'd just left. What to do?

"Okay, then. I'm going inside," I said. "You are staying outside." I turned and walked to my front door. The cat stayed under the truck. I fumbled with my key in the lock, then wrenched the door open, hurried in, and slammed it behind me; as if the cat would make a mad break for the door. *Yeah, right.*

I peered out the front window between the slats in the

blinds. The feeble beam from my porch light didn't reach the driveway. I needed a motion sensor light on the carport.

I watched. Nothing. *Stop being stupid, Kaitlyn. It's just a cat for Pete's sake.*

A cat hadn't killed the man in the yard. I didn't know much about serious crime--except for what I got from all the *CSI* and *Law & Order* reruns, but I knew enough cops to know those shows weren't reality.

The body in the yard was very real. The man had been shot, I felt pretty sure of that. Or maybe stabbed and the killer pulled the knife back out? Bloody shirt... Or maybe.... There had been a lot of blood. Stabbed. Probably stabbed. Someone would have heard a gunshot, right?

I stripped out of my work clothes and into my at-home bra and flannel pajamas printed with penguins. I slipped on fuzzy purple slippers. I wasn't cold but the outfit wrapped me in a comforting feeling. The work shirt, with the fake blood and who knew what else on it, I left to soak in cold water and baking soda in the bathroom sink. In the kitchen, I put on the tea kettle. When it whistled, I poured hot chocolate into a mug and topped it off with a handful of mini marshmallows, then added a few more for good measure. My stomach felt raw and empty, but the meager fixings in my refrigerator didn't offer any satisfying options.

I stood with the refrigerator door open, contemplating having a large bowl of double fudge ice cream for dinner. My cell phone rang and I jumped, my heart suddenly pounding.

Irrational. *You're not in danger, silly. It's just the phone.* I checked the caller ID before answering.

"Rosie," I said with relief, seeing my best friend's name.

"Kaitlyn, are you okay? I heard on the news there was some kind of disturbance. They said a female Code Enforcement officer found a bunch of animals in cages. Was it you?"

"Unfortunately, yes."

"And a... body?"

"Yes."

Rosie sucked in a breath. "A dead body?"

"Yes. Very dead."

"Damn."

I went to the couch with my steaming mug, sat down and told Rosie the whole story.

Rosie McCallum is my best friend. She's put up with me since we were in high school, she the girls' basketball star, and I a failed clarinetist, hanger-on with basketball team. I'm 37 so that was a long time ago.

Rosie has always been a great friend; sometimes low energy but always a good listener--when she's not involved in a crisis herself. Lately, she's been hung up on a former boyfriend, Mac, who dumped her for a Sea Gal (that's a Seattle Seahawk's cheerleader). Her adventures of trying to get him back consumed our conversations lately, but tonight, she listened without comment.

"That's horrible," she said when I finished reciting my story.

"It was horrible," I replied, embarrassed to hear my voice quiver.

Rosie works in the filing room at a humongous engineering firm in downtown Seattle. Her job sounds more boring than watching grass grow. She never leaves her building during the day, spending eight hours moving in and out of racks and drawers of files and online databases. She's smart. Every time I encourage her to expand her career horizons, she tells me she likes the peace and quiet. We are opposites, but it works.

Me, I like getting out of the office. My job keeps me outside. I like to move around and get bored easily so I need a job with variety and challenge. I certainly got both today.

"Are you okay? Do you want me to come over?" Rosie lived only a few miles away.

"No. I'm all right. Just a little shaken. And the weird thing is the white cat sorta followed me home. It must have hopped in my truck. What do I do?"

"You could hold it for Animal Control, but I bet they're going to be overwhelmed for a while," she said. "The news said this was the worst animal hoarding incident to happen in Snohomish County in years. And besides, you said he was fat. Doesn't sound like one of the deprived ones."

"He certainly isn't starving. And he was loose. I'm not sure where he came from. I mentioned him to one of the neighbors, and she said she'd never seen a large white cat around the place."

I heard some crackling before she said, "Make some of those lost pet flyers and hang them up. Then if he's missing, you'll find his owner."

"He doesn't seem lost."

"Don't assume," Rosie said. "You hate it when people assume."

"You're right."

Rosie crunched into the phone. I would be offended, but Rosie is always eating something.

"What are you eating?"

"Veggie chips from Trader Joe's."

"Potato chips?"

"No, veggie chips."

"Isn't potato a vegetable?"

"These are good for you."

"Sure."

"They are!" she said, and crunched some more. "Remember that time we were at Lake Ballinger and there were Canadian geese everywhere. All that goose poop!"

"Not helpful, Rosie."

"...and the geese tried to attack us 'cause they wanted our potato chips?"

I sighed. "I don't want to talk about animals at all right now."

"We're still on for dinner tomorrow, right?" she asked.

Rosie and I had a regular dinner date every Saturday night. Because eating is practically a religious experience with Rosie, you don't cancel a meal—not ever. We moved it to Sunday if either of us was dating, for me not very often. A lack of single men in Cedar Grove and I never went anywhere. How would I meet new people?

"Yes," I replied. "Right now my gut is just a little wigged out. I'm sure I'll be okay by tomorrow."

"Okay. Pizza Pizzazz at six."

"I'll be there. Thanks for calling, Rosie. Nice to know someone is worrying about me."

"That's all I ever do, worry about you. You don't get out enough. You need to enjoy life more. Live a little. Not every guy is going to be like Ben."

"I know." I'd heard this argument from Rosie before—a lot. Rosie also bugs me about my love life and what she calls "pinching pennies"--what I call financially cautious. You wouldn't know it on the surface, but the two issues are related.

My ex-husband, Ben, was a sweet guy with a cute smile. He loved me for more than my boobs (although he certainly appreciated them) and I assumed we'd be together into our graying years. Unfortunately, what I didn't know before we married was that Ben had issues with keeping a job. He couldn't settle on a profession and hated being told what to do. He'd get bored and frustrated, sending him off in a new direction. His new "self-employment" always cost money. "Gotta spend a little to make a little," he'd say. Only thing was, he never made any. I was the one with the government job, so guess who ended up paying the bills?

For several years that was our pattern. We'd have loud fights about money. He accused me of not being supportive of his visions. Hell, I'd have supported any vision as long as it didn't mean I had to write a check.

I sighed.

"Holy Hamburger! Stop it," Rosie said. "I know you're reliving it. Let it go."

I wanted to, I really did. I knew it was over when I caught him using my ATM card (I took his away), draining our bank account (before I paid the rent) for a "once in a lifetime business opportunity." His excuse was that he didn't tell me because I never wanted to take chances. In the end, Ben loved the pursuit of his vision-of-the-month more than me.

After we divorced, collection agencies hounded me trying to recover money to pay the debt he accumulated during our marriage and separation. Government collectors called to collect back taxes on businesses I didn't even know he had owned. But because Washington is a community property state, no one cared that the businesses weren't mine. So sue me if that whole experience has made me a little tight with money.

"Thanks, Rosie. Thanks for checking in. I feel better. I'll see you tomorrow at dinner."

"Okay. Go have a glass of wine."

I chuckled. "Take care."

***

After the call, I drank my hot chocolate and grabbed the last Hunger Games novel, the one that I kept meaning to read even though all the movies were out. I snuggled down in my bed, but I couldn't concentrate on the book, my eyes kept closing.

However, when I turned off the lights and tried to sleep, the scene in that backyard haunted my thoughts. What would happen to those little dogs with the sad eyes? Who would do something like that? And why? Were the people who lived in that house crazy? They had to be.

And why was that guy dead? Had he discovered the animals and had to be stopped before he told? Why kill him? There were no answers.

Then I started worrying that Ben would show up again and try and manipulate his way back into my life. I was just lonely enough and self-conscious enough to be swayed by him. I'd heard nothing from him in a long time so I was safe, right?

Somewhere a dog barked and it gave me the chills. At one

point I got up and checked all the locks on my doors and windows. I started at every creak of the house and slap of the wind in a tree.

It was several hours before I truly fell asleep.

CHAPTER 4

Saturday, September 16, 2017

Climbing out of bed on Saturday morning is always tough. I love to sleep in. Today there was a chill of fall in the air that made leaving the cocoon of my warm bed especially challenging. Early morning, I'd dreamed of a time when I was a kid, maybe five or six, and we'd had a pet dog named Beaner. He had been old and slow, but when Beaner died, I'd cried for days. My parents refused to replace him and I never had or wanted a pet again. In the dream, Beaner was white and fluffy... Odd, he had been a black, short hair.

I gave myself extra time that morning, till eight o'clock, then I got up, took a long shower. I dressed in jeans, a navy CG polo shirt, and sneakers. After a quick breakfast of a bagel and salmon-flavored cream cheese, I filled my red and white cooler with water, Diet Sprite and Gummi Bears and prepared to head out. Glancing through the front window, I saw that a spider had spun a web across my window. Pretty, but the big ugly thing hung in the middle. *Eeww!* My city truck still sat in my driveway where I had left it. Hopefully, my tools were safe as well.

Jacket, cooler, keys. Check. I opened the front door and let out a loud squeal. The massive overweight cat sat, calm as you please, on my front porch, a pile of white fluffiness. It looked up at me with its slitted green eyes. Its furry cheeks pooched out like they were filled with air. Filled with fat more like it.

"Meow."

"What do you want?"

It didn't move. I'd have to walk past it to get out. *Shit!* The thing was as big as a small pony!

Okay, I was exaggerating but he was big.

"You cannot come with me."

What to do now? I had to go to work. Leave the feline thing here in my yard? We were a good two miles from the street where I'd picked up this shadow. Holding my little cooler low by my knees, thinking I could use it as a shield if the cat took a swing at me, I side-stepped around the animal, jogged to my truck, opened the door, and climbed in. My heart pounded irrationally in my chest.

The cat yawned, stretched, sauntered over to the truck, and dropped its butt on the cracked pavement next to the driver's side. I clicked the key and rolled down the window. "If you want to come along, you have to get in the back. You've done it before."

The cat didn't budge.

"Okay, then." I started the engine and gave it a moment to warm and defog the windshield. The damn cat still didn't budge.

After another pause, I put the truck in gear. "I'm leaving now. Don't go running under the tires, okay?"

Freakin' really? I was talking to an overweight, head-full-of-cotton cat! As I hit the button to roll up the window, the whizzing sound seemed to spur the cat to action. It leapt into the bumper of the truck, jumped over, and disappeared. Crazy animal. I'd have to call Animal Control later. Maybe drop it off....

I pulled out of my driveway and drove, very carefully, to work. I parked at the Public Works building and got out. The cat was hunched down in the truck bed, pushed up against the wheel well. "Are you planning to stay in there until I come back?"

It didn't move. Nothing I could do. Maybe the thing wanted to come in and make a complaint. Whatever.

***

The lobby of the Public Works area was spacious for a city building. Cheryl's desk filled the space directly ahead of the door. Navy-vinyl waiting chairs lined the wall to the right under a bulletin board extolling the city's wonderful projects, lists of public meeting dates and times, as well as requests for citizens to join city boards and committees.

Cheryl wasn't behind the desk, it being Saturday. Another receptionist was on the phone. Most of the city departments were closed, but Public Works kept a small crew on the weekend. I didn't know this gal very well so I just waved and moved past the counter to the door that led to the hallway and my office.

I use the word office loosely. I have a cubical with gray walls and about as much space as a phone booth. I checked my voice mail—nothing. I went back to our tiny kitchen and, low and behold, someone had started the coffee. Thank you, coffee gods! I poured the hot liquid into a green mug with the Cedar Grove logo on the side (an intertwined C and G with some little ivy-looking leaves). I added a liberal amount of creamer from the fridge and returned to my desk.

First, I logged onto the computer to clear my email. Most citizens quickly figured out that all city employees have basically the same email address—the first initial of our first name and our last name@cityofcedargrove.gov. So pretty much any citizen can send you email.

I had a few follow-up messages from previous cases but nothing urgent. I opened a form and started the report on the Maddens. Bile rose in my throat as I relived my discovery. I described the smell and sounds, and the cages.

I documented everything I could remember about my first visit and all the notes from my subsequent visits, including my personal observations of the people and their reactions. The smells and sounds that drew me into the backyard. Something in all of this would help. The distraction of the dead body meant I hadn't done most of the tasks I usually do when on a complaint. I'd have to go back and find the homeowners to discuss the mitigation.

By the time I completed my review, I felt less confident in its value to the lead detective. My back hurt from sitting too long and my fingers were numb from typing. Could any of this mess be helpful? What did I really have to offer? I packed up all the sheets of paper and sealed them in a manila folder.

The exercise if nothing else was cathartic. I felt like I'd opened up a little more space in my mind. Should I just waltz over to the police station and give it to whoever was assigned. I started to get up, planning I would drive over, then thought better of it. What if he wasn't there? For a weird reason, I didn't want to just leave it with anyone, perhaps have it read by someone else. I dialed the police non-emergency number. A female voice answered. "Is the detective assigned to the animal hording murder available."

"Let me check." The line went silent then she was back. "I'm sorry, he's out for the afternoon. Would you like his voice mail?"

"No thanks. I'll catch him later."

Then I dialed Joshua's cell. I'd make nice with him and give him the notes and he could make sure they went straight to the detective. Maybe I could also find out what had progressed on the case last night, see what new info they may have uncovered. Joshua was bound to know something. I mean, what's the use of having a cop in love with me if I didn't pump him for information?

***

I walked the two blocks to the CG police station. A few bigleaf maples along the street had begun to turn yellow and orange. The air was cool, but today the sun had pushed away yesterday's hint of a storm. That's weather in the Northwest—blink and it changes. With the fluffy white clouds and clear blue sky it felt like a summer day in August. The kind of day where we say, "Yeah, this is why I live in the Northwest." It makes up for the other 300 days a year when it's gray and rainy.

A one-story building with a large gated parking structure in back housed our police department. Cedar Grove had 20 officers for the city of about 18,000 residents. The building's glass front doors led into a small lobby area. The reception desk behind the bullet-proof glass was empty, but I could hear activity in the back room. I'd been there before so I knew the door into the offices was locked.

A warning bell had chimed when I entered, so I didn't wait long before someone came forward, a woman in her 40s with short frosted hair and a wide mouth with deep red lips. She smiled. "Can I help you?" she called through the glass.

"I'm looking for Joshua Caperelli. Is he on duty?"

She shrugged. "I think so. I'm Sandra, the records clerk, but I'll check for you. You with the city?" she said pointing to the logo on my shirt.

"Yes. Kaitlyn Willis, Code Enforcement."

She disappeared into the back. The soft murmur of voices, the click of fingers on keys, and general activity drifted into the lobby. After a moment, the woman returned. "You can come back."

"Thanks."

She buzzed open the door.

I followed her into a short hallway. At the end of the hall, we turned into an open area with tables and a large white board. Stations with computers and phones lined the wall on one side. Rows of shelves on the left wall had twenty or so small cubbies labeled with names of forms; a cop's job included a lot of paperwork. On the other side of the hall, I saw a door leading to a lunchroom.

Near the back, Joshua stood with a couple of other cops in uniform, their thick black belts strapped on their waists, their shirts buttoned up tight. He turned as we approached.

"Katie! Hi!"

He was so enthusiastic that sometimes I almost felt sorry for the guy. Almost. "Hi, Joshua." I nodded to the other officers. "Hello."

"You the one that found that mess yesterday?" a young cop asked. To me he looked all of about 15, but since I was getting close to forty, a lot of people looked young.

I nodded. "Unfortunately."

They shook their heads. "A real nasty one," the older, paunchy one said. He had white-blond hair and a hint of a Scandinavian accent.

Joshua looked at me expectantly, a goofy smile on his face. He wasn't a bad-looking guy. Just too overzealous for me.

He smiled. "Do you want to go to lunch? I could take a break…"

"Ah, maybe, okay, I guess. I did want to ask you guys what happened last night on the case. I've been working on my statement and my code enforcement report," I added lamely. I was curious. I had to get the image of those animals, of the body, out of my head. Maybe if I knew more. If I found out the reason behind the insanity…

"I heard nothing much was found at the scene," the older cop said. "State Crime Lab guys were out all night. But they probably wouldn't tell us anyway."

Now I saw that he had *L. Jorgenson* stitched on his right

pocket. To give him credit, he did his best to not look anywhere in the vicinity of my chest. "You want coffee?" Jorgenson asked.

"Sure."

We all moved across the hall to the lunchroom. A coffee station was set up on the counter. Along one wall, a series of hooks with clipboards held wanted posters and patrol information. A large, old-style TV with a built-in DVD took up another part of the counter.

I leaned my hip on the table. *Appear casual when digging for info.* There was something about that in the Nancy Drew Detective manual, right? "What about the homeowners? Have they been located?"

The other cop, who was pretty cute if you liked them dark-haired and really young, answered, "Nah. They're MIA." I moved so I could see his name tag. *E. Heineken.*

"Have they released the crime scene?" I asked.

Joshua replied eagerly. "Not yet, not all of it anyway."

Jorgenson handed me a steaming mug. "Thanks." I took a tentative sip. *Yuck.* But I smiled broadly anyway.

"I've never seen animals like that. So many animals." I shivered. I didn't have to fake a face on that one. "Nothing I could do for them."

"I know! What possible reason could someone have for doing that?" Joshua said. "Creepy."

"Ya, I went to a house once that had a basement full of dead animals." Jorgenson had poured himself a cup of coffee. He drank with gusto. "Just bunches of bones and half rotten carcasses lyin' around. I guess you get used to the smell after a while."

Guess you got used to the taste of the coffee. Where was Starbucks when you needed one? "And did they arrest someone in that case?"

He shrugged his big shoulders. "Nah, just sent the old lady who lived there for a mental health eval."

"Joshua, you were first on the scene, you see any reports yet?"

I said. "Anything about the dead guy?"

Joshua did that weird tongue-in-the-cheek thing. If he ever wanted a girlfriend, he'd have to do something about that tick. "Nope. Hispanic guy. Probably hired help. The landscaper or something."

"Why do you say that? I didn't notice he was wearing a uniform."

He looked a little uncomfortable. "Well, I mean, the rest of the block is older white people. I just assumed he wasn't a resident."

"But they haven't found the homeowners, right? Maybe he lived with them."

Joshua reddened. "Well, their name is Madden. Doesn't sound very Hispanic."

I wasn't pushing his buttons on purpose. Or maybe I was. Not because he had made a un-PC comment, but because I hated it when people made assumptions. Like the one that says big-boobed blonds are dumb.

A rattling noise coming from the back of the small building caused Jorgenson to down the rest of his coffee. "Let's go, Heineken. We need to get back out."

The two officers departed just as two others I didn't know entered and went straight for the coffee.

"Where's Brad?" I asked Joshua.

"Ah…" His voice dropped to a whisper. "He's on the night shift for a few weeks." He looked at his watch. "I need to get going too."

"So lunch?" I tried to throw him a bone once in a while.

"Of course, Katie!" he replied.

Such an eager beaver that I let the "Katie" go; didn't want to offend my "source." "Has a detective been assigned?"

"Suspicious death, so yeah."

"Homicide?"

He shrugged.

"Didn't you see the big hole in the guy's chest? He was

probably stabbed or shot, right? But there wasn't any weapon lying beside him so I don't think it was self-inflicted."

"Suspicious." Joshua said. "Evans was assigned." He smiled, not concerned or unaware I was grilling him.

I nodded. I didn't know Detective Evans. A man was dead, very upsetting, but the eyes of those dogs had gotten to me. "What about the animals?"

I swear I thought I saw Joshua's eyes get misty. It had gotten to him too. "Many were DOA. I heard they put down five cats and six dogs. PAWS didn't have room to house all of the others, so some went to the Humane Society in Seattle, and other places. I think the raccoon went to the Wildlife Rescue in Arlington."

"A couple of those little dogs were cute, but their eyes were so sad. Who would do that?" Just because I didn't want a pet didn't mean I didn't care about animals. I set down my still full mug. "So how about the teriyaki place over by Pizza Pizzaz?" Can't go wrong with chicken and rice drenched with sauce.

"Sounds great," he said. "I'll meet you there."

***

After my chat with the cops, I walked back to the office discouraged that I hadn't learned much. The sky sparkled bright postcard-blue and the air smelled crisp, cool, and clean. But the sun didn't hide the cracks in the sidewalk or the run-down look of some of the buildings around the corner from City Hall. I headed straight to my truck to check on the cat. Cautiously, I peered into the bed. Empty. *Well, crap.* Where did the freakin' thing go? And how was he getting in and out of the truck so easily?

Joshua beat me to the restaurant. We ordered, waited for our food to arrive in big Styrofoam containers, then took them to a small table on the sidewalk outside the restaurant. "How have you been?" I asked politely as we started to eat.

"Good. Work is crazy, kinda stressful right now." He started with his "salad," which in the teriyaki world is one section of the container filled with iceberg lettuce and a few strips of carrots.

"How come?"

He looked at me like I was dumb, then stage whispered, "Murder investigation."

"Oh, sure. That makes everyone on edge?"

He nodded. "Most of the time we deal with natural deaths or suicides. Maybe a gunshot wound here and there, gangs fighting. Homicide is different. Gets everyone riled up. The chief gave us a firm talking to. Stay on task, help where you can, that sorta stuff."

Wow. I hadn't thought about it that way. I didn't like a murder in my city, but it hadn't jumped out at me that it would cause extra stress on the police. It made perfect sense. A breeze whooshed past us and I had to grab for my napkin before it was sent flying.

I decided to get off that subject. "How's your mom?" I'd met Joshua's mom when we were ten and she invited me over for cookies and milk.

Joshua brightened. "She's great! Still cooking all the time. I gain ten pounds every time I go home."

I looked down and realized I'd practically inhaled most of my food. "How is she doing, with you being a cop and all? I remember she wasn't very happy about your career choice."

"She doesn't like it." He wiped his mouth, smearing sauce across his cheek.

"You're good at your job. She should be proud of you."

His smile just about ripped open his face.

"You've got some sauce on your cheek."

"Oh, dear!" He wiped it away.

It was easy to fall into the routine he and I have had for years. For all the crap I gave him, he was still a rock, always there when I needed him. We'd known each other so long, he felt like family. "I need a favor." I pulled out the manila envelope from my large purse.

Joshua looked wary.

"I just need you to be sure this gets to Detective Evans," I said offering him the envelope. "It's my statement about the... incident."

"Oh, yes!" He took it eagerly. "So sorry you had to deal with all that."

"I want to be sure it goes straight to Evans and I knew you'd handle it for me."

"Of course, Katie! Ah, Kaitlyn."

I smiled. "Thank you."

As he drove off in his police car, I had to breathe deep and remind myself not to give the guy so much shit. He was okay. Over eager and clingy, but I can deal with that to have someone always watching my back.

***

Back at City Hall, I paused before entering the building, looking around for the fat white cat. Where was it? And why did I care? "Here, kitty, kitty."

"Who ya talking to?" John Tsai asked.

I started, surprised. I hadn't heard him approach. "No one." I turned and walked toward City Hall. "You on today?"

"Yep." John followed along beside me, his worn Doc Martens clomping on the pavement.

John was tall and dark-haired. He wore a beige trench coat that disguised his thin frame. Underneath he wore jeans. His slicked back hair looked wet from a shower. He was getting in late for the weekend shift.

"You hear about last night?" I asked.

"Of course," he said shaking his head.

"Anything interesting from the gossip wire?"

He shrugged. "Not that I heard."

Real helpful this guy. I followed him to the front door. He

53

opened it and held it for me then followed me in. Chivalry isn't dead. I scurried down the hall toward my cube.

The Public Works office was often quiet on the weekend, easy to get a lot of work done. But today I couldn't concentrate. What went on in that backyard? Why would someone hoard animals like that? If you liked animals so much, wouldn't you take care of them? Like the crazy cat lady who lived on our block in North Seattle where I grew up. She had twenty-some cats living in her house. She treated them like they were her children. They were fed and watered and probably better cared for than most kids.

I looked down at my report and saw more questions than answers. I couldn't really wrap up the complaint unless I knew the problems had been resolved. And just removing the animals from the cages wasn't solving the problem. The smell might take more mitigation.

I needed to go back to the scene and talk to a few more neighbors. Then I'd try and reach Detective Evans. If he found the Maddens and was finished interrogating them, I needed to chat with them about how they would clean up their yard-- assuming they hadn't been arrested for murder. I went to the vending machines in the kitchen down the hall and bought a bag of pretzels.

John wandered by the kitchen. "Working hard?"

"What are you still doing in the office? Quiet weekend?"

"So, so. I'm just leaving. I've got two live ones. Graffiti on the side of the Albertsons Grocery and a house with two cars parked on some overgrown grass," he said. "You wrap up the Tolefson's dying tree?"

"Damn! I was on my way to do that last night when I got waylaid by the other thing."

The Tolefsons had almost certainly phoned the Mayor at home after I didn't show. He probably hadn't called the City Manager on a Saturday but still...

John looked at me with a smile. When he smiled, I could

forget his grandstanding ways.

"You want me to take it?" he asked.

I stared at him. "You would do that?"

"Hey, I hear last night was pretty rough. You hit the lottery on that one, big time. I mean, I know you can handle it, but still." He paused. "I can take the Tolefsons's complaint. Use my natural Asian charm."

"Thank you, John. Really. I owe you."

A grin tugged at his lips. "You can fill in and do the report next time we're called to a Council Meeting."

I nodded. It *was* a fair trade and would allow me to concentrate on the Maddens.

"Give yourself a break, Kaitlyn. You do good work. You don't always have to prove yourself." He smiled and left.

It was time for me to get going too. Nothing else I could do hiding in the office. Out in the parking lot, I got into my truck and started it up. Then, remembered the cat. I twisted in my seat and gazed into the bed. A huge white ball of fur was curled in the far corner. One green eye opened and looked at me. The cat was back.

"We're heading back to your neighborhood," I said aloud as if it could understand me.

***

I drove to the block off 235th and 50th streets. I parked a few houses down from the Maddens' and sat in my truck. Even having been down this street before, my super code enforcement eye was always working. This time I noticed a couple large RVs and automatically checked whether or not they were parked on an approved surface. Today they were okay. Who could afford an RV with the price of gas these days?

The sun was high and my stomach growled, announcing lunchtime. I took a handful of Gummi Bears from my stash and munched. The day was shaping up to be quite nice. Maybe we did have a few more weeks of summer. I rolled the window down part-way and the air that flowed in felt warm.

Chewing on my snack, I looked around the neighborhood. I glanced at the Pitowski's house and the Wyman's. Between them, a smaller beige house perched back on the lot with simple, but nice-looking grass in front. I'd needed to follow up with the mystery neighbor. The Maddens' house looked quiet. Still no cars in the driveway.

I waited another minute. My heart actually started to quicken as the vision of *that* backyard flooded through me. The memory of the smell still lingered. An irrational fear of the place welled up inside me. *Don't go there!* my brain screamed! Even though I knew the animals were gone, and the dead body had been taken to the morgue, I felt paralyzed. I was rational enough to know it was irrational.

Better to procrastinate. Another neighborhood canvas was the best way to start. *Darn.* I should have picked up Marcus's interviews from the south part of the block. Then again, he probably hadn't gone back to work last night. I hadn't seen him at the office, so he might still have his notes with him. I scribbled on my legal pad to follow up with him on Monday morning, early.

First stop, the brown house. Stanley Pitowski had said a man named Ralph lived there. I knocked twice, but again no answer. Probably another old guy who didn't wear his hearing aid or couldn't make it to the door. I noted that I needed to get a phone number. If he wasn't mobile, he probably spent his days in front of the television and wouldn't have seen or heard anything anyway.

I looked at my notes from my conversation with Stanley. He had been a jerk, but he was the complainant. I needed to talk to him again and possibly to his wife. *Shoot*, I hadn't asked her name. I stopped at my truck, grabbed another handful of Gummies, and headed for their house enjoying the short walk in the sun.

It was a long rambler like the others, but without the weird addition the Wymans had. This house had white paint with blue trim. The yard was tidy but lacked the symmetry of professional landscaping. Healthy beds of petunias, yet zapped by over-night frost, lined the walkway. I rang the bell and waited. A white aluminum screen door covered the front door. I pulled it open and knocked on the door. I didn't hear anything so I knocked again.

The woman who answered the door was a bit older than Mary Wyman, and she was Mary's polar opposite. This woman was plump with graying hair cut short and permed. She had probably never even heard of Botox. She sported navy polyester pants and an over-sized purple sweatshirt with those funny red hats all over it. She had a warm, welcoming smile. "Hello. Can I help you?"

"My name is Kaitlyn Willis. I'm with the Cedar Grove Code Enforcement Unit. I was here last night and talked with Stanley. Are you his wife?"

"Yes, I am. Estelle Pitowski." She extended her hand and I shook it. Her grip was firm and friendly.

"I'm following up on the *problem* from last night. Could I ask you a few questions?"

"Well, I guess so. I'm not sure how I can help. Stanley really deals with all the city stuff."

"Is he home?"

"No. He went off to golf today. At the Shriners Club, I think. He'll be back later if you need to talk to him."

I really didn't want to talk to Stanley again, but knew I should. It was hard to connect Mr. "you should be dancing at Sugars" with this nice woman.

"You can come in, but could I see your identification first? Can't be too careful, you know."

"Of course." I showed her my city badge and she gestured me in.

An L-shaped huge brown sofas took up most of the living

room. An old wooden coffee table decorated with water rings filled the space in front of it. On the opposite wall, a petite wooden table was dwarfed by the humongous television, the only new-looking item in the room.

"Stanley likes his football," she said noticing me glance at the TV.

The house was stifling hot, so when she offered me coffee I politely declined. She perched across from me on the pillowy floral-patterned side chair and smiled. She must have no idea what a sleezeball her husband was. How did he hide it from her?

"Do you know the Maddens?" I asked.

"Of course. I'm close to all my neighbors."

"I heard that Mrs. Madden was a bit odd."

"I think she does have some medical problems. But you can't hold that against her. She just needed a little kindness."

"You befriended her? Did you have any problems with her husband?"

Estelle squirmed a bit but kept smiling. "I know Stanley complained about them. I think they had some issues with housekeeping. But I don't think either of them had a real job so they probably have money troubles. You can't blame someone for that."

"What made you think they didn't work?"

"Well, Rhonda is around most days. Dave, he may work at night, but their cars are often there all day. I'm home during the day. I don't need to work since my Stanley does so well. He sells those copying machines, you know."

"I do." I smiled to keep her relaxed. "Neither of the Maddens can be located right now. Do you know where they might have gone?"

"I don't. Rhonda would go off sometimes…"

I needed to approach the real subject. I didn't think she'd know much, but I wanted to ask. "What did you know about…," I hesitated. "Their backyard situation?"

"Oh, dear! Stanley talked to some of the animal control men

last night. And then on the news they said that there were mistreated animals in that yard!"

I nodded.

"I would have never guessed. The Dave and Rhonda weren't mean to anyone. And I didn't see any animals over there, not a one. Sometimes Rhonda would unload boxes and bags from her car. I assumed she was a compulsive shopper. I heard about those on *Ellen*. Can't help themselves."

"Did you ever see a big white cat hanging around the neighborhood?"

"A cat? No. Mrs. Carmacelli over in the next block has a black cat that gets out sometimes but not a white one."

I had my legal pad out but had made very few notes.

Estelle popped up, her face flushed. "Are you sure I can't get you something? Tea? A cookie?"

My hostess was so eager that I relented. "A cookie would be great." We weren't supposed to take anything from residents but a cookie couldn't hurt, right?

She tottered off to the kitchen. I heard cupboard doors opening and closing. On the far wall hung an 8 X 10 photograph of a smiling Mr. and Mrs. Pitowski. Judging by the quantity of hair on Stanley's head, it had been taken several years before. There were also high school posed graduation-type photos of two different boys. They looked very much like their father. I hoped they hadn't inherited his personality.

"Have you lived here long?" I called out.

"Almost 30 years!" she called back, and then returned with a plate of what I assumed were homemade peanut butter and snicker-doodle cookies.

Yum! I carefully selected one of each. I took a bite of the peanut butter. Soft, buttery, wow.

"Oh, goodness!" Mrs. Pitowski cried out and jumped up from the couch.

I just about choked on my cookie. "What is it?"

She held out a wrinkled finger and pointed toward the

window like someone in a horror movie.

I followed her gaze and saw an older black Jeep parked in the driveway of the house across the street.

"Rhonda's home!" she said.

***

Well, how-dy. "I better go talk to her."

Estelle nervously pulled at the front of her sweatshirt. "What will she do when she finds the police have been in her house? Poor woman."

I was on my feet, my cookies still clutched in my hand. "I better go."

"Here." She was suddenly by my side pressing a zip-lock bag of cookies into my hand.

I got a whiff of her light, flowery perfume. It reminded me of my grandmother.

"I know you probably work too hard. And you might need these after you talk to Rhonda."

"Thank you." I tucked the bag into my vest and jogged across the street just as a woman I assumed was Rhonda Madden, climbed out of the Jeep in the Maddens' driveway.

Even in a coat, Rhonda looked thin, her face lined, pale, and very gaunt. She was tall for a woman, with a frizzy black/gray mess of hair that hung in clumps off her scalp as if she hadn't combed it since George W was President. I could see twigs and pieces of leaves stuck to the strands. She wore a long gray trench-coat that had seen better days.

"Mrs. Madden?"

Even though I'd tried to make some noise as I approached, she jumped at the sound of my voice. "Whaaat? Who are you?" she said.

"I'm Kaitlyn Willis. I'm with the city's code—"

She glanced around nervously at her Jeep then back to me, tugging on her faded pink t-shirt. "I can't talk. I need to go in my house. I need to go to… I need to…" She wrung her thin, dirty hands and looked at her car.

"Can I just ask you a few questions?" I said. "There was an incident here last night."

"Incident? What?" Her voice was high and light. Her eyes darted back and forth like a trapped animal. "Where is Dave? Do you know where Dave is?"

"No, ma'am. Where have you been?" I said softly hoping to calm her. People have been looking for you."

"Looking for me!" Her voice rose to a shriek. "I need to go… in back." She wrung her hands, her gaze still ricocheting around us.

"Mrs. Madden. You can't. See." I pointed. "There's crime scene tape on your fence." I had an urge to pat her arm and tell her it would be alright. "There was a police incident here last night. They were looking for you. Where have you been?"

"Wwwhat do you mmmean?" She began to stutter. "Wwwwhy wwwould the police come here?" She seemed to realize she was squeezing her hands so she shoved them in her jean pockets kneading on something there.

I could see why she had been described as a nut case or more nicely put by Mrs. Pitowski, someone with a medical problem. Her face was read and blotchy. "Mrs. Madden, is there someone you can call to come over? I'll have the police come and talk to you."

"This is my house!" She wrapped her arms around herself as if she was cold. "I need to go into my house. I need my things."

"The police will help you get what you need."

She glanced wildly around, back and forth, her gaze never resting her gaze on one thing for long.

I knew I really shouldn't push her, hell I shouldn't be here at all, but I continued. "Mrs. Madden, do you know a young Latino man? About 30 or so, nice looking."

"What?" She focused back on me, suddenly meeting my eyes. Hers were very white with small dark pupils. "Who are you?"

"I told you, I'm with the city."

"The city doesn't like us. Carlos told me that. They won't like it."

Ah, hah! Carlos. A tight, excited feeling gripped my gut. Now I was getting somewhere. "Tell me about Carlos," I said trying to be calm.

"No! I need to get inside. Please, I have to go inside. Where is Dave? Do you know where Dave is?"

I was in over my head. I needed to get to my truck and call this in.

"Mrs. Madden, I can call and get someone to help you."

"No. No. Maybe I should go." She looked back at her Jeep.

The thought of her behind the wheel terrified me. I needed her to stay.

"I'm going inside. I've got to go into my house." She turned and ran toward her house.

I hurried back to my truck. I jumped into the driver's seat and grabbed the radio from its cradle. The pile of white on the passenger seat moved and I jumped, banging my elbow on the door handle. "Damn!"

The cat was in my truck!

"What in the hell are you doing in here?" I glanced at the half-open window and wondered how it had made the leap.

The cat stretched as if it didn't have a care in the world. It stared at me expectantly.

The radio crackled. I spoke, "Dispatch, this is Unit 12."

"Dispatch to 12."

"This is Unit 12, Code Enforcement. I'm at the location of the incident from last night." I repeated the address. "There's a car in the driveway of the scene—the wife is home."

"Ten-Four. We will call SNOCOM and have them notify the Detective."

"10-4, Unit 12, over." I clicked off.

The cat stared at me and I stared at the cat. "You can't be in here. You can't. This is where I work."

The cat bent its leg in an awkward yoga pose and started licking its hind quarter.

I got out of the truck and went around to the passenger side and opened the door. "Out!" The cat turned and looked at me, but didn't move. "Out!"

I took my pen and poked at the cat's huge back end. "Move!" The cat hissed at me. This was never going to work. I poked again. It hissed but finally jumped out of the truck. "Go home!" I hollered after it as the cat lumbered away, a roll of fat under its belly swinging like a pendulum.

Moments later, a police car came around the corner in a hurry but no lights or siren. It parked length-wise behind Rhonda's Jeep. Jorgenson and Heineken got out.

"Something wrong with your truck, Willis?"

I moved around to the street side. As I walked toward Jorgenson, I glanced back over my shoulder, but I didn't see the cat.

"My truck's fine. Just heard a noise," I said. "You two ride together?"

Jorgenson hooked a thumb toward the young guy. "I'm his TO. He's only been on the job a couple weeks."

Ah, a trainee.

Jorgenson continued, "We're supposed to secure the scene, see if we can make sure the wife doesn't leave before Evans gets here."

"Good plan."

"I'm Jim Jorgensen by the way. We didn't officially meet earlier."

"Kaitlyn Willis."

The young blond cop joined us.

"This here's Elliott Heineken."

Heineken nodded.

"What you doing here again?" Jorgensen said.

"Finishing my report on the initial complaint. I'll need to

talk to the homeowners to talk about cleanup."

Jorgensen cleared his throat and spit off to the side. Yuck. Why do men do that?" "You talk to the wife?" he asked.

"Briefly."

He nodded. Another car came around the corner. We all looked up. The car was a dark sedan, like an Accord or Camry. It pulled into the Pitowski's driveway across the street.

Stanley got out.

He looked our way and headed over. He wore striped brown pants and an untucked orange polo shirt with some logo over the pocket. As he got closer I could see the logo was not a man on a horse playing polo, but a donkey with big teeth and the words "*Don the Dentist*" underneath.

Stanley smiled his big fake smile. "What's going on here, officers?"

Jorgenson and his partner looked at each other. Jorgensen took charge. "You are?"

"I'm Stanley Pitowski. I made the complaint. Didn't Blondie here tell ya?"

Jorgenson raised his eyebrow.

I shrugged. "He's the neighbor, the complainant."

Stanley shifted uncomfortably. "I see the crazy lady's home. You guys gonna take her away? Lock her in the looney bin?"

"Waitin' on the Detective," Jorgensen said calmly.

Stanley jutted out his chin and put on an air like he was just one of the boys. "Yep, you need the big guns to deal with her. You think she's the killer?"

"Don't know, sir." Jorgensen was looking off down the street, clearly not impressed by Stanley's exuberance.

"We weren't involved in working the scene," Heineken said.

Jorgensen gave Heineken a squinty-eyed look and the young cop shut his mouth.

"Mr. Pitowski, have you ever seen a young Hispanic man around the Maddens'?" I asked.

Stanley perked up. So happy to be helpful. "Sure. We got a

whole team of them Mexicans who do the yard work on the block. They do my yard. Good job, too."

Clearly Stanley hadn't attended any of the government mandated sensitivity training. "Anyone in particular work on the Maddens'?" I asked.

Out of the corner of my eye, I saw Mary Wyman come out of her house and check her mailbox. She lingered on her porch, watching us.

"There's a whole truck full of them that show up. They work on all our houses. At first they didn't work on the Maddens', but we... well, the rest of the neighbors wanted our block to look nice so we persuaded Dave to go along."

"Who's *the rest*," Jorgenson asked without much interest.

"Well, me and Randall mostly. The Smiths and the Turners. And Ralph. You know, the whole happy block."

I smiled trying to keep my tone light. "You and Dave get along after that?"

"Sure." Stanley shifted a little. His eyes shot up and to the right and then back to my chest. "Dave and me are buddies. Sure, we get along."

"No problems with them as neighbors?" I was remembering Mary Wyman's comment about the neighbors from hell.

"We had a few minor disagreements. Wanted them to clean up the house, you know. But Dave was an okay guy. I felt sorry for him being stuck with a crazy wife."

"Why was he stuck with her?" Jorgensen asked.

Just then, Estelle came out onto the Pitowski's front porch. "Stanley!" she called. "What are you doing?"

"Coming, dear," he called in a kind voice, then turned back to us and rolled his eyes. "Gotta go. My Old Lady needs me."

None of us said anything. I waved to Estelle.

Stanley turned toward his house, wearily and just a little nervous. Of us? Or of his wife? Estelle was watching his every move. "Well, then. If you need anything officers. You know where I am. And here." Stanley dug in his pocket and produced a pile of business cards. He handed each cop a card. "If the department ever needs a copier, you call me. I'll fix you up." He went down his driveway and into the house.

"Anyone else feel like they need to wash their hands?" I said.

"Real nice guy, don't you think... Blondie?" Jorgensen smirked, but there was a twinkle in his eyes.

"You guys want some cookies?" I took out the bag.

"Sure!" Heineken said.

A car rounded the corner and stopped behind the patrol car. A man in a dark suit climbed from the black Dodge Charger with a long antenna and strolled toward us.

Detective Evans was tall, well over six feet I guessed, certainly he towered over my 5'6" frame. He looked older than me, not as old as Jorgensen, probably in his early 40s. I liked his short auburn hair, which was cut short, but stylish like he got it cut in a regular salon, not at a barber like my dad did.

His dark suit, with a bright white shirt and no tie, gave off a sense of power. It was perfectly tailored to fit an obviously well-kept physic that I sure wouldn't mind seeing more of. I'd bet a bag of Gummi Bears he looked fabulous in a uniform. I tried to glance at his hands for a ring, but he held them behind his back. His nose was long and slightly pointed, but it went with his narrow eyes. A small scar pointed up from the corner of his full lips. His eyes were kind and strong, and the tiny lines around their edges said this was a man who had lived awhile and enjoyed it. Not movie star handsome, but overall he was easy to look at, very easy.

"Jorgensen. Heineken." He nodded to the officers and gestured to Heineken. "Can you get me a box?"

Heineken nodded and jogged back to his cruiser.

Evens turned to me. "And you are?"

Evans spoke in an exceptionally deep voice that vibrated in my chest and made me go weak in the knees. I had a sudden feeling of shame. What was I doing here? I needed to make myself valuable. *I am valuable! They need me!* "Hi. Kaitlyn Willis,

code enforcement," I sputtered and reached out my hand.
He shook it with a warm, firm grip. "Ah, Ms. Willis. You
discovered the victim yesterday." His eyes did not leave mine. I
felt my face go warm. "Sam Evans."

"Yes, I'm the lucky one." He had a penetrating stare along
with a deep male voice, and I found myself shifting from one
foot to the other.

"First homicide in Cedar Grove in quite a few years," he said.

"Just my luck," I replied stupidly.

Jorgensen spit again and Detective Evans gave him a look
that said, "Have some manners." Jorgensen actually looked
sheepish.

"And you were here again and discovered that the
homeowner, who we have been unable to locate, had returned?"

"Yes." He paused, so I continued. Sometimes I forget to
engage my brain and my mouth just goes on its own. "I talked
to the neighbor," I said and pointed to the Pitowski's. "What
happened to the animals? I mean I know you're working the
homicide but thought you might know." *Lame.* I didn't want to
be the "girl who worries about animals" in the presence of all this
testosterone. But I was. I had seen the little faces of the dogs.
Even the raccoon had looked me in the eye and burned an
impression on my soul. But why did I care? Animal Control
found animals all the time and sent them to the shelter that
worked to get them new homes. Heaven forbid some weren't
adopted, they probably took care of that pretty regularly too.

Heineken returned carrying a small plastic box.

"And what about the victim?" I almost slipped and said
Carlos but realized that would look bad. Like I'd been snooping
in things I shouldn't have. Which was true, of course.

Heineken returned with a small box of latex gloves.

"Ms. Willis," Detective Evans started in his deep, rumbling
voice that made me want to beg him to say my name over and
over.

"Kaitlyn, please."

He nodded. "Did you speak to the woman who came home?"

"Just briefly. I tried to encourage her not to go into the house. She was sort of incoherent."

"Did you confirm it was Rhonda Madden?"

"I asked and she nodded. She was rambling and nervous. I didn't ask for ID -- she wasn't making a lot of sense."

"Did she indicate where she'd been?"

I thought of all the questions I should have asked Rhonda specifically where she had been. Not that she'd really answered any of my questions. I shook my head. He'd probably have better luck.

Evans smiled. "Thank you for your assistance, Kaitlyn. We'll take things from here."

"Can I come with you to talk to her?"

"No." Strong, firm. No wonder the others respected him.

Evans turned to Jorgensen and Heineken. "Jorgensen, you come in with me. Heineken, you stay outside and make sure no one tries to enter the house or the yard." He pulled a pair of gloves out of the box. He wasn't looking at me when he said it, but I knew I was included in the statement.

"Detective, the animals?" I said.

"Animal Control has taken care of them. They've been transported and those that could be were saved. You saw them, you know the situation was grim for many."

"Yes. I was just wondering... There was one cat that wasn't in a cage. It seems to have followed me. I'm not sure what to do with it."

He smiled. It was a warm, sweet smile, but I saw a hint of humor lingering at the corner of his eyes. "I'd suggest lost pet posters."

"Thanks a lot," I said unable to keep the sarcasm out of my tone.

"Protect and Serve. That's us. A pleasure to meet you, Kaitlyn." He offered his hand and I shook it. His eyes never left mine. He never looked at my chest. Not once. He snapped on the gloves.

I turned away and wondered if he might be looking at my butt as I headed back to my truck. Heck, I hoped so.

CHAPTER 5

After I left what I now thought of as the *Death Street*, I had an urge to drive by the nearest animal shelter and find out what to do with the white cat. It had been in the bed of my truck again when I drove away. Since it was late afternoon on a Saturday, I didn't know if shelters were still open. I'd driven the thing back to its own neighborhood, but the cat had decided to stay with me. Go figure. I'd never really *got* cats. Maybe it was homeless and picked me out as some kind of free meal ticket.

I'd have to stop calling it *The Thing*. At a red light, I looked through the back window at the white ball of fur and said, "Hey, Wally."

The cat stirred and turned its bright green eyes at me. He probably couldn't actually hear me.

"Okay, then. Wally it is."

I drove back to city hall to drop off the paperwork I'd completed so far. Even with the animals gone, the smell was still nasty. Rhonda certainly wasn't in any condition to deal with cleanup. On Monday I'd stop back to check on progress. I'd logged more than enough overtime and was thinking of heading home to relax before dinner with Rosie when I realized I had a dilemma. Wally seemed quite attached to my truck. But now I needed to take my own car home. What should I do with him?

In the city vehicle parking lot, I checked the back of the truck. The cat was curled up against the wheel bump. "Hey, Wally. We have to change vehicles now."

The cat looked at me and cocked its head.

"Yeah, that's right. A different car. And this one doesn't have a bed." I wondered if it would be inhumane to try stick him in the back. I drove a *Rav4*, so I didn't have a trunk. He'd have go inside the car. *Dang.* I couldn't leave him the CG parking lot. He wasn't acting like he had rabies or anything. Was it safe for him in my *Rav*?

"Come on." I waved an arm, gesturing for the cat to jump out. He didn't move.

Okay, fine. I went to the other side of the lot, got my car, and drove it up next to the truck. I left the passenger door open and went over to the truck bed. "Wally, let's go. You can't stay in the truck."

The big blob of white fur started licking its front paw then rubbing it over its ear.

I tried opening the bed of the truck and banging on the side. The cat hissed at me and stood his ground. Then I had a flash of brilliance. I ran back into the office and rummaged around in the employee kitchen. Ah, hah! Someone had left a can of tuna. I opened and drained it, then hurried back out to the truck. Wally had to be starving by now, right?

I put a little blob of tuna on the tail gate. Sure enough, Wally sauntered over, acting all nonchalant. He gobbled it up.

I set the smelly tuna can on the ground by my open car door. Wally jumped down and hunched over the can.

Now I had a little problem. The bait was under his nose. I needed to move it into the car. Putting on my work gloves, I reached for the can. Wally hissed. I jumped back a little. Then I wondered if that was just his way of communicating.

"Yeah, yeah. You're eating. I get it. But you just need to eat in here." I reached over and whisked the can out from under his nose. I set the can on the passenger seat, then came to my senses and moved it to the floor of the passenger side of my car. Wally jumped in after it and I slammed the door. Success!

I got in and started the car. Wally continued to chow down on the tuna. "We're going to drive home. You need to behave while I drive, got it?"

Wally looked at me like he thought I was nuts then went back to licking out the can.

The smell of tuna fish permeated the air in the car until I had to roll down the window. Before I drove off, I took a moment to really study this animal. He had no collar, no distinctive marks—except that fact that he was really, really fat. That alone should make him recognizable on a "Lost Pet" poster. I'd have to try it.

Driving carefully, Wally licking himself the whole way, we arrived home without incident. I left the car door open and went in the house, figuring I could keep an eye on my car while I got changed—and air it out at the same time. I went back out to the driveway after exchanging my work clothes for jeans and a long-sleeved black hoody over a hot pink tank. Wally was nowhere to be seen. I checked inside my car and he wasn't there.

This was starting to be a pattern for him. Get some attention then disappear. Sounded like a few men I knew. I had a dinner date with Rosie so I didn't have time worry about an over-weight ball of fur.

***

Tucked into the corner of a strip mall in what could be called downtown for Cedar Grove, Pizza Pizzazz was a small but busy Italian restaurant. There wasn't much around it, a Thriftway Grocery, a miniature-sized post office, a dry cleaner, and Bartells drug store. Across the street another strip of buildings held a small pub, a boarded-up gift shop, and one of those ubiquitous Northwest teriyaki pick-up places. I think they're really more common than Starbucks. Cedar Grove is an older Seattle suburb that hadn't grown up much. Until now.

The CG City Council was currently pursuing a huge redevelopment plan for our city, a controversial issue among residents, but the Council kept plugging forward. I thought it was a good thing. We lived in a world constantly changing and Cedar Grove needed to keep up with the times. A few multi-story buildings, some condos, maybe a brand name variety store, some sidewalks and trees seemed a small price to pay. Would be nice if everything stayed the same but that's not reality.

A light mist sprinkled the parking lot as I arrived. I left the chill in the air behind and slipped into the warm restaurant.. I shrugged off my jacket and approached the hostess, Michelle, a 40-ish woman with dark blond hair pulled back in a messy bun and a friendly smile.

"Hi-ya, Kaitlyn," she said. "Rosie's already here."

"Thanks." I moved toward our regular booth at the back.

Despite the jazzy name, the restaurant sported decorations like most generic Italian restaurant I'd been in, dark wood tables, red and white checked cloths, and old wine bottles with candles in them. Heavy wooden booths ran along two walls with groups of tables for two, four, or six scattered around in the center of the room. The kitchen was in the back with the wait station hidden behind a folding screen with a picture of Tuscany painted on its panels. Rosie and I came here because it was old and comfortable, and they made fabulous pasta. Who can pass up wonderful comfort food on a cool night?

My friend stood to greet me. Rosie towered over my 5'6" frame. Her hair is that real flaming red hair that's never been near a bottle, the kind that other women try to imitate. She'd pulled her long bob into a tiny ponytail revealing a pale swan-like neck. A light dusting of rust-colored freckles dotted her nose. She gave me an exuberant hug and I could feel her shoulder bones poking through her t-shirt.

Rosie has more than once been accused of being anorexic, but anyone who knows her knows that's a load of crap. She eats more than anyone I've ever known, men included. It's like there is a hole at the end of her big toe and everything she puts in her mouth just flows right back out. We're an odd couple--a six-foot tall redhead with barely-there boobs and a significantly shorter, flaxen-haired, triple D-chested sidekick. I'm not fat, just a little curvy, but next to Rosie, I felt like I'd qualify for some reality TV weight-loss show.

"How are you?" she asked sincerely, as I hung my coat on the hook on the end of the booth and sat down.

"I'm doing okay."

"You sure? You had a crazy experience. Tell me everything."

Since we were regulars diners, we hardly had to look at the menu. Ramon, our waiter, recited the specials and we ordered quickly. At the same time, we reached for the freshly-baked sourdough bread from the basket on the table. Rosie slathered butter on a large slice, devoured it, and took another. I longed for her metabolism. All those carbs and fat, my thighs would swell two inches before I left the table. I took a tiny bit of butter and ate slowly, enjoying it.

While we waited for our food, I filled Rosie in on the last two days. "I can't get the vision of those animals out of my mind. It was just so... real. Not like seeing it on TV at all. I can still smell it, hear the whimpering. And then the dead guy..." I shuddered.

Rosie grimaced. "It sounds horrible. Who would do something like that?

"The lady who lives there, I guess. She's definitely not quite right." I tapped a finger to my temple.

"Do you think she killed the guy too?" Rosie scrunched up her freckled nose.

"I don't know. I mean, she seemed a little odd but not really violent, more confused."

Our wine came, deep burgundy tranquilizer swirled in large goblets. We clicked glasses in an unspoken toast.

"Maybe…" Rosie said, "the dead guy was trying to free the animals and she got mad."

"If he had been whacked over the head, I might buy it. But I think he was stabbed or shot. I don't really know."

"Lots of people have guns."

"I don't have a gun. My parents don't own guns."

"Kale might."

I had to nod to that one. My brother was the stereotypical 34-year-old frat boy who couldn't or wouldn't grow up. Kale never kept a job very long because it interfered with his partying. I often didn't hear from him for weeks at a time. When he did call, it was always a relief to know he was still alive.

"I guess she could have shot him, but what was he doing there? If he was part of the landscape crew, why was he there alone?"

Rosie shrugged. "No idea. But everyone has secrets. Who knows what was going on in that house." Her eyes lit up. "What if he was her lover?"

I hadn't thought of that but having met Rhonda Madden it didn't seem to fit. "The neighbors are a little odd, too."

"Aren't we all." Rosie laughed.

"Maybe if I go by again and talk to them. They might let something slip. Maybe if I…"

"What's this "I" thing? This is a police matter. Your part is done."

I shook my head and sipped more wine. "I need to follow-up on the clean-up, that' my job. And I need to know what happened, why it happened."

Rosie said, "The police will figure it out. Then you can ask the cute detective and he'll tell you who done it."

Had I put too much emphasis on Detective Evans's looks when I relayed my meeting with him to Rosie? I sipped my wine and kept quiet.

"Kaitlyn, what gives? Why are you so interested in this mess?"

"I saw that yard, those animals. I found this guy's body, all pale and creepy, and I don't even know who he is."

"The paper said they're withholding his name pending notification of his family. So it sounds like the police know." She reached over and covered my hand with hers. "They'll sort this out. It's their job. Let it go."

"I can't. I see that yard every time I close my eyes. And then there's Wally to remind me in case I forget."

"Wally? Holy cheese fries! Who is Wally?"

I guess I left out that part. "Wally's a cat."

"A cat?"

"He sort of adopted me."

She looked at me quizzically. "You don't like cats."

"Well, no. And I don't really like him. He hisses a lot." I told Rosie Wally's attachment to me and my vehicle.

"He must belong to someone. You need to do lost pet flyers."

"That's what Detective Evans said."

"In his low and sexy voice?" Rosie teased.

Our food arrived, plates steaming. It smelled amazing, like garlic, tomatoes, and comfort. Ramon also refilled our basket of just-from-the-oven bread. I had linguine with white clam sauce and Rosie lasagna with meat sauce. We were quiet for several minutes while we dug in.

Rosie got an orgasmic look on her face. "Heavenly," she said.

No matter how often I eat here, it's always perfect. I took a bite of mine and pushed half to the side to save for tomorrow's lunch. "So, maybe I'll go back to the neighborhood tomorrow. Talk to the neighbors again. See if I can learn any more about the Maddens."

Rosie put down her fork. Not a good sign. "Kaitlyn, are you listening to yourself? You need to let this go."

"No, I..."

She started at me. "It's not your problem. Leave it to the police, to Detective Evans."

I shook my head and opened my mouth to argue, but she interrupted.

"Can we talk about me now?" her voice caught.

Now I put down my fork. "Rosie, is something wrong?"

"It's Mac."

The ex-boyfriend again. "You said you were over him? I thought you were moving on. That's what you said," I tried to sound supportive, not exasperated. I stabbed a bite of pasta again and wound it around my fork.

"I know," she whined and her eyes filled with tears. "But he's going to marry her. He's going to marry the cheerleader."

I just about choked on a clam. "What?"

"They're not supposed to marry cheerleaders," Rosie cried. "The cheerleader was just supposed to be a mistake that would make him come back to me."

"Oh, Rosie. I'm sorry." I wanted to say he wasn't right for her. That he was jerk and he wasn't worth it. He didn't deserve Rosie. But advice from me, a divorced woman who hadn't had a real date in two years, might not go over very well. I held my tongue.

She swiped her forearm across her eyes. "I just thought, you know, that you and I would both be happily married by now? I thought... I don't know. It's dumb."

I knew what she meant, but I'd been married and it hadn't turned out so great so I guess the romantic mystique was gone for me. "We're doing okay, aren't we?"

"Don't you get lonely?" she said scooping up traces of lasagna with a bread crust. "Don't you wonder what it will be like to be old and alone?"

I thought of Stanley Pitowski's living room, years of worn furniture and pictures of the kids on the wall. And Stanley making obnoxious comments to me. Is that what long-time marriage was? My parents were happily married. Or as happy as you can get. They finished each other's sentences and carried on the same arguments year after year. But they loved each other, I knew they did. And even liked each other too.

"You won't be alone. Don't worry," I said. "And you'll always have me. If nothing else I'll be there to get you out of bed, help you to the bathroom, pull out your chin hair. And of course we'll hire us the best puree chef in town!"

Rosie said, "I don't want to be a spinster. I don't know exactly what it is but I don't want to be it." Rosie smiled and wiped her mouth on a red cotton napkin.

Ramon left the check then with a big smile showing his very white teeth asked, "More wine, ladies?"

"Absolutely," I said.

***

We finished dinner and Ramon swept away our dirty plates. "Lemon cheesecake today, Rosie," he said.

"Bring it on," she replied with a grin. Like she would ever say no to dessert.

While we waited for cheesecake, I felt a burst of cold air as the front door opened and a couple of diners entered. I couldn't see the door but heard the murmur of their voices. The chatter grew louder as the newcomers were escorted into the booth behind us.

Ramon appeared with a plate and I forgot about the other diners while I watched Rosie demolish her dessert. I only asked for one small taste. Okay, three large bites. So sue me.

We were finishing up when the voices in the booth behind us came into focus. A man and a woman. The man had a loud voice and I could hear every word. The woman's replies were soft and muffled.

I put a finger to my lips and gestured to Rosie. "Listen," I whispered.

The man was boisterous. "I don't care what you think. He

was a nasty little bug and deserved to be squashed."

A mumbled reply.

"He thought he was a player. Probably involved in drugs."

Mumble, mumble.

"They're a menace to the neighborhood. If this gets them out of our hair, well, good."

This time I don't even think the woman bothered to respond.

"Why're you defending them? You didn't like them either. I've been saying for years that something funny was going on over there. I've said that, haven't I? You bet I have."

"I think they're talking about the murder," I whispered to Rosie.

"You're eavesdropping," she said in a normal voice, using her finger to wipe the last of the cheesecake crumbs from the plate. "How would you know…?"

"Shhh…"

The man was mouthing off again. "That blond bimbo from the city isn't going to do anything. And the police are focused on their work. No one cares about us. Or him, right?"

The woman spoke louder, but I still couldn't make out her words.

"Do you think he's talking about me? He must be," I whispered. It didn't sound like Stanley. Maybe it was Randall Wyman. Or the mysterious Ralph.

"Things are looking up, don't worry. Everything'll be better now."

Pause and mumbling.

"It's under control. After the City Council meeting Monday night, you'll see."

"Let's go," Rosie said loudly and started to get up.

I rose too, slipped on my jacket, and headed for the door. There wasn't a way I could look at the couple without being obvious. Rosie followed. Right before we exited, I peeked around her to see if I could catch a glimpse of the people in the booth. But my view was blocked by a large man who had just returned from the restroom and was passing the booth on the way to his own table.

"Darn," I said as we left the warm comfort of the restaurant. The nip in the fall air bit my cheeks and making me consider hauling out my box of gloves and hats.

Rosie had slipped into a large, puffy white jacket. She crossed her arms over her chest and hugged herself. "Why are you so caught up in this mess?"

She sounded really concerned so I bit back the automatic reply of "I already told you." I shrugged.

"Kaitlyn, a man is dead. You do realize that, don't you?"

"Oh, come on. Of course I do."

"Well, just remember that okay? Someone got angry enough to kill a man. Right here in Cedar Grove. Don't go getting in the middle of this. I couldn't stand it if something happened to you."

I gave Rosie a big hug. "Thanks, Rosie. Thanks for worrying about me. I won't do anything crazy. I promise."

She still eyed me with concern. "Plans for tomorrow?"

"None. Except try and figure out what cats eat. If Wally won't leave, I need to feed him."

"And make those lost cat posters."

"That too." It was funny though. As much as I wanted to find out what Wally's story was, how he ended up where he did, I didn't really want him to have a home. As irritating as I found the animal, I had started to like having him around. I wasn't ready to let him in my house, but I hoped he would be there when I got home.

***

Sunday I slept in late, all the work on Saturday had worn me out. For me, late is anything after seven AM. About eight, I climbed out of bed, and headed to the shower. I'd slept well most of the night, but sometime in the early morning, probably when the sun had come up, I started having odd dreams. As I showered, I tried to remember them, piece together what had left me feeling like I'd woken up late for an important work meeting only to remember it was Sunday and I had nowhere to go. But I couldn't catch hold of any of the dream fragments.

After drying my hair and slinging it back into a ponytail, I dressed in old sweatpants and a gray zip-up sweatshirt, with my oldest, comfiest bra. Sometimes I wished I could go braless, but it's never going to happen, strap 'em in and out of the way, that's my motto. I usually ended the day with large red welts on my sides from the rub of the bra wires, but it was better than in summertime when heat and sweat left bright red itchy rashes under by breasts. I cannot for the life of me figure out why any woman would want to surgically enlarge theirs.

Chewing on my breakfast bagel, I went to the front porch for the Sunday *Seattle Times*. The sky outside looked like ash, and the grass glistened with dew or overnight showers. Tentatively, I opened the door and looked for Wally. I hadn't seen him around last night. Granted it was dark and he could have curled up just about any place and I would have missed him. This morning, there he was, sitting on the porch right next to the plastic-wrapped newspaper. I eased open the door. "Hi-ya, Wally."

He looked at me expectantly.

I pushed the door a bit farther and slowly reached for the paper. He hissed and backed up. "It's okay," I said in that high silly voice people use for pets and children. "I'm just going to grab my paper. You can't come in, but I'll find you something to eat."

I reached down and snatched the paper.

He watched my actions but didn't move. Then he let out the weirdest noise. Almost like a chirp, an *ack* sound from the back of his throat.

"What does that mean?"

He lifted his hind leg and began licking it.

It was damp out, lightly misting, but he didn't seem to

notice. I had an idea. Back inside, I found the lid to a computer paper box and lined it with old towels I'd saved to use as rags. He was so fat he would barely fit if he lay down, but it was something. Back on the porch, I slipped it under the eaves up next to the house. "That's for you. Keep you warm. Not that all that fat you've got shouldn't do the trick."

Maybe that's why he was fat because he had been living outside. But he still needed food. What had he been eating? He started on the other hind leg, licking it and ignoring me.

"All right then. I'll just leave you to that."

I spent the rest of the morning cleaning house. I can do all my cleaning with just bleach and baking soda. My mother had taught me that there is no need for a hundred different cleaners and all the scented bottles they try and sell you in the store. Even without it my house smelled clean but not too sterile. It was a fine art, cleaning. And I was the master. Granted, my house was only about 900 square feet with one bathroom, so it wasn't too difficult.

After the burst of cleaning energy, I plopped down on the sofa with the newspaper. As much as I'd like to be knowledgeable about current events. I also wanted to support print newspapers. I'd never read them every day, they'd only fill up my recycling bin. I flipped through today's but didn't see anything about the murder. I guess a homicide in Cedar Grove wasn't big enough for the *Times* or it was covered earlier and I'd missed it.

I went back and read through all the grocery ads, carefully making notes on where things were on sale and listing them on a pad of paper. Always in order of where the stores were located. That way I could make a circle and not go too far out of my way. I also clipped coupons for everything I might buy and if any of those matched the sale items, I put them in order.

I often shopped three to four different grocery stores. I was never loyal to one. Whoever had the lowest prices got my business. I'd combine this Sunday list with the new grocery ads that came in the mail on Tuesday and do all my shopping on

Wednesday. It was a system that worked. Rosie often told me I was way too anal, but I really hated paying $2.50 for a jar of peanut butter only to find it on sale for $2.10 the next day.

Finished with that project, I moved to the computer. I searched Google and read a number of note-worthy articles on what cats should eat. One of the first things I learned is that tuna isn't all that good for them, too much mercury. Well, damn. I hadn't started off very well. I'd need to make a trip today to pick some up real cat food.

I knew I should get going on that, but my fingers inched back over the keyboard and I mysteriously found myself searching for articles on animal cruelty. That brought up more than I ever wanted to know about humans mistreating animals. I read articles about dead horses found on a trail up near the mountains—slaughtered horses. I read about animal sanctuaries gone wrong. I read about some place in Idaho where they found a double-wide trailer with several deer living in it, alongside the human owner.

The ASPCA had lots to say on the subject of animal cruelty. Surprisingly, only two states, Illinois and Hawaii, have language specifically addressing animal hoarding. What was described in the articles was certainly what I saw. From all that I read, animal abuse was very prevalent. Yuck.

I didn't find much about the *why*. What would make someone horde animals? Articles mentioned depression and other mental disorders. Rhonda Madden had seemed a bit off, but was that enough? My mind spun with ideas, thoughts, and questions.

More importantly, who was the dead guy? Was it Carlos who Rhonda had mentioned in her rant? Was Detective Evans making any progress? I wanted answers. I needed to know why someone died, why the animals were there, otherwise the experience had no meaning. Maybe the answer was that humans did things for reasons that couldn't always be quantified. But that wasn't enough for me.

I ran searches on Randall and Mary Wyman. Not much on either. Randall held a partner title at an actuarial company. According to LinkedIn, Mary worked as a consultant and had also sold some paintings in the past. I searched Stanley Pitowski too. Not much, just the copier company he worked for and a mention that he was a Shriner. I considered looking them up on social media but decided I didn't have the time.

Honestly, I wouldn't mind seeing Detective Evan, Sam, again. Maybe Joshua could tell me when he was in the office.

A trip to the store first. I almost grabbed my keys and took off but decided a change of clothes and a bit of make-up were in order even if it was Sunday. Sometimes I ran across citizens I'd worked with on my day off. Best to not look like something out of a horror movie. I choose black jeans, a turquoise t-shirt, khaki jacket hanging open, and white sneakers.

After a PB&J sandwich, I headed out. The sky had turned dark and the pavement was now black with moisture. Fall in the northwest--damp, damp, and damper. A light dusting of rain drops sifted from the clouds and landed lightly on my shoulders as I ran to my car with my purse over my head. I have an umbrella, but I'd conveniently left it inside the car.

I jumped in and started it up, cranking the defogger to high. As I waited for the windshield to clear, I looked back toward the house and saw a large white ball of fur sleeping in the make-shift bed I'd created. Well, good. I must be doing something right. I headed off for my first ever trip to Petco.

***

When I exited the store it was after two o'clock. The pewter sky hung low. Rain-filled clouds swirled as if gathering rage. Dry cat food, wet food, and a bowl, cat toys filled the back of my Rav4 and my wallet was substantially lighter. Who knew this pet stuff was so pricey? The clerk had happily explained to me why the cheap food in the grocery store was actually harmful for cats and how the twenty dollar-a-bag stuff gave them 100% of their daily vitamin requirements. At one point, the eager young girl started to talk about clipping nails and examining teeth. I stopped here there. The cat may have adopted me and I would feed it, but no way was I sticking my fingers in its mouth.

I was headed home when my cell phone rang. The caller ID said Cedar Grove police. Was Joshua calling me? I fumbled to remove it from my purse, looking for a place to pull over.

"Hello," I said as I pulled to the side of the road in front of a storage facility.

"May I speak to Kaitlyn Willis please."

Not Joshua. It was the low, earth-shaking tone of Detective Sam Evans. Not quite as powerful on the phone but just as sexy. My heart felt suddenly heavy and my heartbeat increased. "This is Kaitlyn."

"Ms. Willis, Kaitlyn. I wonder if you could make time to meet me at the crime scene on 50th street, to review your statement."

Review? "Ah, what do you mean?"

I thought he hesitated but maybe that was just his way of speaking. He spoke slow and methodically. "I have a few scene-related questions to ask you, to clarify things for me."

"I put everything in the report."

"Yes, it was extremely detailed. However, as first on the scene, you may have noticed things we missed. And since then, you may have remembered details that aren't in your statement."

"I don't know..." Go back to the scene with the cages and the body? I felt repulsed and yet super curious at the same time. And get to see Detective Evans again? That was a no brainer. "Sure. I can do that. When?"

"How about this afternoon?"

"It's Sunday."

"No rest for the weary or the detective when there's been a homicide."

That made me smile. "Okay. Can I ask you something?"

"Sure." The word deep and low reverberated through the phone line.

"How did he die, the man?"

"Cause of death was a multiple stab wounds to the chest."

Crap. "I just wondered…"

"How about three?" he said. "Does that work for you?"

"I'll be there."

He hung up and I sat for several moments trying to still my pounding heart. Fear? Excitement? Lust?

Luckily, I'd cleaned up a bit that morning and nothing from Petco needed refrigerating. I turned the car around and headed back to the *Death Street*. I'd be early but that was fine. I wanted a little time to steady myself before I saw Evans and we got to it—viewing of the scene of the crime. The images from the backyard swirled ominously in my mind like fog in a horror movie.

A soft wet mist dripped from the sky. A bit of rain and people stayed in so the block was quiet. Smoke rose from a few chimneys a sure sign that fall was approaching. I pulled over across the street from the Maddens' and gazed at the neighborhood.

Inside, men had their feet up watching football while woman like Estelle baked cookies and prepared a big Sunday dinner. That's how I imagined family Sundays at other homes. They'd never been like that during my childhood.

The street I grew up on had looked similar, nice, simple middle-class. Sunday was the day mom nagged us into the never-ending cycle of cleaning. I'd be assigned to scrub bathrooms, my brother got a list of work to do in the yard, and dad would have a long *Honey do* list of fix-it projects, like the toilet that always ran and the light in my bedroom that flickered for five minutes when you turned it off.

Dad hid in the garage and rarely did any of the projects. He liked chess over sports and Mom didn't cook on Sunday nights. My brother and I learned to finish our work as fast as possible and escape to various friends and neighbors' houses. I learned a lot about quick cleaning. Now I actually liked putting my physical space in order. It felt good to be in control of something. Maybe that had been her goal all along.

It wasn't like I bought into the *Leave It To Beaver* mentality or thought all nice neighborhoods in Cedar Grove were simple respectable homes without conflicts. My job taught me the magical ideal wasn't true.

The Maddens' house stood quiet and dark. I could see the crime scene tape along the side fence, blocking access to the backyard, fluttering slightly in the breeze. Other than that, there was nothing to see and no one stirred. Rhonda had either been arrested or had left again. I wished I had my clipboard, ticket book, and vest. They made me feel professional and knowledgeable, even when I wasn't.

I waited for Evans and hoped that by visiting the scene I'd have some revelation that would help him solve the case. Close off the awful swirling images that made me feel slightly dizzy and off kilter. And Evans would be grateful, right? If I solved the case? That thought made me smile. A date with a detective...

I pulled out a new bag of Gummi Bears and threw a handful into my mouth. A group of teenagers sauntered by, several with blue or pink hair. Lots of baggy shorts, tank tops, and Birkenstock-clad feet--summer clothes even though the temps were slopping toward fall. They walked to the end of the street and turned east into the next block.

I'd downed half of a five ounce bag of Gummies. I was feeling a bit sick when Evans pulled up. He got out of his car and headed toward me. Damn, he was good looking. More than looks, he just carried himself well—very masculine. I climbed out of my Rav to meet him.

He wore dark navy Dockers, a blue button up shirt, and a black corduroy jacket with a fleece collar. I'd heard once that corduroy meant *the clothes of kings*. He wore it with a royal air, even dressed casually he commanded respect—authority emanated from him.

My simple dark jeans, tee, and khaki jacket were comfortable, but I still felt self-conscious. Thank goodness I had on a decent bra and the jacket covered most of my chest. I liked the guy. I wanted him to pay attention to me, not my chest. Just two people hanging out on a Sunday afternoon. Except we were here to talk animal abuse and murder.

"Hello," he said.

I was once again stunned by his deep baritone. "Hi."

"Ready?"

"Detective Evans, is it still a crime scene?"

"Only the backyard." He didn't smile, but I thought I saw the corner of his mouth twitch as if he was holding back. "Call me Sam."

Was he enjoying this? Dragging me through, making me relive it? I hoped not. Or did he suspect me of being the killer and was playing with me?

I followed Evans—Sam, to the side of the house. *He had a great ass! Focus Kaitlyn!* "Did you speak to Mrs. Madden?"

"Yes, she wasn't coherent. I'll go back."

He moved aside the yellow tape and used a key on a new padlock to open the gate.

I felt sweat bead at my temples. "It's all gone, right?" My voice cracked and I swallowed hard. I really didn't want to do this. Logically, I knew the animals were gone, but my body didn't believe it. What if I lost it in front him?

"The animals are gone. And the body was removed as well, of course." He smiled warmly. "I just want you to tell me what you remember, step by step. Something you saw before the troops arrived could be important. It will really help."

I nodded, not trusting my voice.

He lifted the yellow tape and we slipped under. I paused, took a deep breath, and cleared my throat. "The original complaint stated nasty smells and strange sounds." I said suddenly feeling the need to talk. "It smells better now."

I hesitated at the corner of the house and he urged me on.

"I remember coming to this fence. No one was home when I knocked. I knew I shouldn't go into the backyard—I know I'm not allowed…"

"Don't worry," he said, not sounding at all like I was a suspect.

"So I came around here—the gate on the other side was locked—and I could smell something horrible. I figured it was garbage or compost." I swallowed hard. "That's what we usually find."

My throat was dry. There was still a whiff of something stale and nasty in the air—nothing like Friday, but still it was there.

"Good." Evans stepped toward the corner of the house. "Anything you remember could be helpful."

The moment of truth. We turned the corner and there it was, the same backyard. I closed my eyes. When I opened them, the scene from Friday was gone. I took a deep breath. *Stay calm.*

"Continue," he said. He had a way of making a single word so powerful.

The cages were stacked haphazardly against the side of the house. Several of them were lying on the ground on their sides. Empty. The canopy the police had erected over the body still stood.

"I wasn't thinking much except that I'd probably have to cite the owners for cleanup of garbage. I probably wouldn't have gone in, but I heard noises. Weird noises, like moaning. I thought maybe someone needed help. Then when I rounded the corner and saw…"

No pleading eyes, no whimpers or hisses. Just empty cages.

I felt my face heat up at the memory. I wrapped my arms around my torso. "When I saw it all, I just couldn't believe it. It was unreal."

He came over next to me and spoke in a soft, low voice. "Let's just walk through it slowly." A stray bit of yellow table on the fence wiggled in the breeze.

He took my elbow and we moved through the yard. I carefully told him about the animals, their looks and their sounds, the ferret, the racoon. I told him about the body, how I noticed it, where it had been exactly, how it was positioned. He asked a few clarifying questions, reconfirming what I saw and comparing it to what he'd seen when he first arrived. He spoke softly and mostly listened. He really did want my opinion. He wasn't treating me like a suspect or was that the point?

Then it was over and we were walking back around the side of the house. I'd survived.

"Thank you," he said. He re-locked the gate. "You sure there is nothing else you want to tell me?"

I shook my head. Was he waiting for me to confess to murder?

His face was blank, difficult to read.

"Did I remember anything helpful?"

"You never know. Might not seem like much now but could fall into place later."

As we walked back into the driveway, a truck pulled onto the street. It rolled along and turned into the Maddens' driveway. We paused on the lawn and watched as a man in a rumpled tan coat stumbled out of the car. He didn't even look at us, just ran into the house. Must be Dave Madden. Interesting. And here I was again! At least glad Sam was along for the encounter.

***

Evans and I walked toward the front door of the Maddens' house. The early fall wind whipping around our legs. I contemplated leaving—just running to my car and driving away. Don't get involved, my mind screamed. But my need to know ate at me like a chocoholic devouring a Godiva bar. Would Evans make me leave?

The man came back out of the front door. He still had on his coat and his keys were in his hand. "Who the hell are you?" he said.

Evans pulled a badge from his jacket. "I'm Detective Evans, Cedar Grove Police. "

Dave Madden glared at me.

"Kaitlyn Willis. I'm with the city."

He barely looked at me and turned back to Evans. "What the hell is going on? There's yellow tape in my yard and things are," he paused and looked side to side. "... missing. Where's my wife?"

Dave Madden sported shaggy hair and a scruffy partial beard. The beard hair was considerably grayer than the hair on his head. His dirty blond hair looked like it needed a good shampoo. From the half-moon circles under his eyes and very red nose, I figured might be a drinker.

"You are Mr. Madden?" Evans asked.

"Ya," he said. "What's going on?"

Evans towered over the man. Dave Maddens' faded and dingy coat hung loosely like he'd recently lost weight. I noticed his brown shoes were scuffed. He looked angry, his pale skin got redder and redder as he spoke. I watched his fists open and close and was ready to jump back if he started swinging.

"There was an incident at your home on Friday," Evans continued. "Ms. Willis responded to a complaint and the police had to be called."

"Oh, shit." The color drained from his face and he sagged a little. "It was those damn animals, wasn't it? One of the nosey neighbors just couldn't keep to themselves."

"You knew about the animals?" I said, shocked.

Dave suddenly looked sunken, like he'd bet his last dollar and lost. "Of course I knew about them. I live here. How could I miss them?" He ran a hand through his hair.

"And you didn't do anything? You left them that way?" I was pissed. I wanted to reach out and shake him. He had known!

"What was I supposed to do? My wife has issues... she's depressed and it makes her do weird things. Those animals were all that kept her from going over the edge."

"Some of them died! Some had to be put to sleep. You let her abuse them and you didn't do anything?" This guy was a real piece of work.

"Listen, I don't know who the hell you are or why you care, but I got my own problems. He sighed. "Where's my wife?"

Evans put his hand firmly on my forearm, then spoke to Madden. "Sir, your wife was questioned and then taken to the hospital for evaluation."

"They hospitalized her for keeping animals?" Dave said.

"I think they're questioning her about the dead body I found in your backyard," I blurted.

"Body? Was it the raccoon?" Dave said. "I knew that one was going to be a problem." He shook his head.

I wasn't sure why, but it seemed like he was relieved the mess had been discovered.

Evans gently but firmly pushed me back. This time I got the message. "Sorry," I whispered.

Dave pulled his neck back, dropped his chin, taken aback. He looked at us quizzically. Either he was a very good actor or he really knew nothing about the dead body.

"What're you talking about?" he said.

"Ms. Willis investigated complaints about smells and, unfortunately, found a dead man in your backyard."

"In our yard? No one goes in our yard... Damn, it wasn't one of my neighbors, was it?"

Evans ignored his question. "Where have you been, Mr. Madden?"

Dave stepped back and flipped his keys from one hand to the other. "I've been... occupied."

"We'll need more than that, Evans said. "Why don't we go over to the police station and discuss all this.

"I'm a suspect? You're kidding, right?"

Evans' demeaner continued in his calm, unemotional way. "Mr. Madden, a body was found in your yard. Neither you nor your wife were home."

"Ya, well, I've got a string of alibis," he said.

I wondered what that meant. Women? Bartenders? Had he been on a 3-day bender?

Before Detective Evans could ask him for further clarification of these so-called alibis, we heard a noise behind us. I glanced over my shoulder and I saw Randall Wyman approaching. He wore tan chinos, a striped button-up shirt, and white sneakers, very 'preppy-gets-old' look. The shirt, although not tucked in, accentuated his gut. The wind played havoc with his thinning, graying hair, wiping it this way and that.

I tried to remember what he did for a living. His wife had mentioned it. Accountant? No, actuary!

"Dave, where'ya been?" Randall smiled. "You got people looking for you."

Dave looked at the ground. "I been around. Whada you care?"

Randall put on a prize-winning smile. "Come on, Dave. Your neighbors are worried about you. There's been some hula-balou at your house while you've been gone."

Randall looked at me, his eyes roamed, then actually met my gaze with a smile that said he thought we were pals. Then he smiled at Detective Evans. "Randall Wyman," he said. He extended his hand and they shook.

Evans was stone-faced, no emotion.

Dave got more agitated. "I gotta go. I gotta find Rhonda. This girl said someone complained," Dave said. "Now the police are here. I need to go to Rhonda."

My face got hot at the *girl* comment, but I let it go. "I was investigating the complaints about your yard. Just doing my job."

Evans had acknowledged Randall with a handshake, but now he ignored him. "Mr. Madden, do you know why someone would kill a man in your backyard?"

Dave looked at us with bloodshot eyes. "Someone really died?"

"How would he know? He's been gone." Now Randall was playing Dave's buddy. "By the way, who was it?" Randall said. "I mean the paper said a body was found but not who."

"We can't release that information yet, sir."

"Did you complain again, Randall?" Dave's voice took on a whiney tone. "I thought you said it was all fine."

"Not me," Randall said. "But Dave, you know we're all just trying to keep our neighborhood a clean, nice place to live. With the redevelopment coming…"

Dave rolled his eyes at Randall. Then Dave turned to me. "Why were you were snooping in my yard?"

"It's my job to follow up on complaints. That's what I do. And based on what I found, I think you needed someone to intercede. What was happening was atrocious!" I knew I was getting riled so I tried some yoga breathing.

"What'ya find?" Randall asked.

Dave shifted from one foot to the other and ran his hand through his hair. "What a mess. I got to go to Rhonda. She's sensitive."

Randall moved to put his arm around Dave's shoulder. "Yes, Dave. Take care of her. If she did it…"

Dave shrugged away from Randall and slapped at Randall's arm. "Rhonda didn't kill anyone!"

This guy was giving me really weird vibes. Maybe he killed the man and was just upset they blamed his wife.

"Listen, Mr. Wyman, go home," Evans said. "Mr. Madden, I'll escort you to your wife."

Randall hesitated. "You need something, buddy, you let me know. I can get your wife a good lawyer."

"She didn't do anything!"

Dave eyed his truck. Heaven help us if he chose to drive in his agitated state. I wondered if Evans would try and stop him.

Randall walked back toward his house. "Good luck, Dave," he called over his shoulder.

Dave muttered something I didn't catch and ran back inside his house.

Evans turned to me. "I'll take care of this. You should go. It'll be easier that way."

I nodded. "You're right. I'm just in the way."

"I appreciate your help today. I really do." That voice. I felt the need to swoon, but I wasn't sure that would be professional. So I hurried to my car.

Dave had known about the animals! Of course, he had. He lived there. But he'd done nothing! And what about the dead guy? No one seemed to know who he was or why he was here. Well, Evans knew but he wasn't saying.

I kept coming back to Rhonda mentioning a Carlos, like she was familiar with him. I couldn't ask her about him because she was probably in a psychiatric hospital somewhere, if she was as troubled as it appeared. I looked down the street before I got into my car. Randall had gone inside his house. The street didn't look idyllic at all. I had a strong urge to go home and take a shower.

CHAPTER 6

Monday when my alarm went off, I reluctantly crawled out of bed and checked my phone. I'd left several messages for Ben. No response. Typical. I stuffed my feet into fuzzy purple slippers.

As I headed to the kitchen, I thought about Wally. He'd been right there in his box when I got home. I'd unloaded all of my Petco purchases and left him a small bowl of dry cat food with half-a-can of moist food on the side. He'd jumped up and dug right in. I hadn't gotten around to making "Lost Cat" signs over the weekend. I'd better get on that. He couldn't live in a box on my porch all winter.

After I woke up and had my shower, I padded to the front of the house to look for coffee. I took a detour and pulled back the curtains on my front window to do a check of the weather. Yes, I could use a number of different weather apps, but around the greater Seattle area, weather varies by location—are you in the convergence zone? By the water? In the shadow of the mountains?

Instead of seeing bright blue sky like I'd hoped, I saw several vans parked on my street—news vans. *Shit.* Yanking the curtains shut, I sighed. It appeared the media had found me. My neighbors must be overjoyed.

Since I'd sworn not to speak to them, both to Richard and to Detective Evans, I was in a predicament. How would I escape my driveway with hordes of reporters waiting to stick a microphone in my face? The Monday morning gods had not shined on me today. Is an easy Monday too much to ask for? Then I thought about Wally again. Hopefully, he'd took off to wherever it is that he goes when he disappears.

After making sure all my doors were locked and all the blinds were closed. I slugged down a small cup of coffee (with a large squirt of hazelnut creamer) and dressed for work. Standing at the front door, I tried to figure out how to escape. I could just make a run for my car, but they'd fill my driveway before I could even start the vehicle. I'd have to "no comment" myself and try not to run over anyone. The news might play reels of me with my coat over my head, but no way to cover my face while driving.

Only one thing to do. First, I dialed Cheryl and told her of my predicament, noting I might be a few minutes late, in case anyone was looking for me. I also asked her to send someone, like the three burly guys that worked in engineering, out front and make sure the vans weren't also in the city hall parking lot.

Then I dialed Joshua.

He answered after four rings. "Katie, hello!"

"I need a favor. My driveway is blocked by media vans."

"That sounds terrible. I can't get away just now, but I'll send someone to cruise your street."

"Thank you. I really don't need this today."

"You didn't speak to them, did you?" He sounded worried.

"No, of course not!"

"Good. The chief wouldn't like it."

Neither would my boss.

Ten minutes later, a black Cedar Grove Police Dodge Charger cruised slowly down the street, lights flashing, and stopped across the street.. My neighbors may never invite me to the summer street picnic again. However, it did the trick and the vans began to depart.

I ran for my truck. Wally was nowhere to be seen. Good, since I didn't need him trying to ride with me today. I backed carefully out of the driveway, making extra sure there weren't any lingering pedestrians, then headed to city hall. At least two white vans followed me.

When I reached city hall, the line of orange cones across the parking lot looked like party lights. I pulled up and one of the maintenance guys moved the cones so I could drive in. I parked and ran for the Public Works door.

"Phew," I said as I closed the door behind me.

Cheryl sat tall at her desk, on the phone, headset bumping with her nods while. She waved a handful of message slips at me. Her counter was covered with papers. Cheryl was a piler but a very organized piler. You asked for something, she knew right where it was. Cheryl smiled.

Cheryl ended her call. She hung up and pushed her long hair back to reveal earrings dangling with suns, moons, and stars. "Man, it's only eight AM and already the crazies are calling. They know it's council day." She swiped at her lips with some cherry lip balm. "You made it."

"Thanks to you."

"This isn't going to be a habit, is it?"

"Let's hope not. Vultures," I muttered.

"I have some messages for you."

"Thanks," I said as I flipped through my messages. Mostly common complaints and a couple of follow ups from previous citations. One new one said: XX AH AV MV Y! I interpreted it to say "An extra assertive asshole wants an abandoned vehicle moved yesterday."

Cheryl cocked her head at me. "You waiting for something?"

"I have a task for you."

She eyed me suspiciously. "Like my desk isn't already full."

"Could you research all complaints received about the street of the murder in the last year?"

"I thought this was a police matter now?"

"It is, but I need to complete my work and monitor the cleanup. And Richard is hot on this one."

"The way it's going I may not get to it until end of day or tomorrow."

I hated to wait, but I gritted my teeth. "Fine."

As I made my way to the door to the offices and swung it open, Cheryl hollered back for everyone to hear, "I got that vest altered for you!"

"Great. Thanks," I said my face burning. "I'll pick it up later."

Someone yelled, unseen, from a back cubicle. "Why did it need altering, Willis?"

Very funny.

Monday was always a busy day at work. The Code Enforcement officer who worked the weekend (we took turns) always left us week-day folks lots of follow-up work. Citizens who were off work Saturday and Sunday spent the weekend driving around the city finding things to complain about. The third Monday was also City Council meeting day. More often than not, there was something on the Council agenda that involved my department. Our illustrious boss wasn't fond of the meeting. He usually made an appearance then ducked out early, leaving his staff (us) to report on the proceedings.

However, today I would have gone to the meeting without being assigned to the topic of redevelopment in Cedar Grove was the focus on the council agenda. As a resident, it mattered to me and could affect the value of my home, more access to stores but also more traffic. Plus any talk of development brought out strong reactions on both sides of the issue, so I expected it to be a lively meeting.

To top it off, the Tolefson's were always there, taking their three minutes of comment time to report what a crappy job we were doing. I could only hope that John had handled their tree issue. Maybe they'd be too caught up in the development debate to think about code enforcement.

***

My office appeared as I had left it, my work surface clear thanks to a two-drawer gray lateral file cabinet and two overhead bins with lift-up doors. I have desk trays for files in progress and IN/OUT boxes. Today my IN box seemed pretty clear. A copy of the September internal city newsletter had made its way to the top. Why we still got a hard copy when it also came via email, I wasn't sure. The front page advertised the start of flu season and the availability of flu shots. All around me, phones rang, fingers clicked on keyboards, and employees called to each other over the cubicle walls.

I made some routine follow-up calls and cleared a few complaints from my open log. There was an email from our City Manager, Mitchum Iles, stressing the importance of tonight's council meeting and asking all city employees who were also residents to attend.

I worked hard, pushing my way through my messages, closing out files and starting some new ones. I looked up when a pair of beady eyes appeared over my cubicle wall, attached to a head of brown hair, shiny with too much gel. "We're going to lunch, wanna come?" Marcus asked.

"I brought a sandwich," I replied.

Marcus put a finger to his temple and shut his eyes. "I see… I see, peanut butter and jelly."

I frowned at him.

"You're so predictable. Come on, Kaitlyn. It's Council day. Don't be such a tight wad. John and Grant are coming, so is

Sharon. We're going to Azteca."

My mouth watered at the thought of tacos. I don't go out to eat very often except with Rosie—it's too expensive. I figured my co-workers wanted to grill me about Friday, but I didn't care. "Okay."

"In the parking lot in five." Marcus's head disappeared.

I finished the file I was working on and grabbed my jacket. As I hurried by her desk, Cheryl waved a bag at me. "Take your new vest."

"Okay, okay." I grabbed the bag and headed out the door.

It had clouded over and started drizzling. Marcus and John were huddled under the awning waiting for the rest of the group. Marcus wore a black North Face jacket. His slicked back hair suddenly reminded me of Randall Wyman, except he had a lot more hair than Randall. John, tall and thin, wore his cream-colored trench coat that probably cost more than my annual clothing budget.

Grant, the Public Works paper pusher/data cruncher, shoved through the doors then held it open for Sharon. She had squeezed her bulky frame into a flamboyant purple coat with a faux fur collar. I didn't think it was quite cold enough for it, but I figured it was a new purchase she wanted to show off. She looked sharp.

We ran across the parking lot and got damp in the process. I stopped to stuff the bag with the vest in my truck then scrambled into one of the city vans. Grant, who'd commandeered the keys from Cheryl, drove.

Azteca Mexican Restaurant stood on a busy corner, on the west side of Cedar Grove. The restaurant was decorated with Mexican flags, sombreros, photos of dark-skinned women in colorful tiered skirts, and a lot of pictures of full and frothy margarita glasses. A hostess in dark pants and a peasant-style blouse ushered us to a table for six near the back.

A young busboy appeared with water glasses, chips and salsa. Then a dark-haired waiter approached our table and took our orders. We passed on the margaritas and ordered food. Sharon, John, and I opted for the two chicken-taco special with beans and rice. Marcus and Grant ordered a double plate of extra spicy burritos.

The bustle of the busy restaurant swirled around us, as diners talked and ate, silverware clicked against plates, voices murmured conversations. Our group chatted about non-work topics for a while, the latest movies we'd seen, books read, concerts that were coming to Seattle. Our food arrived and we dove in. But as always, the conversation turned to work.

I said, "John, how did it go with the Tolefson's tree?"

John wiped salsa off his face with his napkin. "I went. I talked. They talked over me."

"And?"

"And nothing. Those two are nuts. They just want what they want."

"They'll get it, too," Sharon added. "So you might as well give it to 'em. Cause Mr. Mayor will cave." Heaven forbid they escalate to the City Manager.

Grant made a spitting noise.

"What are you gettin' on about?" Sharon said, glaring at him.

"You work inside," I said to Grant. "You've never had to go visit them."

He grinned. "Nope, not yet."

"Well, good luck if you do."

Marcus, chomped the last of his burritos, said, "So, Kaitlyn, tell us about Friday."

There it was. I took a swig of water and chewed on some ice, wondering where to begin.

"Spit it out, Willis," Grant said.

Sharon nodded her head, her many braids shaking. "Yeah, girl. You haven't shared any of the gory details." Then she paused, looking sheepish. "I know that one should have been mine. Sorry."

"It's okay, Sharon." I glanced around the group. All eyes were on me. I didn't want to go over it again. "Really, it wasn't any fun," I said. "It was appalling."

"So did you touch the body?"

"Did you see a gun?"

"Who do you think did it?"

I put up my hands. "Whoa! Slow down. I didn't have anything to do with the body. He was on the ground. He looked dead. Kinda white and stinky." I floundered. I didn't want to relive finding a body again—and didn't want to say Evans asked me back and maybe suspected me too.

"Shot? Stabbed?"

"Decomposing?"

"He was just there. But the animals… that part was awful. Really, really horrible."

"But there was also a dead guy," Marcus said.

I frowned. "I don't know who he is or what happened to him. I heard he was stabbed. I felt bad for Carlos, but was overshadowed in my mind by all the animals."

I chastised myself for not paying more attention. Someone was dead! "There was a lot of blood and bad smells. Like he lost control of his bladder… I was kinda worried about not throwing up."

"When I canvassed part of the neighbors, no one knew anything about a young guy hanging around," Marcus said. "No reports of fights,"

"And no reports of animal abuse," I added. "Neighbors didn't know about it."

Sharon jumped in and kept me from feeling like a total idiot. "Were the animals really all caged up?"

"Yes! And so mistreated."

"Probably strays anyway." Grant picked at his teeth with his fingernail.

"Even animals deserve to be treated with respect," Marcus said.

John snorted. "I didn't know you were one of those ASPCA people."

"Hey," Marcus said his face scrunched in annoyance. "I have a dog."

I looked at Marcus. I wouldn't have pegged him as a compassionate animal person. Maybe I was a crappy judge of character.

"It wasn't your dog in the cage, now was it?" Grant said, picking at the other side of his mouth. "Like I said, it was probably a bunch of strays. Tell us more about the dead guy."

The waiter saved me by approaching with our checks. We all whipped out our debit cards. The waiter gathered them and disappeared.

"I wonder what happened to the animals they collected?" Sharon said.

Grant spoke up. "Gassed I'm sure."

"Grant, have some class," John said. "The ones that survive Animal Control will turn over to the Humane Society who'll try and get them adopted."

"That's what I'm saying," Grand said. "They're toast."

Sharon shook her head at Grant. "Maybe you should adopt one, Kaitlyn. That might help you get over all this."

I cringed. "I'm not much of a pet person."

"Then why do you care about the animals?" Marcus asked.

"Because I saw them. There were so many. And they had such sad eyes. Like they'd given up. It was just horrible!" I paused. "Besides, there is a cat that has sort of adopted me. I don't know what to do with it."

Everyone shrugged. Even Marcus didn't comment.

"What would possess someone to cage animals like that?" I said.

"Or kill a guy," Sharon said.

"I can think of lots of reasons to kill a guy," Grant said. "A drug deal gone bad. Or maybe a loan shark from one of the casinos didn't get paid."

We all looked at Grant. "What?" he said like he truly didn't know how crass he was.

John shook his head. "I doubt it was a drug deal in that neighborhood."

"Hey, there're gangs everywhere," Marcus said. "The guy was Hispanic, wasn't he?"

"I guess. What does that have to do with anything?" I asked.

"Well, he could be in a gang." Grant squirmed. "And gangs sell drugs, right?"

"That's racist," Sharon said. "You think I'm in a gang 'cause I'm African American?"

"No, I…. I was only saying it was a possibility."

We all frowned at Grant, but the conversation was going in a bad direction so I changed the subject. "The neighbors were kinda weird," I said.

Marcus laughed and the mood lightened. "Most of the residents of CG are weird."

The waiter returned and distributed black leather-like folders to everyone except me. He leaned low and turned his head away so he wasn't looking down my shirt. He whispered something.

"What?"

"I'm sorry, ma'am, but your card has been declined."

"Declined?" I squeaked loudly before realizing I should shut up. Everyone at the table turned and looked at me.

"Yes, ma'am. Do you have another card?"

"I do, but—how could it be declined? I got paid last week. Would you try it again?"

He shrugged and departed.

"You doin' a little too much shopping, Kaitlyn?" John said grinning.

"No! It's a mistake."

Marcus laughed. "Poor girl can't balance her checkbook!"

Just when I was starting to think maybe he was an okay guy.

The waiter came back. "I'm sorry, ma'am," he said in a soft voice.

"Oh, for heaven's sake!" I grabbed my purse and looked in my wallet. A few dollars... "Can I write a check?"

He looked like I was nuts. *Your debit card doesn't work so why would we take a check?* "I'm sorry, ma'am. We don't accept checks."

I felt like a dinosaur. I liked checks. Checks were tangible. They weren't declined for no reason.

"Need us to cover you?" Sharon asked.

If it had been just her, I would have said yes. But not with the others watching.

"No, I got it." I thumbed through my bills again. All ones. Damn. I rarely carried cash. I could charge it on my emergency VISA card, but I hated to do that. I'd have to remember to pay this off as soon as I worked out the problem with my bank.

I reluctantly handed over the card and the waiter disappeared. I crossed my fingers under the table that there'd be no problem with that one. Now I would have to find time—during the work day—go to the bank and straighten this out. I hated banks except when they were paying me interest, which wasn't very often considering I was on a meager government salary.

The group chatted some more while putting on their coats, eager to get back to work but waiting on me. The waiter returned and said, "Thank you. Come again."

Thank god it worked. I quickly signed the receipt, added a generous (okay, probably not the best) tip.

"Everything okay, sugar?" Sharon said quietly as we walked back to the car.

"I have no idea what the problem is. The bank should have covered it with overdraft if my checking account really was low—but it shouldn't be!"

"Probably just a stupid bank mix up."

"I'm sure you're right." I really, really hoped it was true.

***

After wrapping up a few more things at my desk after lunch, it was time to head out into the field. I decided to swing by my bank on the way to my first complaint. I pulled my truck into the *Bank of Cedar Grove* lot and parked. Some longtime residents with money to burn started the bank a few years ago. I had no idea how one starts a bank, but they did it. "B of CG" as citizens called it. They had good service and decent interest rates so I'd given them a try. I had no complaints, until today.

A young woman with jet black hair, dark make-up, and very pale skin smiled as I approached the window. I had the feeling the large Band-Aid on her neck covered a tattoo instead of a wound.

"How may I help you?"

I pushed a blank deposit slip from my checkbook over to her. "There seems to be a problem with my account. You've made some kind of mistake. My debit card was declined."

"Well, let's just see what's up." Her fingers flew over her keyboard. "Your account is overdrawn by $593.42."

"What! That's impossible!"

"Oh, I see the trouble." She lowered her voice just slightly. "There was some sort of garnishment taken out of your account Friday. For $1,272.81."

"What! From whom?"

"Why don't I have you speak with the assistant manager, Mr. Ramacussi. If you just step over there, I'll call him for you."

Embarrassed beyond words and sure my face was the color of my grandmother's pickled beets, I silently did as I was told. At first the word *garnishment* had shaken me, but once it sank in, I knew. My ex-husband haunts me again. I just knew it. The one with a job gets punished for the slacker who spends money but doesn't repay it.

A gray-haired man that my mother would have called an old-fashioned gentleman approached. He wore a sharp black suit and a navy plaid bow tie over a white shirt. He had a strong chin and thick gray eyebrows. His wire rimmed glasses made him look extra distinguished. I bit more formal than most bankers these days. "Hello. I'm Mr. Ramacussi. How may I be of assistance?"

"There seems to be a problem with my account."

"Come over here to my desk and we'll see what we can do." His big smile was warm and comforting.

I wasn't comforted. My stomach was in knots, the tacos from lunch churning. His desk was in a corner of the large lobby and provided only slightly more privacy than the teller's window. He asked me my account number, clicked a few keys, and scanned his computer screen. "Yes, yes. I see the problem. There was a garnishment that caused your account to become overdrawn."

Caused my account to become overdrawn! Someone stole my damn money! "That must be my ex-husband, not me," I said in my most polite voice. "I need my money." I sounded so desperate, which just pissed me off more. What would I do without any cash until next pay day? And how many auto-payments would bounce?

"I'm very sorry. We only deal with the transactions. You'll have to sort out the details with the requestor."

"And who requested that you drain my account and leave me penniless?"

He clicked a few more keys and frowned. "Washington State Department of Revenue. Not very easy to work with, I'm afraid, but here's a number for you." He wrote something on a piece of paper and passed it to me.

Great. "What do I do in the meantime, until I can get this straightened out? I have a lot of auto withdrawals."

"I'd suggest you cancel any automatic withdrawals for now. We cover your insufficient funds up to $500.00. But that's our limit, unfortunately."

Oh, how nice that they covered some--and charged me $30.00 for each one. "But now I owe you $800 and my payments will keep bouncing! And when my next paycheck gets automatically deposited, you'll keep it!" I tried to keep the slight hysteria I was feeling out of my voice. I don't think I was all that successful.

Mr. Ramacussi pursed his lips. "I'm afraid I cannot help you there. I wish I could. I'm sure it is a very frustrating occurrence. I can wave half the NSF fees as you are a longtime customer. We'll allow the account to stay as it is, but we'll need you to bring it current within two weeks."

I was starting to think he didn't believe me about my ex. "I always pay my bills ON TIME. This is a nightmare."

He smiled a weak smile.

"Oh, you've been so helpful." I couldn't keep the sarcasm, a by-product of my frustration, out of my voice. I grabbed the piece of paper and left.

Back in my truck, I leaned my head against the steering wheel and tried not to cry. I divorced the lazy son-of-a-bitch over a year ago and still he haunted me! I didn't have time to deal with the Dept. of Revenue right now. I had to get back to work. I grabbed my Gummi bear stash, had one handful, then took a second. Then I backed out of the bank lot and headed to my complaints on the east side of the city.

***

I dealt with two homeowners who had left rusty, abandoned vehicles in their yard for too long. I gave a warning to one, whose small RV might be in running condition but wasn't parked on an approved surface. The other vehicle, and old TransAm had expired tabs, a rusty muffler, and obviously wasn't going anywhere any time soon. They got a citation. *Move it now.*

Depressed about money or lack of it, I drove to the far eastside of the city, taking a detour through the movie theater lot to see what was playing, but nothing grabbed my attention--the end-of-the-year flood of new releases hadn't started yet.

As the day slipped by, I felt run down. But amidst my melancholy, I kept running through the craziness of the last few days I needed the answers about and the dead man. I wanted to know the reason all this happened, I felt a burning to know the "why" of the crime. What had happened in that house? Why had Dave ignored his wife's hoarding of animals? Why had she done it in the first place? And what did the dead guy have to do with it all? I strongly suspected his death was tied to the animals in more ways than we knew. It had to be.

I looked up my next complaint and noticed it was just two blocks from the *Death Street*. A sign?

I drove to the house on the form. It had a rickety fence that hadn't seen paint in years. It would probably have been okay for a while, but some kids had tagged a corner with graffiti then kicked a hole in the bottom. I felt for the homeowner who probably couldn't afford to fix it. But I had to cite them anyway. They could at least tear it down so it wasn't an eye sore to their neighbors, although most of the block was boarding on having their own citations.

Done with my work, the *Death Street* called to me. I wished Detective Evans would still be there on the street, interviewing and looking for clues. Maybe if I just drove by the street, I'd spot him and invite him for coffee. Evans seemed sharp and good at his job. Had what I told him helped? Was he working as hard as he could on this case and not suspecting me? Should I stop by the police station again and see what they'd learned was a thought. It went on my mental to-do list.

I motored onto 235th and turned onto 50th Street. The Wyman's driveway was empty. Mary must be working in the office today. Same with the Pitowski's. Estelle was either out and about or her car was ensconced in the garage. No Evans in sight.

I looked around and spied a landscaping truck parked up the street a block or so. I remembered the comments about the dead man and how he might have been a yard worker. I didn't want to buy in to the assumptions, but it was a possibility.

I parked north of the Maddens' and put on my new vest. I took my clipboard, got out of the truck, and walked up the street with my best professional swagger. *Project confidence!*

A grayish-blue landscaping truck was parked up the street. A picture of a tree and the words "Evergreen Landscaping" were stenciled on the side. An assortment of equipment, rakes, buckets, weed-whackers, and other implements filled the truck bed. I heard the roar of an electric lawn mower coming from somewhere I couldn't see.

As I approached, a short, compact, dark-haired man in dirty jeans and a red-plaid flannel shirt came around the side of the house and headed for the truck. I walked toward him, smiling. "Hi. I might be looking for a yard service for my house. Can you tell me about your company?" Damn. The lie came so easily. Too easily.

He studied me for a moment, briefly glancing at my orange vest. He said nothing.

"I work for the city, but I live not far from here. Do you work over all over the city?"

He nodded and fiddled with his heavy gloves. "We can work there. Write down the number and call?" He gestured toward the side of the truck with the phone number printed in large black letters.

"Sure, I'll write it down. Do you work on all the houses on this block? Maybe they'll talk to me about your services."

Hot diggity. We may be getting somewhere. Maybe he knew the dead guy.

He leaned over the side as if looking for something in the bed. Then he turned and looked at me again with a wary gaze. "We do most of the block, *Sí.*"

"Great. Do you have a large crew? Could you start right away?" Like I could afford a lawn service.

"Only four men now. We're very busy. You can call and make an appointment."

"Only four? Did you used to have more?"

He nodded, pulled a large set of clippers from the truck and walked away. It was clear he was uncomfortable talking to me. His eyes darted around. Was it because he knew the dead guy? Or because I worked for the city and he maybe wasn't completely legal? Should I have said I didn't care about that?

I thought of Stanley Pitowski and his uncomfortable un-PC talk. I'd bet he would have mentioned it if he saw "non-whites" just hanging around. Thinking about him and how out of touch he was gave me a shiver of frustration.

Another guy, a lot younger than the first, came around the side of the house and met the man I'd been talking to. They exchanged words in Spanish. I tried to listen. I took two years of Spanish in high school and regretted not taking more. It would have been smart to know another language. Needless to say, today I couldn't have followed what they were saying even if I had been close enough to hear it all.

The first man disappeared around the side of the house and the younger man came toward the truck. I pretended to write the phone number from the truck on my clipboard. Then I realized I should actually write it down. I might be able to call and get more info about the crew.

The younger man opened the truck's passenger door and rooted around inside. When he stood back up, I decided to take a chance. "I understand you lost a member of your crew. What happened?"

The young man looked startled and I saw sadness cascade across his face, then something else.

"Was your co-worker the one who died at that house?" I said pointing toward the Maddens' house. The man's eyes got wide and he sputtered something in Spanish. Before I realized it, he had pulled a huge pair of pruning shears from the truck and pointed them at me. "No."

Stepping backwards, I said "I didn't mean... I was just asking..."

He yelled at me in Spanish and I turned and ran back toward

my truck. *Not too subtle, Kaitlyn. You are not cut out for snooping.*

Still, I was pretty sure they knew the dead guy and maybe he'd been a member of their crew. And they were scared. But what did that mean? Just that a murderer was running around town? If this Carlos was on the crew, it gave him a reason for being in the neighborhood but didn't get me any closer to knowing the *why* of his death. The Maddens didn't appear to be folks who would hire out yard work. Had the dead man stumbled on the animals and was going to tell? Dave hadn't even tried to hide the fact that he knew about the animals. He almost seemed relieved that it had been discovered. What about the animals would make a murder worthwhile?

I didn't have any more answers than before. Instead of driving away, I walked back toward the Maddens' then saw smoke curling out of the chimney at the Pitowski's. Maybe Estelle was home after all.

Before I talked to her again, I stood at the Maddens' driveway and looked around. I'd seen the empty cages, what was left, but it hadn't decreased my bad visions. Maybe I should do like Rosie said, try and forget the whole thing. But how?

The wind picked up as I watched the Maddens' house. I intended to head across the street to Estelle's, but then I noticed my truck was leaning, off kilter. *What the...?* I hurried over. As I got close, I could see that the tires were flat. *What the hell?* And the passenger door was open. The glove box hung open, its contents spread across the floor. The items I kept stored behind the seat were scattered on the floor mats. *Damn!* Hadn't I locked it? I couldn't remember. Anger and frustration pulsed through me. Why hadn't I seen someone by my truck? I'd been too wrapped up and focused on the landscapers.

I reached under the seat, cracking my knuckles against the hardware in the process, but luckily my toolbox was still there and seemed untouched. My little cooler sat open on the passenger seat and my Gummi Bears were gone! *For Pete's sake! Who would steal Gummi Bears?* I thought of the teenagers I'd see on the street last time. Must have been them. Must have been. I had only been gone a few minutes. *Damn it!* I'd been so engrossed in this *Death Street* drama I hadn't paid attention to my surroundings. Code Enforcement 101—pay attention.

I pushed things onto the passenger seat, got in, and slammed the door. *Freakin' kids.* I was going to have to call this in. I hope whoever did this hadn't damaged my radio. The handset hung to the floor but appeared to still be attached and working. I called in to dispatch. Red-faced and pissed off, I asked for a tow.

"It may be 15 to 30," the dispatcher said. "Don't leave your vehicle."

So I couldn't even go and talk to Estelle while I waited. Oh, well, what could she have told me anyway. I sat in the truck for 10 minutes fuming and berating myself for getting involved. I was getting too side-tracked by this mess. What reason did I have to be here?

I knew the reason, I couldn't get the vision of that body out of my head. Plus I was a bit obsessive and be in control. I had a need to know what upset the order in this neighborhood. Now that Evans may or may not think I had something to do with it. It wouldn't hurt to stay connected, right?

Suddenly, I noticed a white piece of paper flapping on the corner of one of my windshield wipers. I stepped out to reach for it at the same time a red tow truck came barreling around the corner and pulled up next to me. I grabbed the piece of litter and jammed it in the pocket of my vest.

"So you're stuck, huh?" a large man in dirty overalls asked, hollering through his open passenger window.

"Obviously."

He chuckled, rubbing a large meaty hand through his short gray hair. He climbed out of his rig and walked around to my truck. "Someone slashed your tires."

Guess he'd never heard of Bill Engvall. *Here's Your Sign.*

He had short sleeves under his overalls but didn't seem to notice that the temperature had dropped below bare arm temperature.

I shivered and wished I'd put on my jacket.

"Someone done you in good," he said.

"Can you drop me at city hall.

He laughed a deep throaty laugh. "Gotta get this vehicle to the city *ge-rage*."

"Yes."

"You piss off someone?"

I rolled my eyes again.

"You can ride with me. I'll give you a lift."

"Lovely." I gathered my personal belongings and stood aside while he connected my truck to his. I was cold and boiling mad at the same time. What was I doing here? Was this neighborhood cursed? Was the world trying to tell me something? Like mind your own business?

My tow-truck driver, Ed, chatted the entire time we drove to city hall. His cab didn't have much in the way of a heater so my toes felt frozen and my nose was red and dripping when he dropped me off.

He waved as he drove away with my truck. *Great.* If it wasn't repaired by tomorrow, I'd be driving Old Yeller. That was the name we gave the city's back-up vehicle. It was old and ugly and a real lemon. Boss Richard frowned at using our own vehicles at work and besides, we didn't want residents to know what we drove so they wouldn't try and find us when we were off-duty.

I trudged to my car and drove home. I wanted nothing more than to crawl into bed and hide, but I had to get ready for the city council meeting.

***

Wally wasn't in his box/bed when I pulled into my driveway, so I assumed either he was out prowling or had gone home. I couldn't decide which I preferred.

Inside, I struggled out of my work clothes and into khakis, a long-sleeved light green t-shirt and laid out a tan suede jacket that played down my chest.

Usually I was frustrated that I had to attend the council meeting I. It cut into my evening but it was also overtime so I was okay with it. Tonight I felt unsettled, a bit rattled. Too much stress and uncertainty for me. I liked mundane and calmness and normal routines. I needed to find a way to get settled and back in control.

I had no energy for cooking so I just heated a can of vegetable barley soup and made a peanut butter and jelly sandwich. I would have added a banana, but the last one in the fruit bowl was more brown than yellow and mushy. Without any cash, meals were going to get worse.

Eating made me feel slightly better. I spent a few minutes in the bathroom putting on some makeup and fussing my hair. Amazing how a little eye shadow, blush, and mascara could make me feel like a different person, more confident. I briefly wondered if Sam Evans would be there. I added wine-colored lipstick. Often having to attend the meeting was something dreaded but unavoidable, might as well find the positive.

With about 15 minutes to go before I had to leave, I realized I hadn't checked my phone when I got home. I'd been too distracted. I picked it up and went to my voice mail—the red circle telling me I had messages. I had five new messages. Wow. I was popular today.

Two were from reporters who had somehow gotten my cell number and three were calls from companies wanting to know why my payments had bounced. One was Cedar Grove utilities saying if I didn't replace the payment soon, my water would be shut off. *Terrific.*

In control, I was not.

***

Cedar Grove City Council meetings were normally held in the

council chambers room at city hall. But when the agenda attracted a lot of interest, like redevelopments, the meeting moved to a small auditorium attached to the south side of the recreation center, across the street and down the block from city hall. I arrived forty-five minutes before the posted start time, but the parking lot was already almost full. Darkness had descended on the city and the streetlights around the lot winked on in random order. The lights around the small park that bordered the recreation center were low, as the park closed at dusk. Just enough light to discourage late-night drug deals and other mischief. I could only just see the swings on the swing set moving slightly in the breeze.

I jogged from my car toward the auditorium. A chilly wind whipped at the hem of my suede jacket. My breath puffed out in front of me and my lips felt chapped by the time I reached the doorway. Throngs of people attempted to push their way through the main entrance, most likely in a rush to get signed up for the public comment period.

I moved around to the side of the building and knocked on a staff-only side door. I waited in the near dark since only a lame yellow bulb lit the area. Behind me I heard something scurrying around in the bushes near the edge of the lot. The hair on my neck tickled, a weird sensation like someone watching. I didn't believe in ESP or anything but the feeling was odd. Then a figure stepped out of the trees. Whoever it was wore all dark clothing, including a dark sweatshirt with the hood up. *Creepy!* I banged on the door again. The figure stood very still. Probably a teen lurking in the dark. If he was trying to creep me out, it worked. I pounded on the door again and resisted glancing over my shoulder.

A uniformed police officer I didn't know finally opened the door and peered out at me. I held up my city ID and he let me in. A small poorly-lit hallway with a concrete floor led to the green room where the city council members waited before entering the meeting. "Keep that door locked," I said to the cop.

"Lots of weird people hanging around out there."

He looked at me with a bored expression and shrugged. Just here for the overtime. I turned and headed toward the main auditorium.

There was a disparity between the icy air outside and the overly warm room. Even with its high ceilings, the auditorium felt stuffy. I regretted my choice of jacket, but I didn't want to take it off because my t-shirt underneath was tight.

In the back hall, I ran into Sharon. We made our way to the side door and peered into the auditorium. A long table with seven plain chairs sat in front of the large room creating the council table. Behind the table, drab beige curtains cordoned off the back of the stage area. A row of microphones on thick black stands lined the table.

"You ever notice what those mikes look like?" Sharon whispered. "Like a row of…," she paused as if pondering her word choice. "…phallic symbols."

I laughed. Sharon, my godsend, helping me relax and feel normal even if the world wasn't. She had dressed for the meeting in a deep red top, with ruffles and dark purple jeans. Long purple earrings dangled from her ears. She looked classy despite the mix of colors.

We moved through the crowd to the small area reserved for city employees. Grant was already there, in the front row seat he took every week. I squeezed into the third row next to John. "Hi," I said as I slid in.

"Some crowd, huh?"

John nodded. He looked stylish in a suit jacket over a t-shirt.

"Well, ya know," Sharon added. "When it has to do with change, all the crazies come out."

John pulled out his phone.

I found mine and silenced it. "Guess you found a sitter?" I said to Sharon.

"Nah, but Reggie said he would stay and keep an eye on things."

I raised my eyebrows. Her husband wasn't much of a firm hand and tended to lose control quickly if Sharon wasn't around.

"Hell, what can happen in a few hours?" she said, obviously not believing her own words.

We both went quiet. I was always struck by the starkness of the auditorium when it was used for council meetings. Off to the far side of the room, a wooden podium and mic stood at the ready for the public comments. To the right of the council table was a smaller table with a laptop for the City Clerk to take minutes of the meeting.

The theater seating in the auditorium had become standing room only. A few people squatted on the stairs. Another line snaked through the seats, waiting to sign up on the comment list. Each person would get three minutes to speak, but they all wanted to voice their opinion. The Council didn't respond directly to the public comment, but it gave the citizens, especially the regulars, a way to be heard, and provide sound bites for politicians to use during elections.

I noticed Richard loitering near the back of the room. He came and made an appearance but didn't stay long after he was sure code enforcement wasn't on the agenda. Tonight, knowing we were going to come up, he made his way down a side aisle and sat a few rows behind us. It didn't bother me he was there, but always adds a bit of anxiety to have your boss watching you.

The City Clerk read the *Call to Order*, then we all stood for the flag salute. I found that tradition comforting. There was a lot of thumping and banging and rattling of chairs as the packed house sat back down. The Council moved through the approval of the agenda for the night and the approval of the consent items, usually boring business items that didn't need discussion and could be passed quickly. The City Clerk did the official roll call, which I thought was pointless but apparently was some Roberts Rules of Order mandate.

As the city's governing body, Cedar Grove's seven elected Councilmembers were the heart and soul (read that bureaucrats) of the city. Their job as part-time politicians was to establish policies and laws, adopt a budget, and approve appropriations and contracts. Since they serve staggered four-year terms, about half the Council up for election every two years. And next year would be an election year for three of them, so their take on the hot topic of the night was extremely important to the future of their political careers.

In a city manager-style government structure, the position of mayor wasn't really all that important or different from the other councilmembers; they all voted someone to be mayor and deputy mayor after they were all elected. Our current mayor, Geoffrey Michelson, presided at council meetings and smiled for the city during ceremonies but that was about it. Everyone knew that Councilman Newman was the real power on the council, the one with the City Manager's ear. The deputy mayor didn't do much unless the mayor got sick or couldn't attend an important function. A good thing since our current deputy mayor, Kenneth Farrington, tended to say things that were barely true or the exact opposite of what he intended. I swear he once quoted Dan Quale—by accident—saying "If we don't succeed, we run the risk of failure." The city's PR person was constantly trying to undo the damage Farrington caused. Poor Gal.

"Look at that tie Farrington is wearing!" Sharon said.

"Looks like a holdover from the '70s. Someone ought to introduce him to an iron."

"Don't he got someone to help him dress?" John said.

I replied, "Let's just hope he keeps his mouth shut tonight."

"No way. I hope he opens wide and sticks his foot in," Sharon said, grinning. "Makes the evening more interesting."

Finally the meeting got down to business. Mayor Michelson pulled his mic toward him and cleared his throat.

Councilman Newman smiled his fake smile and leaned back in his chair. His narrow face and sunken cheeks made him look slightly sick under the harsh auditorium lights. His perfectly starched shirt and suit gave him a step up from the other slightly less-formal council members.

"We'll start with the reports," Mayor Michelson said, and the crowd collectively groaned. They were here for the Big Show and weren't happy to have to sit through the mundane first. I sent telepathic waves of "be brief" toward the head of Parks and Recreation and the Director of Information Technology who both had reports on the agenda.

"Ms. Dietz," Mayor Michelson said. "We'd like to hear your report."

Lynn Dietz, a tall red-headed woman with a strong voice and a warm smile, launched into a detailed but succinct report on the wrap-up of the Off-Leash Dog Park project and the plans for next year's annual city celebration, *Celebrate Cedar Grove.*

Sharon whispered out of the side of her mouth. "You think they'll try and make us patrol the dog park?"

I shrugged.

"I ain't ticketing people for not picking up poop, no way."

The IT Director started on about his five-year technology upgrade plan and the attendees groaned.

I tuned out and scanned the crowd. Stanley and Estelle sat together in the third row in the middle, her bright pink sweater covered with bunnies literally made them stand out in a crowd. I wonder what he'd been like 25 years ago. Maybe there had been something appealing about him then. Had he changed drastically? Really changed? Could Stanley be a murderer? It was a thought, but I couldn't picture it.

As I scanned the room, my eye caught a mousey-looking woman. She held my gave and frowned. I looked away quickly. I spotted Randall Wyman sitting with Mary in the back. He wore a dark shirt and a frown. I didn't like him. He was a narcissist, but could he be a murderer? Had he known the dead guy? Even if he had, I had no motive for the murder so speculating didn't really accomplish much. Would he really have walked right up to Evans if he was?

Our regulars, the Tolefsons, were seated in the front row. I saw quite a few of my other regular *customers* mixed in the crowd.

The audience began to fidget and whisper as Mr. IT droned on. A sharp look from the Mayor got him to wrap it up.

"Dang." Sharon said. "Someone should tell that man that none of us care. Long as our computers work when we need them to."

"Which isn't often," I replied sarcastically.

Sharon snorted and a guy from maintenance in the row behind us cleared his throat, loudly. Sharon turned around and glared at him.

Finally the City Planner, along with a trio of consultants hired to work on the development plan, took center stage. Just as they were getting started my pocket vibrated and I yelped. Silence rushed over the room like a tsunami and I'm sure my face turned the color of tomatoes. Then, just as quickly as it had rushed in, the silence broke and the sounds in the room resumed.

The Planners launched into their PowerPoint presentation and all eyes were fixed on the renderings of the new look for our city. Blocks of buildings five stories tall, idyllic-looking sidewalks with border trees, and apartments above new retail. "Property values will rise" was the message. They used the word *vibrant* about eight times. Development was on the way. Councilman Newman smiled his false smile through the whole presentation looking like a proud parent at an elementary school band concert.

As they droned on, I carefully checked my phone. A few missed calls from earlier--I suspected more calls about bounced checks, but one was from Rosie. Weird, she knew it was council night.

The energy in the crowd felt palpable, heavy with emotion. It was like anger boiling under the surface as people tried to behave in public when they really wanted to scream and shout.

The presentation took less than twenty minutes, thankfully.

The Mayor called for open comments. One by one, average citizens took to the mike.

"*I've lived here for 50 years, why do you want to change things now?*"

"*You want five-story buildings in the downtown area? I like the idea of more retail shops, but all the people who live above them will crowd our streets and cause traffic and noise issues.*"

"*Development is a great idea. Time to move into the future I say.*"

"*I own a small store. I'm losing money every month. We need revitalization to bring in more customers.*"

"*The congestion will ruin our peaceful neighborhoods.*"

"*Why don't you put the money into green spaces and parks instead of a downtown?*"

"*My home value has plateaued. This new plan is great if it will raise my property value.*"

"*Raising property values will raise our taxes. I'm against it. No more taxes!*"

On and on it went. More people tonight seemed to be against the proposal. Neither Randall nor Stanley commented, and the Tolefsons were blissfully quiet. However, as I kept my peripheral vision scanning around, I watched Randall and Stanley both get riled up. In different ways I saw strain on their faces. Stanley got red and sweaty and fidgeted. Estelle looked calm and I noticed a ball of yarn in her lap; she was knitting. Randall crossed his arms over his chest and scowled at the commenters. Mary looked bored. The most interesting ting to her was examining her manicure.

I watched my co-workers too. Sharon's face lit up like she thought the whole thing was funny. John looked stoic, hard to read. Marcus was going for bored but his deepening frown said he didn't like what was being said, but I couldn't tell which side of the issue he fell on.

I knew there was a limit to the total amount of time public comment could last. A juggling act for the Council—let as many people as possible express their opinions without keeping us all here until the wee hours of the morning. And as more people approached, emotions ratcheted up along with the overall tension in the room.

It was after ten when the mousey-looking woman I'd noticed earlier approached the mic She had plump arms sticking out of a dark teal shirt with a large turtle on the front. "I want to discuss the animal hording situation that happened in our city." Her voice was soft at first but grew stronger and more confident as she continued. "The shelter is full of these poor neglected creatures and I call on all the citizens of Cedar Grove to step forward and adopt one. No animal should lose its life! You can make a good home for one of these poor souls!"

The crowd erupted in loud murmurs of ascent and someone in the back yelled, "Hear, hear!"

I turned and scanned the crowd. Attendees appeared to be riveted. My eyes caught Randall. His scowl had turned to a full-on glower. Mary seemed to be trying to calm him, but he pushed her away. Suddenly, the couple of reporters who had been standing against the wall, bored and dozing, jumped to attention. They scribbled notes and urged their camera operators to get pictures. Growth and development, slightly boring. Saving the poor mistreated animals, something everyone could get behind.

I couldn't help but think of poor Rhonda Madden. She was mentally ill or, at the least, depressed, some kind of imbalance that made her feel the only way she could control the world was to control the animals. I knew about control. Now she probably wasn't controlling anything.

The Council, who weren't supposed to respond, gestured the Mayor to his microphone. "A wonderful suggestion," he said.

Deputy Mayor Farrington, his partially bald head shiny, jumped in. "Be assured that we will give this issue our full attention even if there are other things we need to attend to."

Mayor Michelson cleared his throat. "One more comment

and we have to cut it off for the night. These chairs aren't comfortable enough to sleep in, folks."

"Ha. Ha," Sharon said deadpan.

The staff member helping coordinate the public comment waved to a small, dark-skinned man who shuffled to the podium. "I am Daniel Garcia,' said the man with a slight Spanish accent. "I want to know what you are doing about the murder in our city."

There was silence for a full ten seconds as the Council glanced back and forth at each other, then to the Genie Dimitriadis, CG Police Chief, who was standing off to the side of the room. She moved toward the stage. The Chief, very reluctantly if I was reading her body language right, approached the council table and leaned toward the closest mic. She had a commanding presence with ink black hair, a straight nose, and large turquoise eyes. "Be assured that my detectives are investigating and will resolve the case in a timely manner."

The crowd could hold it in no more. People leapt to their feet. Above the loud conversation that rose in a crescendo, I heard yells of "Development brings death!" and "Serial killer on the loose!" Mayor Michelson banged the gavel and yelled "meeting adjourned" into his mic. He strode away from the table and made a quick escape out the side door. The rest of the council except Farrington scurried after him to their locked green room.

Farrington held back and tried to say something to the audience, but everyone was yelling and several police officers had appeared to try and control the crowd as they exited. Farrington finally gave up and was escorted away.

I saw Officer Heineken gesturing a line of people at the door. Sharon and I sat unmoving.

She shook her head. "Council meetings are always such fun."

"You said it."

CHAPTER 7

The phone was ringing when I walked through the door. I hesitated, wondering who was calling so late I almost didn't answer. I was tired and unsettled after the council meeting. I grabbed it up and stepped back out onto my small front porch for some air. The sky was dark, the air cool. For just a moment, I thought I caught a whiff of salty sea air blowing up from the Sound. Wally sat in his box, looking up at me expectantly.

"Hello?" I said into the phone, carefully keeping my tone neutral.

I could barely hear Rosie's soft voice. She mumbled something I couldn't understand. "What? Rosie, speak up."

"I can't," she whispered. "He might hear."

"Who?"

"Mac."

"Mac?" I thought she was over him. "You're with Mac?"

"I'm not <u>with</u> him. I'm following him."

"What? Rosie, are you out of your mind?"

There was some rustling as if she were shifting positions.

"Rosie, where are you?"

"In the bushes outside a restaurant in Fremont. He's inside. With <u>her</u>."

I sighed. My friend was always a little eccentric but this was over the top. I glanced at my watch. Already ten thirty. "Let me come and get you."

"No. I've got my car," she whispered. "I just want to see where they're going."

"Rosie, you can't follow them."

"I need to catch them, confront him or...."

"That's stalking," I said. "Rosie, please don't do anything crazy. "

"They don't know I'm here. Oh, here they come! Gotta go."

She hung up on me!

Rosie was crawling around in the bushes stalking her ex-boyfriend! Had she gone insane? "What should I do?" I asked Wally.

He looked at me unblinking for a good five seconds then went back to the intricate process of licking his paw.

"Some help you are," I muttered. I called Rosie crazy, but I was the one talking to a cat.

Maybe I was going crazy. Or just crazy lonely. "You don't think you're coming inside do you?" I asked Wally.

He turned around and stuck his rear end up in air.

"I'll take that as a no."

I went inside and opened a can of cat food and took it back to the porch. A thank you for his good listening skills. As I set it down next to his box, he hissed at me. "Fine!" I stomped inside and slammed the door.

***

I didn't sleep much that night. I tossed and turned worrying about Rosie and feeling an overwhelming sense of being unsettled. And broke. When I left for work the next morning, there was an empty cat food can and a dead mouse on the porch. I guess Wally loved me after all.

I settled into my desk and readied myself for an uneventful day. I held a firm resolve not to think about the murder, the animals, my bank account... After shuffling papers for a bit, I looked at my phone. Why hadn't Rosie called me back? I was hesitant to call her since she should be at work. I checked my voice mail. There was a message from the garage saying my truck would be ready tomorrow. Today I was SOL.

There were several other messages from the media. Delete.

There was also a message from Detective Evans. I smiled, listening to his soothing voice until he got past the pleasantries.

"Ms. Willis, if you could come to the police station today, we'd like to ask you a few more questions about your presence at the crime scene. We need to discuss your involvement in the crime."

Great. They wanted to question me? Did he think I murdered the man? No way. He couldn't. But he hadn't used my first name. *Shit.* What if he did suspect me? I was just doing my job! What else was there to say?

I should never have gone into that backyard. If only I could take back that one stupid decision! If only... Right then, the country group, She Daisy's *"Don't Worry About A Thing"* came up on my playlist. Yes, life is sticky, but I don't think they had getting interrogated on the list of things you shouldn't worry about.

I stomped through reception area, my face scrunched into a sour look.

"What's wrong with you?" Cheryl asked. She sat calmly behind her counter, wearing a cheerful lemon-colored sweater. Large yellow pineapples hung from her ears. I guess she decided to stretch out summer a bit more.

"I'm on my way to the police station. If you don't hear from me in 20 minutes, you can assume I've been arrested."

Her eyes got wide. "What for?" She asked looking alarmed.

"Who knows?" I said and grabbed the door.

"Kaitlyn?"

The voice was not Cheryl's. I turned away from the door, still holding it open, hoping to escape. My boss, Richard, stood next to Cheryl's desk. He looked very serious in a dark suit, white shirt open at the neck, and a file folder in his hand.

"Yes?" I asked dumbly.

"Did I overhear that you were going to the police station? Is this in relation to... one of your cases?"

I dropped the door and took a deep breath. "Yes, it is. The odor complaint that turned out to be animal hoarding and murder."

"I thought we were... about done with our part in that. "

I appreciated the use of we. "I'd like to be done with it, sir. I told the police everything I knew but was asked to come in and answer some additional questions."

"Ah, hah." He paused. An irritating habit designed to make big-mouths like me fill up the silence with self-incriminating babble.

"Sir, I met the detective at the scene yesterday in an effort to assist them," I said. "I guess they need more clarification."

His face got tight. His brow creased. "You still have a full case load to attend to today."

"Yes. I know." *Don't piss off your boss. Don't piss off your boss.*

"I'll expect you to finish your caseload," he said. "Without overtime."

"Yes, sir."

His brow released. "If they give you any trouble, or keep you more than 30 minutes, call me. I'd be happy to get the City Attorney involved."

I nodded but didn't reply. No way I'd call him to bail me out, figuratively, I hoped.

130

***

On the drive over to the police station, I tried to calm down and get my head squared. I didn't want to look like a fool in front Detective Evans--or like someone who needed anger management. But my body wasn't ready for calm. My heart pounded like I'd been exercising. My hands shook. I felt afraid and excited at the same time. Scared that someone really did think I had something to do with the murder. Excited at the prospect of seeing Evans again.

My new vest, which did close over my chest, made me look like a giant pumpkin with denim legs. I switched to a CG jackets over my loose black t-shirt and gray zip-up. I thought I looked pretty good, chic government worker style.

The lobby of the police station was empty but this time two people occupied the desk behind the glass. On the walls, signs advertised safety programs, applications for reserve officer programs, and the citizen patrol. A large poster, *Drive Hammered, Get Nailed,* hung next to the bulletin board next to a faded *Click It Or Ticket* seatbelt poster.

One woman in civilian clothes looked up from her computer and waved at me. I didn't recognize her but thought she was the other records clerk. She finished typing something then came up to the glass. "Can I help you?"

"I'm here to see Detective Evans. He called and asked me to come over."

"Your name?"

"Kaitlyn Willis."

She smiled. "Just a sec."

She disappeared into the back, returned shortly, and buzzed me in. The hallway smelled of beef soup and cilantro, as if someone had recently eaten Pho.

A uniformed officer I didn't know waved for me to follow. His heavy black belt sat solidly on his hips like a weight keeping his feet on the ground. We didn't head to one of the small offices along the corridor or to the lunchroom with its bad coffee, but to a small room at the back of the building.

"Just have a seat and someone will be right with you," he said.

The space was most likely an interrogation room for nonviolent offenders. Was that a good sign or a bad sign? I took off my jacket and tugged my hoody across my chest. I dug my phone out of a pocket in my jacket and glanced at it a few times while I sat, waiting. The room had yellowy colored walls and utilitarian carpet in a green/gray. There were no pictures on the walls and no windows. A video camera hung in the corner near the ceiling. Were they recording me now? Could they do that?

I sent Rosie a text message. I really wished she'd get back to me. I was just closing my phone when Sam Evans entered along with another man. Sam wore dark dress pants, and a white button-up shirt, no tie. He looked classy and expensive. The other man wore all black, pants, t-shirt, shoes.

"Sorry to keep you waiting, Ms. Willis," Evans said. "This is Detective Sheehan."

So we really were back to last names.

I cleared my throat as they sat down, Sam across the table from me. Detective Sheehan pulled a chair away from the table next to Sam and sat so his back was against the wall.

Sheehan was a large man, broad-shouldered with a massive chest, and a rugged, lined face. Bet he had the same problem I did getting things to close over a huge chest. He looked exactly like you'd think a tough detective would look. Nothing like Evans or TV cops like Chris Noth, Jesse Martin or Benjamin Bratt, not to mention Adrian Monk or Shawn Spencer.

Maybe Sheehan was here to play bad cop. Eek! That meant I was really in trouble. I decided to be up front. "I believe I told you everything." *Damn.* I sounded whiney. "I haven't remembered anything new."

"We'd like to run through your story again," Detective Evans said. He looked at me and smiled.

My heart jumped around in my chest and I suddenly felt sweaty. I would have liked to think I was turned on, but I was actually terrified although I wasn't sure why. I hadn't done anything wrong.

"And we're filming ya," Sheehan said in a gruff voice.

"You are? What for?"

"Just for the record," Evans said.

And so I ran through it one more time.

"Tell me why you were in the backyard when it's against policy for city employees to enter a private yard with the homeowner." Sheehan said it in a way I wondered if I would still have a job when I got back to work.

"I told you, because of the smell and I heard noises, moaning. I thought someone was hurt or needed help."

"Why didn't you call 911?" Sheehan leaned his chair back on two legs. I wondered if the chair would support him. He had to weigh 275 or more.

"I didn't yet know there was a problem."

Sheehan frowned. "You should have called it in before you… investigated."

"I worked with you guys a few times. You would have laughed at me if I'd reported *funny noises*."

"We ain't laughing now," Sheehan said.

Sam cleared his throat audibly. I could swear I could hear the video camera working.

"So you knew you weren't supposed to be there and you went in anyway."

"Yes," I said. My arm pits and the trench under my boobs were wet with sweat. The room felt like it was shrinking. I was hot and felt self-conscious. I wished I could put my jacket back on.

"And you didn't recognize the victim," Evans asked.

"No."

Sheehan jumped in. "And you didn't touch the body?"

"No."

"And you didn't see a weapon?" Sam said.

"No."

"And you didn't hide a weapon?" Sheehan added dropping his chair back onto four legs with a thump.

"No!" I squeezed my hands together. My palms were clammy.

"And you're sure you didn't know the guy?" Sheehan leaned toward across the table. "Didn't have a beef with the guy?"

"No!" Sheehan was excellent in the bad cop role.

Sheehan leered at me and leaned in so I could smell his nasty cologne.

Suddenly, I was done being scared and I was pissed. I sat up straight. "Do I need a lawyer? The City Attorney?"

Sheehan opened his mouth, but Detective Evans jumped in. "No, Ms. Willis. We are only asking questions."

Sheehan scowled. "Homicide is a very serious crime."

His intense stare made me squirm. I was tired of this. "And you have no other suspects besides me? You've got both of the residents of the house, right? Have you questioned them? "

"Of course," Evans started, but I kept going.

"What about the neighbors? I've talked to all of them and I'd say you have a couple of viable suspects. None of them liked the Maddens and Mr. Pitowski is especially creepy. He's probably guilty of something. And what about the animals? Animal hording is serious and often caused by depression. Maybe Mrs. Madden is sick and she killed him!"

"Listen," Sheehan raised his voice. " If you are involved in this, we'll find out!"

"You listen," I said. "I'd say they everyone else has better motives than me—a dedicated city employee who was just doing her job. And now…" I stood and grabby my hoody. "I need to get back to that job. So unless you plan on detaining me, I'm leaving."

Detective Sheehan's jaw went slack with surprise, then quickly he recovered his tough bravado. I thought I saw a little tremor of a smile in the corner of Detective Evans' gorgeous lips.

"I'll show you out," Sam said.

"I think I can find my way." I threw open the conference room door which banged against the wall. I stalked out. I probably should have let Sam walk me out, but I was too pissed.

***

I drove my Rav slow and careful back to the office, then took my anger out on the pavement by stomping my way to the front door. Cheryl looked up as I entered. She opened her mouth to say something, but I shot her a look that said, *speak at your own peril.* She shut up.

In my cube, I grabbed my clipboard, cooler, case log, and keys. I trudged back out to the parking lot, only to remember that my truck was still at the garage. *Crap.*

I went back inside and walked to Cheryl's counter. "I need the keys for Old Yeller."

"Uh, huh," Sweet, sugary smile, yellow pineapples bouncing.

I took a calming breath and tried not to roll my eyes. "Please."

She handed me a ring of keys and smiled sweetly. Sheehan had put me in a truly sour mood, but I wasn't it talking it out on others.

Old Yeller lived up to its lemon reputation by coughing and sputtering before it started. My anger sputtered too, suddenly diffused. Really, who would think I would have anything to do with a murder? Detective Sheehan apparently.

I drove out of the city hall lot and headed to a neighborhood on the east side of the city, far away from the *Death Street.* The sky had turned blue with lots of fluffy light gray clouds, like dryer lint in the air. I rolled down the window as the cab of the truck started to warm. The heater was stuck in the on position, great in winter, a little stuffy for early fall.

As I drove, I thought about Sam. Looking back with more

of an open mind than I'd had at the time, I believed that he didn't think I was guilty of anything but others, like Sheehan, must be pushing him to cover all bases. At least I hoped so, because I was starting to like the guy. It figures, I come off a nasty divorce and dating dry spell and the first guy I'm interested in is a cop who's investigating me for murder.

Turning onto 34th Street, a busy thoroughfare, I saw a group of people standing on the corner by a gas station and holding picket signs. The corner usually held an assortment of used vehicles for sale; today it was full of people. As I neared, I read their signs, "Save the animals" and "Animals have feelings too." The public cry, rallying for the animals in the cages. One sign even said, "Just say no to euthanizing." It felt good that someone else cared about the poor creatures besides me. Odd, me caring about animals and giving a thumbs up to picketers. I usually pitied them, not ever quite passionate enough about anything to stand on the streets with signs.

I drove down a residential block and slowed. It was a plain but clean street with sidewalks. A white-haired man walked a large black lab on a leash. Several of the homes had small signs staked in their yards. "Redevelopment will cost us too much." "Save Cedar Grove's history. No redevelopment." A young woman pushed a double stroller with two dark-haired boys sleeping inside.

Today I wasn't on the hunt for a specific violation. I was just covering my assigned area for the annual city-sweep. Once a year, code enforcement tried to cover every block in the city doing a visual inspection for code violations. It was a good way to keep our presence out in all the neighborhoods, not just the ones with abuse. I stopped, hoping Old Yeller would start again, and wrote a warning for a boat and a box trailer parked on the street—not allowed. All vehicles must be on approved surfaces on the owner's property. The warning gave them 72 hours to move their items.

My heart wasn't really in my work today. I sat in the

unsightly yellow truck and opened a Diet Sprite. Even a handful of Gummi Bears didn't lift my spirits. Worry for Rosie filled my brain since she hadn't returned my calls or texts.

I hoped she hadn't been arrested for stalking. Or worse, that she had confronted Mac and his fiancé. That could have been ugly and probably demoralizing. Either way she'd be feeling lousy and needing comfort. I'd tried her cell many times since she'd hung up on me. There was nothing else I could do.

To distract myself I again thought about Sam. He really was good looking, hot. And, so far, he seemed like a nice guy too. But a cop! That was alright I guess. It wasn't like Cedar Grove was a huge city like Seattle. This week's death was the first homicide in five years. Chances of working together again were slim.

Since my disastrous marriage and subsequent divorce, I hadn't thought much about dating or relationships. I'd enjoyed being alone and immersing myself in my job. But lately the nights felt long and lonely. Maybe that's why I hadn't taken Wally to the Animal Shelter. I just wanted someone, something to talk to.

I imagined Sam holding my hand, his arm across my shoulder, then sighed. What was the point? He wasn't interested in me. Why would he be? I didn't sky dive or bungie jump. I didn't run marathons or publish best-selling novels. I was just a lowly code enforcement officer with a few close friends and not much else except the baggage of an ex-husband who was about to run me into the poor house. Tomorrow I'd have to call Ben again and find out what was going on and when (or if) he was going to pay me back. I wasn't holding my breath on that.

Depressing. I thought of Sam again and a warm tingle zapped through me. Was there any chance? I drifted off into a daydream, arms around me and well, more creative variations of intimacy. Did Sam wear boxers or briefs? Did he have chest hair? Did he have a secret tattoo?

My guy-picker radar had never been great. I was usually so worried that every man who wanted to be with me was only

interested in my boobs that I tended to be a little standoffish—
or so I've been told. I took a big risk with Ben. He'd been cute
and charming and affectionate. And pretty good in bed. I
thought I'd hit pay dirt.

I'd left the marriage feeling used, abused, taken advantage of,
and hurt down to my core. How long did it take to really trust
again? Was it worth it to try? But something in my heart and I
admit, in my loins, was telling me it might be time.

Suddenly, my cell phone rang, startling me. I fumbled for
the phone and in the process spilled Gummi Bears into my lap.
Dang! I checked caller ID and smiled.

"Rosie! Hi!"

"Hey, Kaitlyn. I got your messages."

How many had I left? Five? Eight? More? "I was worried
about you."

"I'm fine. I came into work late since I was out after
midnight last night."

"Rosie, what in the world were you doing? What were you
thinking?"

"I was thinking it ain't fair! Mac and I had a good thing. He's
not supposed to be with her. He's not." Her voice cracked and I
felt her hurt pour through the phone.

I wanted to give Rosie comforting words, but I didn't know
any. She was hurting. She had really loved Mac and thought he
was the one. I hadn't agreed at the time, but who was I to say? I
kind of liked having her boyfriend-less again so we could be
single together. But that was selfish.

"Rosie, you have to let him go," I said in a whisper.

"I can't! I have to fight for him! I think he's worth it. She's
not right for him."

"I don't..." There was nothing I could say that made any
sense. I didn't have any idea how to manage a relationship. I only
dated a handful of men before I married Ben and in the last year,
I'd shut myself off from even thinking of boyfriends. Well,
maybe the thought of a one-night stand might have passed

through my mind once or twice. Or three times…

"Kaitlyn, you have to help me. I have a plan."

My best friend wanted my help. What could I say except yes?

She said, "Meet met at McGrath's Pub at eight."

"I'll be there, Rosie."

"Thanks, K. You're the best."

I hung up and sat for a moment wondering what I was getting into with Rosie. What kind of a plan? Absent-mindedly, I shoved my hands into the pockets of my vest. My right hand touched something paper. I pulled it out. It was the note I'd found on my truck the night it got towed. The slip was a regular sheet of 8 ½ X 11 white paper like in every printer, ripped in half and folded twice. I opened it and read the hand-written note, *"Leave it alone or else!"*

Cryptic. But not very original. Who would have left this? What were they referring to? And what was the *or else*? I thought of the figure loitering outside the council meeting and a chill of fear tingle my spine. Was someone threatening me? What did they think I knew?

I took a deep breath and got a hold of my feelings. Being fearful pissed me off. "Screw 'em!" I said aloud as I fired up Old Yeller. The truck sputtered then purred.

I pulled away from the curb and headed back to city hall. No one was telling me what to do unless they were my boss. If I wanted to crawl around in the bushes and support my friend, I would. If I wanted to investigate animal hording or murder, no one was going to stop me.

***

McGraths was your standard dive bar. Dark wood bar with battered stools. A few scattered tables and a TV in the corner tuned to football. A digital juke box played classic rock just a little too loud. A musty smell hung in the air—too many bodies, not enough air flow. And a hint of someone enjoying the now legal marijuana. Low lighting except in the corner where a lively game of darts was heating up. Beer and darts. Who came up with that volatile combo?

Rosie waved to me from a table in the corner. She had a glass of dark beer in front of her. As I approached, she stood and gave me a hug. I hugged back, hard. Her tall lean frame seemed too thin and vulnerable. I held her arms and stepped back. Her red hair curled around her shoulders a little mussed. She looked tired, a little pale. Not crazy, just broken-hearted.

"Thanks for coming, Kaitlyn. I didn't know if you would." She looked a little sheepish. She knew what she was doing was nuts, but I guess she couldn't stop herself.

"So..." I started.

"Let's get you a drink." She stood. "Beer?"

"Sure. Something light on tap." I reached for my purse.

"I got it."

Rosie ambled up to the bar. She wore black straight-leg jeans and a neon blue top. She flashed a thousand-watt smile at the bartender and he quickly poured my beer.

She returned and I took a long swig. It felt good to relax a little after the stress-filled day. "So what's the plan?"

Rosie fiddled with her glass. "Nothing specific really. They'll be here about nine. I thought you could distract the cheerleader and I'll try and talk to Mac before he starts the dart tournament."

I didn't even want to know how she knew they'd be here. "Distract her? Like how?"

"Maybe you could accidentally spill something on her fake boobs."

"Are you kidding? Why don't you just call him?"

"I have! He won't return my calls!" She sounded panicky.

"Meeting him head-on in a bar—in front of his friends—does <u>not</u> sound like a good plan."

"I don't know what else to do."

We sat in silence for a moment sipping our beers listening to

Bon Jovi.

"What if we follow them home—" she said. "Or better yet, we can sneak into his house while they're here and put itching powder in all her underwear."

I frowned at her.

"I know. I know. She probably doesn't wear underwear."

I laughed! It felt good.

Rosie laughed too. "Thanks, K. For listening to my crazy ideas."

"Of course. I'm sure you'll repay me sometime."

"What if we just key his Mustang?" Rosie grinned. "It would sure feel good."

"We don't want to be too childish," I said, then thought *Why the hell not?* "Maybe instead of desperation..."

I thought about being almost 40 and about being single. I couldn't envision either Rosie or me being patient enough for online dating. How did you get a guy's attention? Not sitting back and being boring. Why not go for the outrageous? I filled Rosie in on my idea.

***

We were each close to finishing our second beer when Mac and Miss Sea Gal came into the bar. She wore skin-tight white jeans and a stretchy peach-colored tank top. She didn't try and hide her chest. Hoop earrings the size of dessert plates dangled from her ears and mixed with her perfect wavy blond hair.

The couple didn't even look our way as they sauntered to the bar. He got a beer and she a glass of pink wine. They sat at a small table near the dart board. Mac was a nice-looking guy. Nothing special in my mind, but he must have something that Rosie liked. It sure wasn't a nice butt like Sam's. Mac's jeans sagged over a flat behind.

Rosie and I went over the plan. "Who should we ask?" she whispered conspiratorially.

I scanned the room and settled on the guy most likely to have been a jock in high school. He was young, maybe early twenties. He had model good looks, deep chocolate skin, and a body that said he spent more time in the gym than with a girlfriend. And he was surrounded by a group of buddies. Lots of ego.

"How about him?" I said pointing.

"Oh, shit! You think he'll do it?"

"Can't hurt to ask."

This was the hard part of the plan. I took off my sweater. Underneath I had on a skin-hugging t-shirt with a low scoop neck. I downed the last of my beer and thought about ordering a shot. I hadn't done anything like this since high school—and not really there either. At that moment, ZZ Top's *Sharp Dressed Man* came on the jukebox. Gave me a little boost.

I ambled up to Mr. Jock and his friends. Predictably, all eyes went straight to my shirt. "Hi, guys," I purred.

Stuttering and drooling followed.

"I need a favor."

Unconscious nods.

A few minutes later, I returned to Rosie's table and slipped on my sweater. She'd ordered another round.

"Well?"

"He'll do it. His name is Dwayne. And his buddies will help."

"Can I do it?" She took a gulp of beer.

"Rosie, yes you can!"

"I'll do it. I'll do it." She smiled. "What did you promise them?"

"I said they could all feel me up in the parking lot after."

Rosie spit beer on the table. "What?"

"I'm kidding. I said I'd pay their tab for the night."

"I'll pay it," Rosie insisted. I wanted to say no, but remembered my overdrawn bank account.

A few more minutes and I gave the high-sign to our new

compadres.

There have been times in my life when I thought of doing mad, wild things—get back at someone things, revenge things. I think everyone fantasizes about doing something like that. But I'd never actually done anything really crazy.

Our plan was not mean or hurtful. More like silly and childish and... what were we thinking! ·

Mac and his date continued to sit at their table looking like they were having about as much fun as someone waiting to be called for a colonoscopy. Apparently their dart team buddies had yet to show up.

At the appointed moment, someone put *Old Time Rock 'n Roll* on the jukebox. Josh swaggered over to Rosie, took her hand, and swung her to her feet. "Babe!" he called in a loud, drunken voice. "Rosie, my darling, dance with me!" He swept her around the tables causing enough commotion that everyone in the bar noticed, including Mac. His date glanced up briefly, then went back to examining her sipping her pink wine.

Josh tipped Rosie back. Her face was red and glowing. She smiled seductively. When they were positioned close enough to Mac that he couldn't miss the show, Josh said, "Man, Rosie, you are soooooo hot!" Then he kissed her long and hard.

"Get a room!" Josh's buddies bellowed, hooting and hollering.

Mac finally clued in. I couldn't hear above the ruckus but saw his mouth form *Rosie?*

I gathered our purses, readying for a quick exit.

Another serious smooch and Rosie came up for air, then pretended to notice Mac for the first time. "Hi, Mac!"

"My ex," Rosie mouthed to Josh.

Josh looked at Mac, incredulous. "You let this hot woman go?"

Mac started to stand. "Rosie..."

The cheerleader shot Mac a look that could have melted glass.

"We've got places to be if you know what I mean," Josh said with an eyebrow waggle. He scooped Rosie up, her long legs dangling over his arm. Then he carried her out the door, his friends hollering after him.

I inconspicuously followed.

The night had gotten cold with a damp chill in the air. In the parking lot, Josh set Rosie down and smiled his prize-winning smile. "That was kinda fun!"

The three of us locked eyes and burst out laughing.

"But seriously," he said. "You <u>are</u> hot. If that guy can't see it, he's not for you."

Maybe jocks do grow up. I thought of my brother and wasn't so sure.

Josh waved goodbye as his buddies filed from the building and climbed into an old green Camaro, their wallets padded for drinks at some other bar.

Rosie and I looked at each other and cracked up again. We laughed and laughed until our eyes watered and my gut felt like I'd just done 100 sit-ups.

"That was ridiculous." Rosie hugged me. "But thanks, Kaitlyn. Thanks a lot. I needed that."

"Me too! I haven't laughed so hard in ages. I guess we both take life too seriously sometimes."

"Yeah, I guess we do."

I hugged her tight.

"You okay to drive?" she asked.

I nodded. "That sobered me up."

"Look out, here he comes!" Rosie and I ducked behind my car. Mac pushed out of the bar with an tight, strained look on his face.

His Barbie Doll girlfriend followed behind and looking hot and bothered. The wind whipped at her perfect blond hair, flinging strands across her face. "Mackey," she whined. "Wait up." She tottered on her spike heels as she hurried after him.

I guess the dart tournament was a bust.

Rosie looked at me and whispered, "Mackey?" We suppressed giggles as we watched them drive away.

When we got to our cars, I noticed two vehicles parked in the far corner of the lot. Only a scattering of cars filled the spaces, and all of those were parked near the door to the bar. These two were in a dark corner without streetlights. Two figures stood face-to-face between the vehicles.

"Come on. Let's go," Rosie urged.

"Coming." I tried to peer through the dusk but the figures were too far away. One of the cars was a dark sedan that seem familiar. The other a large dark SUV. Both common in Cedar Grove.

A group of people poured from the building, laughing loudly.

When I glanced back at the cars in the dark, the drivers had disappeared, presumably back into their cars. A drug deal? I didn't like that in my city.

"Kaitlyn, what are you doing? Let's go to your house, make Margaritas, and watch Casino Royale again," Rosie said.

I nodded. "If you promise to freeze frame when he comes out of the water."

Rosie was still smiling when we drove away. My friend would be all right.

***

I woke up suddenly with my heart pounding, but my pitch-dark bedroom was silent. A thick fog clouded my brain. Vaguely I remembered my dream. Sam Evans was there. He was scrutinizing me, looking and looking. I felt exposed. Then he leaned toward me... and kissed me!

I shut my eyes and tried to return to the dream, tried to get back that luscious warm feeling of lips touching, sparks flying... I turned over and heard the wind blowing through the trees outside my window. something, probably a raccoon, scurried around outside.

But Sam... I snuggled under the covers, relaxed, and tried again to recreate the feeling. We were on the beach, the sun going down, tan skin glistening in the dusk...

BANG!

A violent explosion rattled the windows and shook the ground, a flash momentarily lit my bedroom window. I sat up straight in bed and glanced at the clock—two AM, then threw back the blankets and practically fell on my face trying to untangle my feet from the sheets.

CHAPTER 8

Tuesday, September 19, 2017

"What in the hell was that?" Rosie hollered from the living room.

I threw an zip-up sweatshirt on over my sleep shirt. In the living room, Rosie was on the couch huddled under her blankets, a pillow covering her head. I hadn't let her drive home after our margarita fest.

"Kaitlyn," she croaked. "What was that? A bomb?"

I hurried to the window and pushed back the curtains so I had a clear view of the front yard. Something was burning in my driveway! Bigger than a breadbox, but smaller than a car. My Rav sat just a few feet away from the burning mass. Luckily, Rosie had parked her car on the street.

"Shit! Something's on fire by my car!" I rushed to the kitchen, snatched the phone off the counter. Sam's business card with his cell phone number sat next to the phone. But I dialed 911.

"Nine-one-one, what is your emergency," a very calm, young female voice asked.

"Help! There's something on fire in my driveway!"

"What's your address?"

I rattled off my address even though I knew they should have it on their computer screen.

"I don't know what's burning—but it's near my car. I need to move my car!"

"Just stay calm, ma'am. And don't go near it. The fire department is on the way."

Adrenaline pumped through my veins like ice water and I started to shiver. Then a sudden thought--Oh, God! Wally!

"I gotta go!" I hung up before they could ask me to stay on the line.

"I have to find Wally!" I said to Rosie as I hurried back into the living room. She lifted her head out of the covers to peer over the top of the couch.

I rushed to the front door and flung it open. Wally's box near the porch was empty. "Wally!" I yelled stupidly into the night.

"Kaitlyn! Don't go out there!" Rosie said. "And who the hell is Wally?"

"The cat!"

Several of my neighbors had come out of their houses to stare at the blaze wrapped in robes and slippers. The distant sound of a siren pierced the still night air.

Suddenly it was as if everything went to slow motion. People moved into the street, light from the fire flickering on their faces. I noticed one gal had fuzzy lion heads on her feet, another had thick combat boots under a floral nightgown.

My neighbor from across the street, I didn't know his name, came into my driveway. "A hose?" he hollered. "Do you have a hose?"

I should be someone who was more prepared. I should have a hose. I should have a fire extinguisher! I think I did, but where was it? "I'm not sure. A hose, yes, somewhere."

I looked up from my bare feet into his face. He was a nice man, dark-skinned and handsome. He played his mariachi music too loud, but otherwise was a good neighbor. I didn't know his name! What a shmuck I was!

Rosie, stood in my doorway now, her red hair sticking up in every direction. The sleep shirt I'd loaned her hit well above her knees. "What should we do?" she said.

My next door neighbor, a grumpy old retiree named Walter, pulled his hose over the fence between our houses, then shot water toward the blaze.

"Do you know who did this?" the across-the-street neighbor asked.

I shook my head. "What is it?" I said.

"Looks like maybe a garbage sack or something. Your trash can is overturned. I don't know what the bang was."

I thought about the empty tequila bottle we'd put in the garbage last night. Great accelerant if any was left in the bottom. "I should move my car."

Where were my keys? Should I drive on the grass to move my car? I could hear the sirens getting louder and louder, then a fire truck swung around the corner.

The firemen jumped from the truck, their bulky pants and large boots making them look like cartoon characters with overly thick arms and legs.

They efficiently wielded hoses and worked on the burning pile, which began to look smaller and less threatening as I watched. Black smoke curled up from the soggy mass and fingers of smoke trailed around my yard. The smell was overpowering, dank and sour. My bare legs and feet started to get cold. I sent Rosie back inside to make hot water for tea.

After a bit, things settled down. Neighbors wandered back into their homes. I convinced myself Wally had run for cover

149

and was just hiding out.

A police car had pulled up during the put-out. Now, a uniformed officer spoke with the fire fighters then headed toward me. It was Brad. "Hey, Kaitlyn," he said with a sympathetic smile. "It looks like it was an elaborate prank. A bag of garbage was lit on fire but didn't have much fuel we can see, except maybe something from the trash. The explosion was a flash-bang. Noise, sonic boom and a bright light, but definitely not damaging. We've used them to clear rooms during drug raids. Think it was just lit for the startle factor in case you didn't notice the fire."

I rubbed my eyes. "Startled me alright. I could have gone back to a perfectly good dream—" I quickly shut my mouth when he looked at me funny.

Brad continued, "Can you think of anyone who would play this kind of joke on you?"

"I'm a city employee. Other than a resident upset with his citation, I don't know who would've done something like this," I said without conviction. I wrapped my arms across my chest, suddenly feeling exposed. I'd put on a sweatshirt but no bra. A gust of wind blew down the block, spreading the foul smelling smoke through my clothes and hair. I thought about the threatening note I'd received. Could this be related? Should I say something?

"How would someone get hold of one of those... flash-bang things?" I asked.

"There are ways," Brad said rolling his eyes. "The Internet..."

"But why would someone have one?"

He shrugged. "Maybe he just gets off on scaring people."

We talked a bit more, but since I had nothing to add, Brad and the firefighters soon left. They took away the burned sack, but a dark black stain remained on the concrete.

The night was again silent. Suddenly I realized how cold I was. I wrapped my arms around my body. Where was Wally? Probably in the next county after that flash bang thing.

I went back inside. Rosie had tea waiting for me. She was dressed.

"I'm up and sober. I might was well go home."

I snuggled onto the couch, covering my cold legs with the blanket and savoring the hot steam coming from my mug. "You sure?"

"Yeah." She sat next to me. Her mug full of coffee. "I have to be at work in the morning any way."

We sat in silence a few moments, savoring our drinks. Then I told her what Brad had said.

"Who do you think did it?" she said, her voice wavering.

I shook my head. "Probably an unhappy resident."

"You don't think it was Mac, do you?"

That stopped me. I hadn't even considered him. But it didn't fit. "If we were at your house, maybe. But it doesn't seem like something he'd do, does it?"

"No." She seemed relieved. "No, it doesn't seem like him at all. He's kind of a wimp." She paused. "That means someone is pissed at you and they know where you live."

We let that lovely thought hang in the air.

Rosie finished off her tea and set her mug in the kitchen sink. "It was a great night," she said. "Sorry it had to end like this."

I got up and hugged her and watched her until she got to her car and drove away.

As I sipped the rest of my tea, I ran through all that had happened since I'd found the animals and the body. I'd talked to Mary Wyman and her husband, Randall. I'd talked to slimy Stanley, and his cookies and cream wife, Estelle. I'd met Rhonda Madden and, along with Sam, talked to Dave Madden. It didn't seem like any of them had said anything related to the murder. But someone, maybe someone named Carlos, was dead. Who was he anyway?

I'd also talked to the landscaping crew. Well, sort of. Since I didn't speak Spanish I hadn't understood much of what they said. I made a leap to believe that Carlos was a member of their crew and based on their reaction I was right. Even if he was, what did it mean? Just that he had a reason to be in the neighborhood. But why kill a landscaper?

He must have known something or found out something. He got dead. I'd been snooping around and had been threatened—a burning sack of garbage in my driveway was a very real threat. What did I know? How did I figure out what I knew if I didn't know what it was? My head hurt from too much alcohol, smoke from the fire, and not enough sleep.

I needed to solve this murder. The police were working on it, but they didn't have a personal stake in the outcome. And suddenly, it felt very personal. I needed to find out who had killed this guy who might be named Carlos and why. It was the only way to get back my sanity and my safety. If the perpetrator was locked up, I couldn't be threatened, right?

A faint howl drifted on the air followed by a scratching noise. Not scary or creepy, just sad. Wally!

I jumped out of bed, ran to the front door and flung it open. Wally sat on the porch. "Yeeeeow!"

"Yeah, it scared the shit out of me too," I said. "You hungry?"

Wally tilted his head and looked at me. I figured he had no interest in my house. Then he flicked his tail.

I went inside, filled a bowl of dry food, and returned to the porch. I set the bowl next to Wally's box.

He looked up at me again with his head cocked to one side. Then, as if he'd lived here all his life, he dug in to the food, his crunching echoing in the dark night.

"Well, okay then."

I went back to bed but sleep was a long time coming.

***

The events of the previous evening left me exhausted. I woke up with a brutal headache—a combo of a hangover, stress, and sleep deprivation—a doozy. Getting out of bed proved a challenge, about like me climbing Mt. Everest. I rolled off the bed and dropped my feet to the floor. Wrenching my eye lids open, was painful, it felt like they were full of grit and sand. In the bathroom mirror, my eyes looked like deep caverns. My hair smelled like burnt cabbage. I popped three extra-strength Tylenol, downed a bottle of water, and called Cheryl. I said I had car trouble and would be in late. I don't think she believed me.

In addition to physical pain, I felt unsettled. Why me? Why my driveway? I took a long, long shower, which helped my mood considerably. I still looked like a zombie *The Walking Dead*, but a clean zombie. I dressed in my comfortable jeans and a soft pink sweater over a white tank that gave the illusion it might still be summer. I shuffled to the kitchen on a mission for coffee. I also rooted in the cabinets for breakfast. A two-week-old box of cereal and plain toast was all I could find—perfect since that was all I thought my stomach could handle.

Wally was curled in his box when I left home. "See you later," I said as I left a small bowl of dry food on the porch.

***

I got into work about ten o'clock. I tried to sneak by Cheryl, but she magically ended her call just as I was passing her counter. "Get your car fixed?" she said, watermelons bobbing in her ears.

"Ah, hah. Just needed a jump." I started to turn away then waited. "Any word on my work truck?"

"I got a call from the repair shop. They'll drop it by here at the end of the day."

"Great." I hurried to my desk before she could ask any more questions about me and my car. The rest of the office barely noticed my late arrival.

I got coffee from the kitchen and tried to settle into work, but I couldn't concentrate on code enforcement. I popped two more Tylenol (it had been three hours), spun around in my chair

153

like a top, and thought about the last week.

My life, before I walked into that backyard, had been simple and calm. I vowed to never again break the rules. But at the same time I realized I'd been living a very safe life. There'd been a time I had been a risk taker. I'd been spontaneous and adventurous. But since my divorce, I'd kept a tight rein on life, a slow gait, maybe a little trot, but never a gallop. Not letting the horse veer off the path, so to speak.

What I thought was me controlling my life, was really life controlling me. The crazy stunt with Rosie had felt exhilarating, as if the fun part of me I'd hidden away finally poked its head out. I'd let my hurt turn into a lack of confidence. Finding those animals, that body, was the world trying to run me off my path, out of the safe zone.

But I could be in charge. I was in charge. Whoever tried to threaten me didn't know they'd unleashed a monster. I was determined to get the old Kaitlyn back. No, a new and improved Kaitlyn, who took chances, confronted conflict and solved murders!

Start small, I thought. I picked up the phone and dialed Ben's cell, half wondering if he'd changed his number. Or if his phone had been cut off for non-payment.

"Yo."

"Yo? Ben, it's Kaitlyn."

"So I guessed. Caller ID said *City of Cedar Grove.*"

"I'm calling about…"

"How've you been?" His voice was cheery, pleasant, nothing wrong.

"I'm fine. No wait. I'm not fine, I'm pissed."

"Of course you are."

"My bank account is overdrawn by over a thousand dollars! I have no money."

I heard a can top open. I hoped it was pop, not beer, since it as only 11 in the morning. "Do you remember why I'm overdrawn?" I said.

Swig. "You've taken up gambling?"

Divorced just over a year and he could still get a rise out of me. "Because the Department of Revenue sucked my account dry. Does this ring any bells?" I didn't give him time to spout a snide answer. "All because you didn't pay your taxes on some business that you started while we were married and now they've come after me. Are you not working?"

"I am. I'm running an espresso stand."

"You're what?"

"Too cool, huh? Here's the best part. The gals serving the drinks all wear skimpy bikinis! Business is through the roof. I'm thinking of expanding."

"I thought that was illegal," I said shaking my head.

"It's still in the courts."

"Well, if you're doing so well with your bikini baristas, why don't you pay the Department of Revenue?"

"Profits are good, but they go back into the business you know and…"

"Ben, I need to be paid--in full--by Friday, one thousand two hundred and seventy three dollars, plus two-hundred dollars to cover just a small portion of the bank fees I'm being charged."

"Kaitlyn, come on," he whined. "Hey! You should come work for me! With your rack, you'd rake in the tips!"

I sighed. "Friday, Ben. I have zero money in the meantime so I'm really being generous."

He tried to speak, but I cut him off. "If you don't show up with cash in hand by Friday before four pm, I'm sic-ing the Health Department and the *Mothers Against Public Shows of Skin* over to your little slut stand. Then I'll call the cops to follow you around. They'll find some reason to pick you up. How current are your car tabs? I'll find out who you're dating and tell her you have a number of ugly diseases." My voice rose and I saw a couple of heads pop up from other cubes.

"Kaitlyn, honey…"

"Don't," I whispered. He must have taken my change in tone

as forgiveness.

"So, K. How are you? Why don't we get together tonight and you know, catch up?"

"You're kidding, right?"

"No. We were good together. Let's just spend an evening and see if the old flame can be relit. I've got a can of whipped cream."

"Ben, grow up. Get a job and leave me alone."

"Ah, Kaitlyn…"

"Friday, Ben. Fourteen hundred seventy three dollars by Friday or life as you know it will be a living hell."

"Where am I gonna get that kind of cash?"

"Take up gambling."

"Come on."

"Maybe your bikini babes can throw a car wash. Fourteen seventy-three by Friday. Goodbye." I stabbed the END button and slammed down my phone.

The exchange sent my blood pressure soaring. My temples pounded with each beat of my racing heart. I swear I felt blood rushing through my veins. Fight or flight. I was ready to fight the next person who spoke to me.

Grant's head popped up over the cubicle. "Personal problems?"

"None of your bees wax."

"Can you at least tell me where the bikini baristas are?"

I rolled my eyes at him, but I doubt he saw or appreciated the gesture. How to better use the energy? I dug through my purse and came up with Sam's business card. I punched in his number and jammed the receiver to my ear. *Calm down before you speak.* I heard my mother's voice. *Don't lash out in anger.* She hadn't said anything about lashing out in lust.

"Sam Evans." The deep voice sent a chill through my body, to my toes, and back up to other bodily regions.

"Hi." I kept my voice soft and calm. "This is Kaitlyn Willis."

"Kaitlyn, hello." He sounded surprised. That was good. Catch him off guard.

"I was wondering if you'd like to go out for a drink tonight."
Pause.

Shit, shit, shit. My temples reminded me the last thing I needed was another drink.

"Well, I guess I could do that. What did you have in mind?" In mind? I had nothing in mind. I was being spontaneous. I blurted out the name of one of the few nice restaurants in our city—The Grove.

"Let's get out of the city where we both work, okay?" he said. "How about something in Seattle?"

Calm. Seductive. How did one talk seductive? I was out of practice. "Ah, sure. That would be great."

"How about I pick you up at home around seven?"

His voice was so sexy. "Sure." Right then he could have asked to suck my blood and I'd have said *sure.*

I suddenly felt ridiculous. After all, I wasn't some high-schooler with their first crush. And he was a cop who may or may not think I had something to do with a murder.

"All right," he said. "See you later,"

"Bye." I ended the call and felt dizzy. I gulped air and tried to slow my breathing.

"You okay, Kaitlyn?" Sharon must have come back in. She filled the opening to my cube, which at the moment felt very small and claustrophobic.

I nodded, unable to speak.

She stepped in and swirled my chair around to face her. "You look pale. Put your head between your knees."

I followed orders, mostly because she smashed her hand down on the back of my head and pushed. Blood drained down to my brain and I felt like I could breathe again. But the pounding in my temples rushed back. I noticed Sharon was wearing animal print ballet flats on her size 11 feet.

"Did you kill a leopard?" I asked sitting upright again.

"Huh? Girl, what is wrong with you? Should we call 911?"

"I asked a guy out."

She looked at me with a quizzical expression. "Good for you."

"A cop."

"Huh. A little close to home but not bad."

"A cop who might think I killed someone."

"What? Girl, you talkin' crazy. Anyone who knows you knows you'd never kill someone."

That stopped me. I stared at her. Her shirt under her CG jacket matched her shoes. "Why not?"

"Why not? Honey, you're way too controlled, kinda uptight. Besides, I ain't never seen you mad enough to even hit somebody, much less kill em'."

"Am I really that boring?"

"Did I say boring? No, I did not. You're just—careful."

I sighed. "I'd like to kill my ex-husband, but then I'd never get my money back."

"Grant said you was exchanging words with someone about money."

I frowned.

"This ain't the most private place for personal calls. Besides, I came by to tell you Richter's got Councilman Newman in his office, and when they're done, he wants to see you."

"I better get outta here." I was not in the mood for talking to my boss. I began to gather my things. "What am I going to do?"

"About Richter?"

"About my date!"

"Go have fun! Have a drink or two and get a good dinner out of it."

I stood up. "Right. I can do this. I can have fun. I'm fun, right?"

"A barrel of laughs, sista."

Sharon hugged me quickly. "Now scram before boss-man comes callin'."

I threw on my vest. Then grabbed everything from my IN

box and stuffed it into my bag thinking I could sort through it in the truck. "Thanks, Sharon." I headed for the door.

She called after me. "I expect a full report tomorrow! All the luscious details! Us married women have to live vicariously through you single gals."

I turned back to wave and saw Marcus peering over the cube at us.

"What're you looking at," Sharon said to him.

***

The day had started cloudy and gray. However, in the way of the Northwest, by afternoon it took a hard right and was sunny and warm. The radio weatherman predicted drizzle overnight with a downpour tomorrow. Tease us with sun then back to rain.

Old Yeller was being cooperative today so I stopped at Little Caesars for a mini pepperoni and olive lunch. Before I ate, I turned off the ringer on my cell phone in case Richard tried to track me down. Avoiding my boss was probably a bad idea, for sure a bad idea. But I needed to sort out my attitude.

Feeling better, I took a quick cruise around the city in my yellow submarine. Not very subtle, but what the hell. Several of the homes on the west side of town had yard signs in favor of redevelopment: "An *improved Cedar Grove is good for all.*" "*Say yes to redevelopment.*" And even more creative ones: "*Don't be stuck in the past--redevelop now.*"

I parked Old Yeller in the lot next to Lowell King Park and killed the engine. I couldn't remember who Lowell King was, somehow important to the city. Tall evergreens surrounded an open grassy area perfect for a game of Frisbee. The play equipment, with red and white striped poles, was the reason many residents referred to the recreation area as Candy Cane Park. The swing set and slide were doing a brisk business with toddlers, as stay-at-home moms took advantage of the September sunshine.

I took a Diet Sprite from my cooler and rolled down the window to enjoy the fresh fall air. With a big sigh, I tackled my in-box detritus, ripping open envelopes and discarding junk mail. I placed the violation-related items in a pile and moved the paper I could recycle off to one side. At the bottom of the stack, was the city's newsletter I'd ignored a few days earlier. I pulled out my phone and made note of the flu shot day on my calendar.

I flipped past the City Manager Iles's column and tips for packing healthy lunches. I stopped at the center section featuring photos of various city departments and employees. Being featured was not always a good thing depending on the photographer and the mood of the City Manager's Assistant who put the publication together. Sharon had the misfortune to have been snapped at the summer picnic gnawing on a giant chicken leg. Cheryl had been prominently featured in the February Valentine issue after she wore giant heart earrings the size of a small country. She had a strange frozen grimace on her face.

I half expected a photo of first aid training, me with my butt in the air. Instead there were pictures from various community meetings relating to the redevelopment. They showed happy citizens standing around eating cookies and admiring presentation boards featuring the redevelopment plan. It included several shots centered on a smiling Councilman Newman.

One photo caught my eye. A good-looking Hispanic man was photographed from the side peering intently at one of the boards. He wore jeans and a tight black t-shirt. It was only a three-quarter shot, but still, one never forgets a face, especially the face of the first dead body you've ever seen. The man in the photo was the dead guy from the Maddens' yard! The caption on the photo said: "Citizens review redevelopment plans on August 20th at Sunrise Middle School."

Yes! I pumped the air. A clue. A real clue! Or it could be, after I tracked down the photographer so I could find out the dead man's name. Make sure it was Carlos.

This was good. If I confirmed who he was, I could find out more about him and that might lead me to why he died. Know the victim, right?

When I finished sorting the mail it was almost two o'clock. I'd managed to piss away most of the day. I called and checked in with Cheryl. Finally, good news. My truck was back so I headed to my last couple of complaints.

The pounding in my temples had subsided into a weak ache, but my gut clenched every time I thought of the evening ahead. What had I done? What possessed me to call Sam Evans? A momentary mental breakdown caused by stress from my ex-husband.

Well, damn. I'd asked Sam out. Did that mean I should pay for dinner? Me of the overdrawn bank account? I needed to find out if I could pull money from my savings to cover my negative balance. I hated to and for sure didn't want to touch my CD. I really wasn't counting on Ben coming though.

I called city hall and asked for the City Manager's assistant, Melinda Golden. Melinda was the *golden girl* of the city. The City Manager gave her a lot of power and she took charge of anything she could and was rewarded for it. Her desk served as the hub of city gossip. She was a bit stuck up and not a fan of Public Works but was a darn good gate-keeper for the City Manager. I got her voice mail.

"Hey, Melinda. This is Kaitlyn Willis from Code Enforcement. I've got a question about the last city newsletter. Can you give me a call?" I gave my cell phone number. "On page 10 there are some photos from the redevelopment meetings. Can you tell me who shot them? Or if you have sign in lists from the event that match up against the photos? Thanks."

Who knew if she'd call back. If she did, I'd need a good story as to why I needed the info. The truth would send her running straight to her boss, who would go to my boss...

I drove by a few houses and made note of the cleanup results of previous citations. Most had been taken care of, although one would require another chat with the homeowner. But not today. I wasn't in the mood.

I headed back to city hall about four-thirty. Through the glass front doors, I saw Councilman Newman loitering in the Public Works lobby. He couldn't still be looking for me, could he? That question was answered when he practically attacked me the minute I entered.

"Ms. Willis, I've been trying to reach you."

I had no messages from him. Wonder how he defined trying.

"I've been working." I smiled, hoping I didn't sound as snide as I felt.

Theodore Newman was tall, six feet three at least. His close-cropped gray hair was always looked perfect. His intense eyes and odd smile, along with his height, gave him an advantage over others. I could never figure out how he continued to get re-elected. But, thankfully, this was his last stint in office due to term limits. He was one of the biggest proponents of the redevelopment of Cedar Grove. I think he saw it as his legacy. Probably hoping they'd name a street after him.

"I need a few minutes of your time," he said.

Not an invitation but an order. Cheryl watched us and I turned to her and said in my sweetest voice, "Is the conference room available?"

Newman cut her off before she could answer. "Mr. Richter has offered his office."

Great. This felt like an inquisition already. "Uh, sure."

We marched past John and Marcus who were entering the lobby as we headed toward the offices. They eyed me suspiciously. I shrugged and followed Newman toward my boss's office.

Richard Richter, befitting his title as Director of Public Works, had a nice-sized office with windows overlooking some greenery planted between buildings. The walls were adorned with photos of Richter golfing with Seattle celebrities, sports players, local politicos, and the previous Snohomish County

Sheriff. The room included a small round conference table with four chairs. I dropped into one of these, hoping Newman wouldn't sit behind the desk. I felt intimidated enough when Richard sat there. My boss was nowhere to be seen at the moment.

I wondered what this *meeting* was all about. It wasn't unheard of, a councilperson talking to city staff. It happened all the time, though not usually at my lowly level and not in private.

Newman hesitated before he chose the chair opposite me at the table. He took a moment to settle in, his gaze held on my face. "Ms. Willis, I want to talk to you about the homicide that you… discovered."

I said nothing, waiting to uncover the point of the meeting.

"Feel free to take off your work vest, get comfortable."

"I'm fine." No way was I giving him a look at my boobs.

He cleared his throat, shifted sideways, and crossed his legs. "Have you been contacted by any media about this case?"

"The local stations were at the scene and I've received a several messages with requests to speak, but I haven't called anyone back."

"I'm sure you remember the agreement you signed when you became employed. It's against city policy for you to talk to the media."

"I haven't forgotten, sir. Like I said, I haven't returned any of the calls."

"We've been getting a lot of calls at city hall and the AP wire picked up the story about the companion animal hoarding, so there's been interest in that as well."

The picketers, with their "no euthanizing" signs, would be a great human interest story for the AP. I could see why it was getting attention. "I won't speak to them," I said. "Is there anything else?"

He looked out the window. So casual. "Were you questioned by the police?"

I hesitated, wanting to say the right thing. I hadn't even

brought Richard up to speed yet.

Newman's sunken eyes narrowed as he turned back to me.

"I gave my statement. Then went back to provide clarification and answer additional questions." Oh, I could talk politic language too!

He glared at me. No longer trying for the friendly approach. "And you would not be trying to conduct your own investigation, would you?"

Interesting. Where would he have gotten that thought?

"I've only done the follow-up required to complete my code enforcement report and citation," I said.

"Ah, hah."

I had the urge to squirm under his gaze but made every effort to stay still, breathing deep and purposefully like they taught us in yoga class. I smiled again just to show I was still friendly and not intimidated by his questions.

"Stay out of the way of the police. Let them do their job." He looked down at his finger nails then up to my chest. "Your report is complete now, I assume?"

"Just about. I'm waiting on the homeowners cleanup plan."

"Ms. Willis, your employment here is as code enforcement only."

What the hell? Had someone been tattling on me? "Sir, I don't know who you've spoken to, but I am only doing my job. That's all."

"And what about the incident at your residence?"

So he knew about that too. "The police believe it was a teenage prank."

Just then the door opened and Richard strode in. "Hello. Hello."

Newman stood.

"How are things going here?" Richard asked.

I stood. "I think we're just wrapping up, aren't we?"

Newman eyed me. "I think we are," he said in a guarded tone. "Remember what I said."

"Back to work then," I said brightly and escaped into the hall, my hands shaking and my heart beating wildly.

CHAPTER 9

Wednesday, September 20, 2017

After hurriedly finishing paperwork at my desk, I packed up my things and called Cheryl.

"Is the lobby clear?" I whispered.

"Huh?" she said.

"Is Newman gone?"

"He left about ten minutes ago."

I breathed a sigh of relief. "What about Richard?"

"He left with Newman. What's up, Kaitlyn?"

"Nothing." I returned my voice to a normal level. "I just want to go home."

She snorted disgustedly. "I've got the report you wanted. The one you were in such a hurry for."

Damn. I'd forgotten all about it. "Thanks. Really, that's great. I'll grab it on the way out." I wanted to add, "don't tell anyone I asked for it," but Cheryl wasn't a gossip and had no love for

Melinda Golden or Newman.

"A call's coming in." She hung up.

I scuttled out of the office, grabbed the report from Cheryl, and ran to my car. I had a big night ahead and I needed to get ready. It was a relief to be back in my Rav4 after a day in the yellow attention-getter.

On the drive home, my phone rang. I pulled into the library's parking lot and answered. "Hi, Kaitlyn," Rosie said with yawn.

"You just waking up from a nap?"

"Yeah. After last night, I needed to rest."

I laughed. "I should have stayed in bed myself." I told her about my visit with Newman.

"Geez cheeze, Kaitlyn. What'd you do? Bad luck is following you like the pretty girl in a horror movie."

"I didn't do anything! I'm a good person." I said hoping to convince myself.

"You are a great person. Most people don't know what a great person you are," Rosie said. "Thanks again for last night."

"That seems like a long time ago."

"Does Newman think you were involved in the murder?" I heard the rattle of a package ripping open. "Does he think you had something to do with it?" She crunched on what sounded like potato chips.

I leaned back against the headrest. "Someone has been telling him what I've been doing. He even knew about the fire at my house last night."

"Who told him?"

"Dunno."

Pause. Crunch. "Is he involved?"

"Newman?" That was something I hadn't considered. Could he have been involved in the murder? "I don't see how. Or why?"

Crunch. "Take care of yourself," Yawn. "This is getting kind of scary."

"It'll be okay. I haven't done anything." A thick gray cloud slid in front of the sun and the sky got darker, all around me things fell into shadow.

"Stay home tonight and lock your door," she said.

"Well, actually… I have a date."

"What!" Rosie broke into a hacking cough, like she choked on her snack. "A date? With who?"

"Sam Evans."

"The sexy detective!"

"Yes," I said.

"Holy Brioche! How did it happen?"

"I sort of asked him. I just blurted it out. I don't know what came over me."

Rosie laughed. "Dang, girl. Last night, then this. You're really coming out of your shell."

"I think I've gone crazy." I sighed. "And I'm tired."

"You'll catch a second wind. You call me tonight with all the dirty details."

"Okay."

"I'll be waiting up for a report."

I groaned.

"Kaitlyn on a date. Wow. Just take care," she said and hung up.

***

I drove the rest of the way home. As I climbed out of the car, a large figure blocked my path. "Shit!" I jumped back and banged my elbow on the car door.

"Sorry. Didn't mean to scare you." It was my neighbor from across the street.

I shook off the startle. "No worries. Sorry, I'm a bit on edge."

"I wanted to check on you," he said. "After last night. That was kinda weird,"

"Very." I leaned against my car feeling exhausted. The darkening sky swirled with clouds now, blocking all traces of the sun. I wanted to get inside before it rained.

"We haven't officially met. My friends call me GC." He held out his hand.

GC was average height solidly built. He had dark eyes, but they were warm and seemed kind. His jeans looked well lived in. He wore a hooded pull-on sweatshirt with a Washington State University logo on the front. *Go Cougs.* His curly black hair stuck out from under a Seattle Mariners baseball cap.

I'd never chatted with the neighbors across the street. My fault I'm sure. I get caught up in my own life. "Hi, GC. I'm Kaitlyn."

He paused.

I took a deep breath and put all my energy into staying upright.

It seemed GC had something else on his mind. I didn't have the energy to coax it out of him. "What's GC stand for?"

"George Carlin." He chuckled. "My mom was a fan." He paused then blurted, "Do you know who set the fire?"

"No. The police don't have many ideas either."

"Do you know why?" He fidgeted, shifting from one foot to the other.

What was up with this guy? "No. The only thing I can think of is that it's related to my work. Or just kids goofing around." Was he nervous? Or just worried about the neighborhood was being targeted? Great. My neighbors would hate me over this. "I'm sure it won't happen again," I said. "I'm so sorry it woke everyone up."

He shrugged. "I don't sleep much anyway." Pause. "You found some dead guy too, right?"

I guess everyone heard the news. "Yes. Unfortunately."

"Do they know who it was?"

Hmmm. Why was he interested? "The police probably do. I was just there on a code complaint. The police..."

"But you saw him, right?" GC's voice caught.

Suddenly the guy seemed like he was about to cry. Should I

offer him water? I turned toward my house. I opened my mouth to offer him a drink, but he jumped in.

"I'm pretty sure it was *mi primo.*"

"Cousin?" I knew a bit of Spanish, just a bit.

"The guy who was killed. I think it was my cousin Carlos, but..."

"I'm so sorry." I didn't know what else to say.

"The fire last night, tryin' to scare you? Why? Do you know?" I shook my head. "I don't I know anything, really I don't."

"But you work for the city, right?"

He knew a bit about me or saw my work truck at home a few times. "Yes I do."

"You could find out what's up with the dead guy?"

"That's not really my area, just code enforcement."

"But you can find stuff out, *sí?*"

"The police..."

GC shook his head and he face got red. "They won't tell us nothin'. My wife, she is very upset." He looked across the street at his house. "You find out what's happenin', who they suspect."

"Why do you think it was your cousin? What would he have been doing there?"

"He was a landscaper, he musta had a job there, and..."

"And?" Now I was curious.

"He had... friends there."

I eyed him. He was acting cagy.

He shifted uncomfortably and looked away.

"If you know something you should go to the police," I said quickly tiring of this.

"I tried, man." He removed his cap and ran his hand through his curly hair. "This big guy, he met with me, but he was a *cabron.* He didn't listen. He thought I was involved."

"Detective Sheehan, right?"

"Yeah. You know him?"

I shook my head feeling the fire incident and the hell of the last few days weighing me down like a concrete block. "I met with him too." I inched toward my door feeling cornered. "What did you want the police to know?"

"Carlos, he was a *mujeriego*. He thought making it with white women made him *muy macho*."

"A playboy? Think he was having an affair with someone on that street?"

"That's what he bragged about. You think that's why he was killed? A *carbon*, a jealous husband?"

"I don't know." I thought for a moment. "What about the animals? Could Carlos have been involved in that?"

"Carlos was a *tirón*. Didn't care about animals, but he didn't deserve to die like that," GC stuffed his hands in his jean pockets. "He had six kids."

Six? *Shit.* I shifted my purse to the other shoulder. That felt wrong so I dropped it to the ground. Maybe if I just laid down right there under the carport I'd feel better.

"Can you find out what's going on?" His eyes were dark and pleading.

"But the police..."

"The police don't care. He was Latino!"

"I don't think they'd dismiss it because of that."

GC frowned and shook his head. "You're kiddin', right?"

I thought of Grant's comments at lunch about drugs and gangs. Discrimination was everywhere.

"Just please see what you can find out. For my wife."

I felt stuck and so tired. "Okay, sure. I don't know what I can do, but I'll try."

"*Gracias,* thank you." He glanced away, started, and jumped sideways. Wally sat on the sidewalk staring up at him. Wally's rear end spread out over half of the walkway. "*Mierda!*"

"That's just Wally."

"Didn't know you had a cat. It is a cat, right?"

I shrugged.

"Nice kitty," GC said in a skittish voice. He stepped around Wally, walked on the grass, and turned down the driveway.

"*Gracias,*" he said again, then scurried across the street to his house. He turned back and waved before he went inside.

***

After that *discussion*, I hurried inside tired and just feeling *off.* What did GC really want? I grabbed a Diet Sprite and settled on the couch. I had plenty of time to get ready for my first date in over a year, right? Recharge my batteries for a few.

At six forty, I stretched, looked at the clock, and panicked! Damn, only twenty minutes to get ready! No time to be undecided about what to wear. I threw on clean jeans, black ballet flats, a black t-shirt, and an army-green blazer. It didn't close in front, but it hung forward just enough to camouflage my chest. I spent the rest of the time on hair and make-up and by seven I was as ready as I would ever be.

I paced across my living room, straightened magazines on the coffee table, clipped the wicks on burned candles, and organized the stack of newspapers in my recycle bin. I paced the kitchen, anxiety swirling in my gut like a hundred moths swarming a light.

At seven ten, I'd progressed to using packing tape to lift lint off the couch. I surveyed my small space and felt suddenly nervous about my mismatched furniture. I wondered if Sam would come inside and what he'd think of my simple lifestyle.

Back in the bathroom, I resisted the urge to curl my hair again. I touched up my lipstick and went back into the living room. My driveway was still dark.

He wasn't coming. I'd gotten all dressed up for nothing. My stomach rumbled. I hadn't eaten since my pizza lunch, which really wasn't all that long ago, but my hangover had finally abated and left me famished.

I stepped out onto the porch. Dark had quietly overtaken the sky, washing it in an inky gray. Street lights glowed pinkish-yellow in the dusk. My porch light lit the walkway. In his box by the door, Wally had curled up to sleep, his head tucked under his paws, looking like a fluffy white pillow.

"How can you sleep at a time like this?" I said.

A white paw slid down revealing one dark green eye.

"Yes, I'm talking to you," I told Wally. "He's not coming. I shouldn't have gotten all worked up."

Wally gave me a one-eyed glare like he wondered when I'd leave so he could return to his nap.

"Where are you from? Why are you here?" I asked him. "I'm not very good with people. And I don't know what to do with a pet. Why did you choose me?"

I'd thought about that. I was good with my customers. Good at my job as Code Enforcement Officer. It was a nice and predictable job, form filled out, boxes checked off, reports written and filed. At the end of the day there was satisfaction in that. Why did that feeling of confidence evaporate when I left work? Why did I struggle with relationships? Was Wally sent to me as a test?

There was no response from the white Cyclops pillow. I squatted down. Wally lifted his head slightly.

"Did you see what happened in that yard? Do you know who killed Carlos?" I wondered if he would let me pet him, but I decided not to chance it. "Damn, I wish you could talk."

Wally's head tilted to one side, then he stood up suddenly, his back arched and hissed.

His movement startled me. I tipped back and fell on my butt, just as headlights swept into my driveway. I scrambled to my feet and brushed dirt off my rear.

A dark non-descript sedan, like every other Honda or Toyota, stopped behind my car. When the door opened, the dome light came on and illuminated Sam Evans in the driver's seat. My heart quickened and I sucked in a breath along with a bug.

I coughed and cleared my throat as Sam walked to my front door. "Hi," I croaked.

"Hi."

Damn. That deep toe-tingling voice got to me even with only one word.

"You need anything before we go?" he asked.

"Nope, I'm good."

He looked good in the dusk, his hair slightly shiny as if it was damp.

"Sorry I'm late. I got caught up at work."

"No problem. You found where I live...."

"A perk of the job." He smiled. His eyes moved down and I felt a moment of panic. Don't be one of those! Don't look at my boobs! But his gaze continued to the ground where Wally was weaving around his feet. "That is one huge cat!"

"Yeah, that's Wally."

Sam knelt down and scratched Wally behind the ears. Wally acted like it was the most natural thing in the world.

Sam wore crisp dark jeans--not the kind you've worn a thousand times and washed over and over. Was he trying to impress me? They fit good over his strong body. Really good. Under a deep indigo jacket, he wore a light blue button-up shirt, open at the collar.

"Some cat you've got."

"Not really mine. He kind of adopted me."

He continued to scratch Wally's head. Wally purred audibly. "I think you need to get him to be a Weight Watchers spokesperson for cats." Sam stood and smiled. The smile illuminated his eyes.

I smiled too, reflexively imitating him.

"Are you ready to go?" he asked.

"Yep. Let me grab my purse."

I opened the front door and gestured him in. Might as well let him see my home, make his judgment and get it over with. Maybe if he saw my humble abode, he'd realize I couldn't be a murderer. Maybe he'd see that I was too boring to have killed someone.

Inside, I grabbed my purse and keys from the little side table. When I clicked off the lamp, the room fell into darkness. Sam stood framed in the doorway by the porch light.

"You should leave a light on," he said. He fingered the door jam. "Your lock is pretty crummy too. You need a good dead bolt."

Cop through and through. But it said he cared, right? I clicked the light back on. Sam stepped out onto the path, waited for me to shut the door and walk ahead of him. He opened his car door for me. As he moved to close it, I saw a small gun nestled against his waist.

On the ride to Seattle, about 15 miles and usually about 15-20 minutes if there wasn't a sports event, I observed Sam from the corner of my eye. His hands gripped the wheel firmly but with his arms relaxed. They were rugged hands, worn as if he had been a blue-collar worker in a previous life or he worked with his hands in his free time. I wondered what he did in his off hours. What hobbies occupied his attention? What was he passionate about? But it wasn't the time to ask those questions.

I didn't remember ever feeling this drawn to another person. Something about his *being*, his aura, or something made me want to move closer and drink in his smell, a combination of soap, a minty shampoo and something else I couldn't place.

I suddenly realized he had asked me a question and I had been so mesmerized, I hadn't heard. "I'm sorry. I drifted off for a moment." Great. Now he thought I didn't pay attention when he spoke.

"I asked if you had been to the Purple Wine Bar before."

"No. I haven't. I don't get to Seattle much."

"I live downtown, so I walk there a lot. I think you'll like it."

Downtown. No doubt his life was much more exciting than mine. He walked places. The most exercise I ever got was from once-a-week (if I made it) yoga.

I watched the lights from Northgate Mall and North Seattle College whiz by as we continued southbound.

Sam's right hand reached toward the space between us.

Oh, crap! Did he want to hold hands?

He pulled it back quickly. "Sorry. Sometimes I forget I'm not in a police car," he said.

"What were you reaching for?"

"The computer. I was going to run the plates of the car in front of us."

"You run plates while you're driving?"

"Patrol does it all the time. Me, not so much, but it's a habit."

"Why that car?"

He shrugged. "Just cop sense, I guess."

"What's the one way you can tell if someone has been drinking."

"Easy. They drive with their windshield wipers on when it's not raining."

I chuckled. "Good to know."

The lights of Seattle twinkled around us. Cars filled the lanes on the freeway, their headlights pinging off concrete barriers. Red taillights blinked on and off all around us like a faulty string of Christmas bulbs. He checked his cell phone, propped in a suction-cup holder on the dash.

"You on-call?" I asked.

"Twenty-four/seven. I'm not up in the rotation, but you never know. Let's hope all is quiet in Cedar Grove tonight."

We crested the hill onto the Ship Canal Bridge and I could see downtown Seattle spread out to our right. The newer buildings dwarfed the well-lit Space Needle. "Do your colleagues know you're with me?" I asked.

He shrugged, noncommittal.

"Sheehan hates me."

Sam chuckled. It sounded nice. "Sheehan is suspicious of everyone. It's a cop's curse."

"But me?"

He looked over at me and flashed a flirtatious smile.

***

Inside, the wine bar was warm and crowded. Ceiling-high shelves of wine formed a square bar area in the center of the restaurant. The hostess smiled at Sam (somewhat intimately it seemed to me) and seated us right away.

We chatted as we waited to order food after we both got a glass of wine, mine white, his red. He made suggestions from the menu but let me choose. I liked that. A gentleman but not overly pushy or aggressive. A few months after my divorce a friend convinced me to go on a blind date. The guy planned everything, ordered all the food and drink for us, and barely let me say three words the entire night. He dropped almost two hundred dollars on a meal I barely touched.

We traded the usual pleasantries and a bit of our histories as we ate. I tried to take it slow, but I was nervous. I wanted this to go well, and I wanted information. Sam was originally from Southern California but came to the Northwest 15 years ago. He had been with the CG police only a few months, a transfer from Seattle.

"So did always wanted to be a cop?" I said.

"Yep. Childhood dream."

"You must be good at it if you've been on the job for over 15 years."

He smiled. It was a really great smile.

"It's a tough job," I said thinking about the way cops put their lives on the line every time they step out.

"It is, but most of the people I work with are great and I feel like I'm making a difference."

Lighten up this conversation, K. I wanted to learn more about Sam, but I was also curious to ask about the murder. I couldn't resist and I wondered if he really expected me not to bring it up.

After we got our food I asked, "Have you ever seen anything like that yard before?"

Sam twirled the wine in his glass. "I've seen quite a few deaths. Mostly natural causes. A few suicides. That yard was pretty bad."

"I'm having trouble getting those animals out of my head."

He shrugged. "I guess in my line of work we get good at not letting it get to us. Compartmentalize. You must see some nasty stuff yourself."

"Mostly inanimate objects. Mistreated cars. Lots and lots of garbage."

He chuckled.

I mentioned the fire in my driveway, but he already knew about it. "Has there been any progress in the murder investigation?" I said. "I mean, do you know who the dead guy was?"

"He's been tentatively identified, but I can't reveal his name at this stage."

I wondered if I should say something, spoil the evening with this shop talk or have him find out later I held back. He didn't seem to think I was a suspect. But Sheehan did. Maybe if I offered helpful information, he'd pass it along. "My neighbor thinks the dead man was his cousin, Carlos."

"Really?" Sam raised his eyebrows but didn't look shocked.

"Yeah. His name's GC. He lives across the street. You should talk to him."

"I think he came in to the station."

I sat up straighter. "He did! But Sheehan…"

"Sheehan's a good cop. A little rough…"

"He's an ass!" My hand flew to my mouth. I blame the wine. "Sorry."

Sam laughed.

I noticed that Sam was a slow eater. He ate lots of his vegetables and only three-quarters of his salmon. My plate of grilled chicken and garlic mashed potatoes had mysteriously disappeared. The waitress sashayed over and took our empty plates, then offered dessert. We both declined. She looked disappointed, which made me feel oddly satisfied. I had Sam's attention.

"What happened to Rhonda and Dave Madden?" I took a swig of wine, thinking a big dinner and wine on top of a lack of sleep was probably a bad combination.

He paused and seemed to be considering how much to say. "They're a pretty mixed up couple. They'll be charged with animal cruelty, but we couldn't hold them on anything. No motive for them yet. And turns out Dave has a great alibi. He's an obsessive gambler. He was on a two-day binge at a local casino. They have him on tape during the time of the murder."

"He lived in the house knowing those animals were there?"

"Seems that's how he coped with his wife's issues, letting her hold the animals. Went to quite a bit of trouble to keep the neighbors from finding out."

Should I ask the time of death? Would that be pushing it too much? Probably. "But Carlos, if he is the dead guy…"

Sam raised an eyebrow but said nothing.

"He probably found out about the animals and maybe he was going to tell," I said. "Maybe Rhonda killed him because he was going to let the animals go."

"Hold on there! Don't go doing my job." I heard light teasing in his voice. "We're checking on the other neighbors. Spent quite a bit of time with Mr. Pitowski."

"But what if…"

"We're working this case," he said more seriously. "All leads. We'll find out what happened."

I fiddled with the napkin in my lap. "I just feel like if I knew more maybe I wouldn't dream about those animals. Or the dead body."

He looked at me quizzically. "You're a pretty complex person, aren't you, Kaitlyn?"

The way he said my name made my pulse race. I smiled and my face got hot. "Just stupidly curious maybe."

Sam waved for the waitress and asked for the check. I

glanced at my watch. It was almost ten o'clock.

"One more question," I said, holding back a yawn. "And if you can't answer, just say so. Has Councilman Newman shown particular interest in this or is he in anyway related to this case?"

Sam studied me. "Why do you ask?"

"He called me to the carpet today about my involvement. Knew a lot of things, even about the incident in my driveway."

"Newman is frequently interested in our cases—as he has a right to be. He has expressed interest in this case, yes, but I figured he just wanted to latch on to the publicity it's generating." Sam paused, thoughtful.

"He thought I had talked to reporters, as if I leaked the story to the media."

"Negative publicity is a big deal for this city," Sam said.

"Maybe that's it." I said.

The waitress brought the check. Before I could even consider what to do, offer to split it? Sam had pulled the black faux-leather folder toward him, inserted his credit card and handed it back to the waitress.

"Thank you for dinner," I said, feeling slightly tipsy.

"You are a charming dinner companion," he said with a slightly flirtatious tone in that deep, deep voice.

I know I blushed again, right down to my triple D boobs.

***

I must have dozed off on the ride home. I came awake suddenly, slouched in the seat of Sam's car. Parked in my driveway. Sam was not in the car. Wasn't I a lively date.

It was dark, but the security light on my driveway illuminated two men. One leaned up against my car—no, faced my car! Was Sam hand-cuffing him? I struggled out of the unfamiliar seat belt and bolted toward them. "What's going on?" I yelled.

"Stay back, Kaitlyn. I caught this guy prowling around your house."

The man facing the car struggled. "Get this jerk off me!"

Sam held him firmly. "He may be the one who set the fire last night. I'll take him in for questioning."

"Kaitlyn, tell him to let me go!"

I recognized that voice. "Ben?"

"You know this guy?" Sam sounded surprised.

I sighed. "Let him go."

Sam didn't move.

"He's my ex-husband."

"He was prowling around..." Sam's deep voice was stern and serious. I bet he could scare the hell out of bad guys.

"He may be a prowler and a no good son-of-bitch," I said. "but I doubt he set the fire. He doesn't like matches."

Reluctantly, and maybe a little roughly, Sam removed the handcuffs. Ben turned around rubbing his wrists. He wore jeans and cowboy boots. Under a gray long-sleeve t-shirt, it looked like his once taut abs had started to turn soft, which made me smile in a mean sort of way. His brown hair was a bit too long and curled over his large ears.

"Jeez, Kaitlyn. You didn't have to sic the cops on me," Ben said in a whiney voice that I hadn't heard before.

I moved closer and stood next to Sam, hugging my arms across my chest to keep warm. "I ought to sic the cops, the FBI, and the IRS on you!"

"You're over-reacting."

"You took all my money!"

Ben straightened up. "I didn't take it."

"You must have received notices?"

He shrugged. I knew Ben's sheepish look—it wasn't genuine.

"What did he do?" Sam said looking at me. "Something I can pull him in for?"

"Only if being a quadruple-sized asshole is a crime."

Ben ran his fingers through his thick hair. A nervous habit

that told me things hadn't worked out like he'd planned tonight. Probably thought he'd find me at home, alone, all ready to be wined, dined, and suckered. Not anymore.

"Kaitlyn..." Ben started.

"Why were you hanging around my house? Do you have my money?"

Ben stabbed at the pavement with the toe of his boot and shoved his hands into the front pockets of his jeans. "Not exactly."

Sam crossed his arms and stood in a police-like stance glaring at Ben. I thought again of Sam's gun. Maybe he had a second one hidden up the leg of his pants. What would it feel like to slide my hand up there...?

"Who is this guy?" Ben said with faked machismo.

"A friend." That sounded weird. "He's a cop."

Ben's eyes got wide. "I'm working on getting the money," Ben whined. "I have to get a few more baristas, maybe a few more good weekends. I'm thinking of trying Yellow Polka Dot Bikini Wednesdays too."

"What in the hell is he talking about?" Sam asked.

"Apparently Ben's latest *venture* is a coffee stand with stripers serving," I said to Sam. To Ben I said, "You do realize that the polka dot thing doesn't make any sense."

"Huh?"

Sam glanced at me with a "you were married to this guy?" look. Aloud he said, "He seems a little loopy. Maybe I should give him a breathalyzer."

"I haven't been drinking," Ben said. "Not tonight. Where have you two been anyway? It's pretty late to be coming home."

"Since when do you care what I'm doing?" I held up a hand. "Don't even answer that. Where's my money?"

"You loaned him money?" Sam asked.

"No frickin' way. I divorced him because he was always spending my money. Only it seems that his screw-ups continue to haunt me. This week the Washington Department of Revenue sucked my bank account dry to pay for his taxes."

"I didn't know they were gonna to do that!" Ben whined.

"You admitted you received notices!"

"I don't pay attention to those." I could tell he realized he'd screwed up. "What're you so sensitive for? It's not my fault."

"Oh, please. It's all your fault."

Ben frowned. "And why have you got cops patrolling around your house?"

"If you must know, we had an incident last night. And if I find out you had anything to do with that..."

"What incident?"

"A fire."

Ben held up a hand. "No way! I was out with my buddies last night. I didn't have anything to do with your, ah, *incident*."

Deep down, I knew Ben didn't start the fire. It wasn't his style, too hands on. And he really did have a strange fear of matches, lighters, and fire starters.

"Listen dick-wad," Sam said in his mean cop voice. "You stay away from this house."

"And who are you? This situation is between and my wife."

"Ex-wife," Sam and I said together.

"Well, aren't you the cutesy couple," Ben hissed.

Sam stepped forward. He was at least five inches taller than Ben. "You don't call her, you don't harass her, you don't even look at her unless you are handing her cash."

"Lighten up," Ben said.

"Listen buddy," Sam said looking quite intimidating. "You need to scram. Now!"

Testosterone flew. I swear both of them puffed up their chests. I stepped between them, facing Ben. It felt good to have Sam at my back. I had a wine headache and was exhausted and had no patience for this. "Ben, go home. We have nothing to discuss unless you have my money."

"I'll get your money," he muttered. Then he strode off down the driveway. I now saw his partially restored '64 Mustang, or as

I liked to call it the *64 Money Pit* parked in front of my next-door neighbor's house.

Sam and I stood in the driveway and watched Ben drive off into the foggy night.

"Well, that was fun," I said.

"Are you gonna be okay? I mean, do you need money?"

"No!" I was mortified that my troubles were now out in the open. "I'll manage. I always have. It's not the first time he's wiped me out." For some reason I felt an urge to defend Ben. "He's not a bad guy. He has great visions, but he just can't follow through on anything." Why was I defending him? Or was I defending the me that had married him.

"But Bikinis Baristas? There've been issues with those stands."

"You ever buy coffee from one?"

"Hell, yeah." He chuckled. The driveway light illuminated his gorgeous smile.

"You were pretty scary. I can see why you're such a good cop."

He shrugged and turned toward me. "Not exactly how I pictured ending the evening."

"I'm sorry I feel asleep. Some date I am."

He stepped forward and my heart hurtled against my rib cage.

"It was an enjoyable evening, Kaitlyn."

I couldn't help myself. I blurted, "You don't think I'm a murderer, do you?"

He grinned at me. A flirtatious grin.

He didn't think I killed anyone. But that didn't mean Sheehan agreed.

"I'll just get my purse," I said feeling suddenly self-conscious. This was only our first date after all. We walked back to his car and I retrieved my purse. After I slammed the car door shut, I turned and Sam was close. I felt his warm breath on my face. A moment before I had been cold. Now I felt like I was on fire.

He smiled his flirty smile, then leaned in and pressed my back against the car. And he kissed me. I mean really kissed me! *Holy shit!*

CHAPTER 10

Thursday, September 21, 2017

I slept like the dead but still my body did not want to get up when the alarm went off at six thirty. Snuggled in a cocoon of blankets, meshed in happy dreams of long, glorious kisses, I felt tempted to call in sick, but my *good girl* side wouldn't let me.

I left a dish of dry cat food and a bowl of water by the front door and said goodbye to Wally.

It was a chilly fall morning. A sheen of dampness blanketed everything in the yard and the pavement was dark as if it had been raining overnight. A light mist drifted on swirling fog giving the morning a gloomy ambiance. But I was smiling. The weather wouldn't dampen my good mood.

While I sat in my car waiting for it to warm up and the windshield to defog, I noticed the large manila envelope that I'd grabbed from Cheryl last night on the way out of work. It held the report of past complaints and violations from the *Death*

Street. I unclipped the envelope and removed several printouts.

Lots of reports from that neighborhood, but somehow I hadn't been called to any of them. Marcus had responded to the bulk of the issues, but that wasn't unusual. Once a code enforcement officer had visited a neighborhood, they tended to get dispatched again for repeat calls. Going back over the last year, there were a rash of complaints made by R. Wyman. Ah, my friend Randall. The ones more recent were mostly anonymous with a couple made by S. Pitowski.

I reviewed the list of who the complaints targeted. They weren't all against the Maddens. Seems old Randall had complained about most of the neighbors on his block and the block behind him, even old Ralph. Stanley's grievances were all directed at the Maddens. The name Carlos didn't appear anywhere on the report.

What did this tell me that I didn't already know? Randall liked to pester his neighbors. Maybe he convinced Stanley to go along and take over as the complainer. The neighbors had a lot of reasons to hate Randall, but why target the Maddens? Why leave the body in their yard if not to cast blame? If Dave didn't kill Carlos, did Rhonda? That didn't make a lot of sense unless he was going to report her animals. The woman didn't have all her marbles, but she hadn't seemed violent. Disturbed, yes. Murderous, no. But if she and Carlos were having an affair and he cut it off? I wasn't going to figure this out right now.

As I backed my car out onto the street, I noticed the dark black spot still marked my driveway like a fresh scar to remind me of the fire. I did my best to ignore it and drove the five miles to the office.

Stanley had taken over the complaints. Could he have been the driver the of the neighborhood strife all along. He was certainly a jerk, but did that make him a killer? Sam said he'd been interviewed. What if he tangled with Carlos over a woman? Someone he flirted with, but who chose Carlos instead? It didn't seem likely that they would be competing for the same woman.

Stanley ran right home when Estelle called. He was a flirt but probably had no follow through.

What did Councilman Newman have to do with everything? I got a strange sense that Cedar Grove's redevelopment had a staring a role in this crime drama. But how? If Newman was doing behind the scenes work to improve neighborhoods and attract retail, why did he care about this street? Because of Randall?

Mist hung in the air and sprinkled my windshield. I flipped the intermittent wipers on and off as I drove to work. I didn't see the police car following me until I turned into the city hall lot. It pulled in behind me as I parked. My heartbeat quickened. Maybe it was Sam. But he didn't drive a patrol car.

I flipped the hood of my jacket up as I climbed out of the Rav. My heart plummeted when Joshua exited the cruiser and walked toward me.

"Hi, Katie!" His perfectly pressed blue uniform looked a little oversized on him. He wore a hat covered by a stretchy shower cap-like plastic. The black microphone clipped to his shoulder reminded me of a pirate's parrot.

His smile was so wide, his face so eager, I just couldn't chastise him for showing up and calling me Katie. "Hi, Joshua." I gathered my things from the back seat of my car.

"What was Detective Evans doing at your house last night?" he asked.

I set down my cooler and looked at him. "How do you know that?"

"You left with him."

"Are you following me?"

"Katie. There's a maniac loose!" He looked at the ground. "I want to protect you!"

"I'm a big girl. I can take care of myself." I grabbed my cooler, and started walking toward the Public Works building.

"But someone is targeting you! The fire!" He jogged after me. The mic on his shoulder squawked. "I'm only keeping an eye on you and your house. But I guess you have Detective Evans protecting you." Joshua's face drooped, sad and hurt.

What was it with the men in my life lately? "Joshua, do not follow me. It's stalking."

"It's okay. I'm a cop. And I don't mind," he said. "I can make sure you're safe. You and your cat. You didn't tell me you got a cat."

We reached the door of Public Works. "I'm going to work now." I reached for the handle and held the door open. "Don't you have things to do?"

He smiled. "Of course. I'm on patrol."

"So go protect and serve." "Bye, Joshua." I pushed through the door.

He smiled weakly and headed back to his car. Maybe I shouldn't be so hard on the guy. He really was a good person, just a bit intense. Like the time in the seventh grade when everyone was catching the flu and he followed me around reminding me to wash my hands.

A dozen or so people crowded the lobby. Cheryl perched calmly behind her desk smiling and directing the visitors to sign in.

I ducked around the swarm and leaned on the corner of Cheryl's counter. Today her earrings were oblong orange disks. They went well with her orange-trimmed black sweater. Pretty tame for her. She'd bust out the fall leaves and pumpkins soon.

"What's going on?" I whispered.

Cheryl smiled a phony smile. "All these concerned citizens are here to speak to Mr. Richter, the Mayor, the City Manager." She played with her earrings. "Or whoever they can get in to see."

I glanced back at the group. "About what?"

Cheryl picked up a piece of paper covered in scribbles. "Redevelopment, animal cruelty by city workers, code enforcement, overflowing sewers, and..." She dropped her voice now. "Any other shit they can make up."

Code Enforcement? Darn it, I'd better scram. "What about my truck?"

"Returned last night."

"Thank God." I handed her Old Yeller's keys then moved quickly away.

"Have a lovely day!" Cheryl called after me.

I hurried back to my desk. Marcus popped in just as I was unloading my papers. He wore a tight black polo shirt and black jeans. His hair was slicked back.

"What's up, Kaitlyn?" he said glancing at my chest then quickly away.

"Not much. Did you see the craziness out there?" I gestured toward the lobby.

"That's why I'm back here."

I sat down and shuffled papers.

He didn't move. "Any updates on the murder?"

I swiveled my chair to face him. "Not really. What have you heard?"

He just shrugged. "Nothin'." He fiddled with a picture of a palm tree I had pinned to my cubicle wall. "You still snooping around?"

I frowned. "I'm not snooping around. I need to finish my report, make sure the yard is cleaned up--that's it."

He nodded. Still poised like some wanna-be super model in the entrance to my cube.

"You got something else on your mind, Marcus?"

"Nope."

"Okay, then," I said. "I'll get to work."

"You out late last night? You look like crap." With that, he walked away.

What was that all about? Mr. Negativity. Guy must be having a bad day or a bad decade was more like it.

I goofed around at my desk for an hour trying to get the nerve to call the landscaping company Carlos had worked for. But I couldn't come up with a story, a reason to ask questions.

Hell, I couldn't come up with any questions to ask.

What did I need to know? GC said Carolos did landscape work. It was clear he worked on that block. *Damn!* They made it look so easy on TV. Just call and pretend to be a family member, ask a few questions, get a revelation that solves the mystery.

I went to the kitchen for coffee and found Sharon and John loitering around the water cooler. The room was small and held the faint smell of fish and burnt popcorn. John looked sharp and put together in his standard slacks and button-up. Sharon wore a black shirt with a giant yellow pineapple on her chest over black jeans. Her version of mellow.

"You see the craziness out there?" Sharon said, gesturing toward the lobby.

"Came through the crowd when I arrived," I said.

"I think it's grown!" Sharon exclaimed. "Every nut job in the city is here."

"Some have picket signs," John added, nonchalantly sipping coffee from a green REI mug.

"They can't picket inside." I said.

"They're not technically picketing right now," John said. "They're waiting."

I filled my mug. "Where's Richard?"

Sharon snorted. "No one knows. He must have gotten word of all this shit and split."

"Maybe Cheryl can send them to the golf course to find him," John said.

We laughed.

"Cheryl sent someone over to main city hall, but Mr. Mayor and the City Manager are MIA also," Sharon said with a knowing smile. "So they came back."

John said, "Figures."

We stood in silence listening to the buzz of voices floating through the thin walls.

"Cheryl said some of them are complaining about code enforcement," I said.

Sharon harrumphed. "Girl, they's always gonna complain about that."

"If you wanted a job where people like you, you should have picked a different profession," John said. "...but don't worry. All of us do our jobs well."

"Thanks, John. I just wonder what they have to complain about."

Cheryl entered the kitchen and the conversation. "That would be you," she said to me as she moved toward the coffee, her long earrings swinging.

"Me?" I exclaimed. "Why?"

"I don't know." Cheryl filled a mug and dumped in liberal amounts of sugar and dry creamer. "I just know I got a big one about you. Anonymous." Her spoon clicked against the mug as she stirred.

"What did I do?"

Cheryl shrugged. "I passed it to Richard—as per procedure."

"Great. Just great."

"Can you guys skedaddle so I can enjoy a little silence while I'm on break," Cheryl said. "That crowd out there is giving me a royal headache."

***

The Death Street shimmered with light filtering through gray clouds and wisps of low fog. It looked so quiet and normal. No sign of animal cruelty, mayhem, or murder.

The Maddens' house was dark and still, the curtains drawn. The lawn was a bit long and starting to turn brown, no doubt from the many police, fire department, and animal control officers who had traipsed across it. Overall, it had a sad, neglected feel as empty houses do.

My visions of the animals in cages returned with a vengeance, yet this time I saw the cages surrounded by a fogy mist that swirled eerily through them. The mist lifted and revealed a human foot.

If I had been in a bad movie I would have shaken my head to clear away the feeling of gloom. Instead I tried to concentrate and wipe my mind clean. I ate a handful of Gummy Bears. I should knock on the door to complete my follow up, but I could tell no one was there and really didn't want another confrontation with the Maddens. Still, I felt the need to take some action.

I got out of the car and walked resolutely to Ralph's house. I hadn't talked to him yet so it would be okay, non-confrontational. And not harassment. I knocked several times, but no one answered.

What next? I decided on the Wyman's. Mary might be home. I went to her front door and knocked. As I waited for an answer, I felt my confidence wane. I half hoped no one would come to the door, that it would be a day that Mary Wyman went to the office.

But just as I was about to high-tail it back to my car, the front door rattled then opened.

A totally different person had taken over Mary Wyman's body. Her face was flushed and splotch, her hair messed, wearing a wrinkled loose-fitting man's shirt. The face that had struck me as so posh and Botoxed when we first met, now looked old and tired. Her eyes, sans makeup, were red-rimmed and bloodshot with dark circles under them.

"Ah, hi." I wondered if she had known Carlos and was grieving. She sure looked unhappy and irritated to see me on her door step.

She put a hand on the door frame and I noticed one of her fake nails had broken. "What do you want?"

"I'm sorry to bother you, but since I knew you worked at home, I thought I could stop by and ask you a few more questions about the *incident* and your husband's complaints about the neighbors."

She frowned and her taunt skin stretched. The veins in her thin neck bulged. I wondered if she would strike out at me or just collapse. "If you want to talk to my husband," she hissed. "You can come back when he's home. I don't need to answer any questions." She looked back over her shoulder. "I have nothing to say."

"I apologize..."

"You apologize! This whole thing is a disaster!" Her voice caught. "A tragedy."

"I'm sorry. I didn't know you knew the man... Carlos."

Her eyes narrowed and she looked very frightening, in a distraught, manic way. "Just leave me alone." She slammed the door.

I stood there stupidly staring at the lion's head knocker for a few moments before I hurried back up the walk. I could have sworn I heard voices inside the house as I left. Maybe she was calling her husband or worse, calling the city to complain about me. Great.

A cold wind whipped down the street and I tugged my coat around me. A light rain softly fell from the sky as if a misting hose had been turned on over my head. Back in my truck, I started it up and cranked on the heater. Was Mary grieving? If so, what did that mean? Or was it something else? Guilt? Could she have killed Carlos? Why? More questions. Always more questions and no answers.

I considered calling Sam and asking him what was new on the case. He probably wouldn't tell me anything, but I'd get to talk to him again and that thought made me smile and sent an angry bee tearing through my gut.

However, when I phoned the station, they said Sam was out. Maybe I could grill Joshua for info. No, there was no reason to encourage his stalking.

As the truck warmed up, I jotted notes on a report form. A form that would, in effect, close the case I opened when I first followed up on the original complaint that set all this chaos in motion six days before. I was involved in my writing so when someone tapped on my window I jumped and pulled the pen across the form.

"Shit!"

Stanley Pitowski stood outside the truck grinning like an over-sexed teenager. I rolled down the window.

"Hi, Blondie." He wore another windbreaker type jacket, this one with an outline of an evergreen and *Lonny's Tree Trimming Service* printed in on the left chest. I noticed his teeth were unnaturally white.

I frowned. "Mr. Pitowski."

"Whatcha doing here?"

"Working," I said curtly. I looked down at the paper in my lap and saw a long black line across the page. *Damn.* I'd have to rewrite the whole form. I set the pile of paperwork on the passenger seat so Stanley couldn't peak in and read it.

He did seem to be standing on his toes trying look.

"Why?" he said. "I thought the police wrapped up everything,"

"I have to finish my complaint paperwork. Make sure the mess is cleaned up."

"Huh."

Take control, K. "Mr. Pitowski, you called in quite a few of the complaints against your neighbors, was it just the smells? Were you aware of other problems or issues that needed to be addressed?"

He stepped away and taken aback by my bluntness. "Nah, just wanted people to clean up their yards. I mean, with the redevelopment coming, we want to look top notch. Keep our property values high."

He sounded like someone who is repeating, word for word, what they've been told. Kind of like the young kids who often knocked on my door promoting some or other church. "So you're for the redevelopment then?"

He shuffled his feet. "Well, sure. It will mean our house will be worth more, right?"

"Could be."

"If zoning changes we could possibly sell part of our lot or... who knows. I mean, Randall says...."

"What does Randall say?" I could totally buy Randall convincing Stanley of just about anything. Stanley would go along if he thought it made him look better. But how did complaining about their neighbors really improve their home values? The block was within the area that could be zoned mixed use. Seemed like murder was likely to be about money. Who would profit from Carlos being dead and Rhonda Madden's animal hording being exposed?

"I gots to be getting home. Estelle will be wondering where I am. I was supposed to be home by lunchtime. We have tickets to some fool-ass play or something tonight."

"If you think of anything that you want me to include in the final report, let me know."

"Sure, Blondie." He looked me in the eye/chest again.

"And don't call me that ever again or I'll add your house to my routine follow-up list."

He frowned and stepped back farther, then turned and walked away, muttering something that sounded like, "just tryin' to be friendly."

***

I grabbed a drive-thru burger then investigated a few other easy complaints writing a few citations, before heading back to the office. At my desk, I mulled over Stanley's comments about redevelop and property values. Was that enough to kill over? A trip to visit our engineering team might help. They could answer some questions about how citizens might benefit from the city's plan.

I headed down the hall toward the back of the building. That's where the bulk of the Public Works employees who weren't code enforcement worked. My intention was to catch one of the engineers and ask some questions about rezoning. As I neared the engineering area, a space filled with low-walled gray cubicles, I heard, before I saw, the City Manager's Assistant, Melinda Golden.

"I don't care what Fred told you, I want it now. It was due yesterday."

Damn. I stopped mid-stride and turned slowly, poised to escape.

"Kaitlyn!"

Caught. Could I pretend I didn't hear? Doubtful, since her high-pitched, scratchy voice penetrated the space. Phones stopped ringing, fingers stopped typing. Heads popped up over cubicle walls, eyes scanning the room. When the prairie dogs saw Golden, they dropped back into their holes. *Crap.*

I turned around. Melinda stood in the center of the aisle.

The Golden Girl was a thirty-something woman, about 5'10" with long black hair and perfect high cheek bones. She was model thin but kept from being exceptionally good-looking by her squinty close-set eyes and permanently turned-up nose. Her nose might tip-up, but she looked down on the rest of the world. Her black suit with pencil skirt and pale green shirt matched her haughtiness. Her huge gold necklace said, "look at me!"

The rumor around city hall was that she was either sleeping with the City Manager or had something on him that gave her power over the rest of us staffers.

"Kaitlyn," she repeated in a serious voice. "Where are you going?"

"Nowhere. Just walking around a little... being social." I forced a smile.

"Uh, huh." She put her hands on her hips. "Why aren't you working?"

I should have just smiled and walked away. Should have. "I am working—" There was a bit of defiance in my voice that I couldn't control.

LESLIE J. HALL

"You were told very clearly not to pursue the homicide."

"Who said I was working on that?" How did she know? It was creepy really.

She frowned at me. "I know."

"Following up on the complaint is my job. I have to get it mitigated and close my report. How come you're working?"

"I'm always working." She paused. When she spoke her voice was tight. "The City Manager made it very clear that the animal case was in the hands of the police."

Sharon appeared in the hall behind Melinda, blocking the aisle. Sharon froze then moved her considerable bulk in a backward tip-toe, looking like an uncoordinated, plus-sized ballerina.

I stifled a giggle and tried to keep my face serious. Sharon disappeared. Lucky her.

"I need to get back to work." I said.

Melinda narrowed her small eyes to slits making her look like a snake. I half expected her to hiss at me. "You watch yourself, Kaitlyn, 'cause I'll be watching you." She stalked away, swinging her hips in her tight pencil skirt.

Great, now I had the wrath of the Golden Girl on top of everything else. I slunk back to my cubicle and slouched down in my chair. I just couldn't focus or think about my actual work. I jiggled my mouse and spun the chair around. When I spun back to face my computer a reminder from my calendar popped up, yoga class—yoga class!

I stopped spinning and almost fell over backward. A glance at my watch said it was 4:11. I had just over 15 minutes to get to class. I quickly shut down my computer and gathered my things. At the entrance to the lobby, I pressed my ear to the door. It sounded quiet so I pushed through. Cheryl sat at the counter. The lobby was empty. Thank God.

"I'm gone for the day," I called to Cheryl as I scurried to the front door.

"Where are you off to in such a hurry?"

"Yoga class!" I stopped halfway through the door. "Richard approved, but don't tell Marcus or Golden that."

She smiled and winked.

"Thanks."

***

I drove the few blocks to the Cedar Grove Rec Center, parked quickly and rushed inside brushing past a group of teenage ballet dancers, dressed in pink tights and black leotards, stretching in the hallway. I changed in the ladies locker room and hurried into class, finding a great spot in the back. After some warmup stretches, I found myself on my back, my legs over my head, toes almost touching the floor behind me, my boobs squished against my thighs.

After an hour of stretching and bending into one odd position after another, I made my way to the door, slipping my winter coat on over the oversized shirt and stretch pants that were my less than fashionable yoga uniform. Who cared what you wore when you sweat that much? Yoga might seem simple, but it sure kicked my butt—yoga was tough. If I did it more regularly, I'm sure I'd feel better. Tonight my legs and arms felt like jelly.

Dusk had fallen while I'd been in class. Shadows shrouded the parking lot, the pinkish glow from the street lights barely lit the rows of cars. The wind felt chilly when it touched my sweaty cheeks. Since I'd been running late to class, I had just tossed my keys into my purse. Now, as I moved across the lot, I dug for the elusive jingle of the keys hidden in all the junk in my bag. Where were they?

I was almost to my car when I heard a rustle and sudden footsteps close by. Before I could pull my hand out of my bag and turn around, someone had come up behind me and slammed me against a sedan.

I dropped my purse and bit my tongue! *Ouch*! My automatic

response was to struggle. Pressure on my neck and a knee in my butt pinned me against the vehicle. My shaky limbs didn't seem to work properly. The pressure forced my face sideways against the glass, constricted my throat and pushed my teeth into my cheek.

I wanted to cry out—someone else had to be walking to their car right? My heart thumped against my chest. I desperately struggled for breath.

"Listen up, you little bitch. You need to stay out of things that don't concern you. Stop nosing around in other people's business."

The words were deep and raspy. I got the sense the guy was trying to disguise his voice. I tried to think, but my brain was in full terrified mode and I couldn't get a clear thought. How to get away. Could I kick back? If I got my head free, maybe I could scream. But if I screamed or ran, what would happen? Did this guy have a gun? He was taller than me—no way I could fight him off.

I shifted my weight for an attempt at a kick.

As if reading my mind he said, "Don't even think of trying to turn around or run, I know where to find you. You won't be safe—neither will anyone you know. I'll find them too."

Oh, God! Rosie! My parents! My brother! I'd never forgive myself.

"What do you want?" I managed to croak. My purse had fallen to the ground. He hadn't grabbed it so this wasn't a robbery.

"I want you..." The pressure increased. "...to mind your own business. Stay away from the things that don't concern you."

Even though I was sweaty, I could feel goose bumps on my arms and I could see my breath in the cold evening air. I forced my mind to calm. *Don't panic! Don't be stupid. Give him what he wants.*

"Do you understand?" he said forcefully, his breath warm on my ear.

I focused on breathing.

"Do you!" he hissed.

"Yes!"

Off toward the rec center, I heard a noise, then the sound of a group of teenage girls laughing. Ballet class had let out.

"I'm going to let you off this time, bitch. Don't even think of turning around until you count to 100—or you or one of your little friends will be sorry."

The pressure on my neck released suddenly, the knee withdrew, and I heard footsteps running away. *Crap*! Had this person been following me? Was he talking about the *Death Street*? Why? I tried to think if I had recognized the voice, but my brain was muddled.

I didn't turn, I just sunk to the ground shivering uncontrollably. The ballet girls came down my aisle and their laughter stopped abruptly.

"Are you okay?" one said.

I shook my head.

They looked at each other. "What happened?" one of them squeaked.

Another one came over to me and put a hand on my arm.

"Be careful, Janie. She might be a crazy person."

"I'm…." I felt my stomach convulse. "I'm okay. I… fell." I didn't want to start a panic and have them call the cops.

"Let me help you up." The girl put a hand under my arm.

In the glow of the street lights, her face looked pale. Her dark blond hair was pulled back in a serious tight bun, but her smile was kind.

I let her help me to my feet. "Do you see my purse?"

Her friends seemed to decide I wasn't a nut case and circled around me. One of them found my purse and keys and handed it to me.

I felt light-headed and rung out and desperately wanted to go home. I spotted my car one aisle over. "I'm okay now. Thanks. Thanks so much."

The girls eyed my suspiciously. Janie said, "Maybe you should go back inside. They have a first aid kit."

"No, it's all right. Thank you so much for helping me. My car's right over there."

They watched me limp to my Rav so I turned back and waved, forcing a smile. As I got into the car, my heart skipped a beat as I realized someone could be hiding in the back seat. I turned slowly to look, but the back was empty. I turned the key, locked the doors, cranked the heater to full, then dropped my head against the steering wheel trying to be calm. *Breath slowly, stop shaking.* It was a good ten minutes before I felt ready to drive home.

CHAPTER 11

Thursday, September 21, 2017

I drove on auto pilot, slow and careful. I parked, went inside, and stripped off all my clothes. I considered a shower, but couldn't summon the energy so, even though it was only six thirty, I put on pajamas and climbed into bed. Burrowed under the covers, I tried to get angry, to understand why I was targeted and what I should do about it. But I only felt numb and defeated. Why had I ever thought I could figure this out? I couldn't even figure out my own life!

As I lay still, cocooned under the blankets, feelings started to come back, mostly fear, along with a real pain in the back of my neck where my attacker had pushed on it.

Someone attacked me! Someone threatened my friends and family! This threat was much more real than it had been with the note or the fire. The voice was deep, but sounded faked. I couldn't place it or even think who it could have been.

Why would someone want me to stop nosing around Carlos' death? It had to have been the murderer, thinking that I knew something or was getting close to something. What was it? Obviously, it wasn't something as simple as Rhonda Madden having a psychotic break or her husband flipping out over the animals and killing Carlos because he was there. Besides, Dave had an alibi. There had to be more to it, a secret that someone was protecting.

According to Golden, someone at the city didn't want info about the death getting out. Why? Because it somehow made them look bad? I thought of Councilman Newman. I assumed he didn't want murder in a city that was looking to attract new businesses. Golden was, undoubtedly, Newman's source. Who else could it be? What could be his connection? Why would he get personally involved by asking me to back off? Could he have attacked me? What was at stake for him?

For some reason, it would have been easier to accept if I thought a hardened criminal, a gangster, or some such person was after me. A gut feeling told me it was one of the neighbors who had been pushed to their limit. Crazy to protect something or gain something. This wasn't an organized assault on me. It was a bunch of lame tries at scaring me. Unfortunately, it worked. I was afraid, beaten down. Why did I keep pushing on this? Why couldn't I just get over it? I should be focusing on my job, cleaning up my finances. And on a very cute detective.

Then there was my neighbor, GC. He'd asked me to look into Carlos' death. Did he really want answers or just to know what was going on because he was involved? I didn't get that vibe from him. But you never know. Did I live across the street from a killer?

***

After two hours of lying still, thinking through the events of the last week and making no progress other than working up a killer headache, I gave up and got up. The clock glowed 8:30.

Darkness had enveloped my house and a lone light illuminated the street and lightly falling rain. I was hungry but couldn't summon the energy to fix any food. I picked my phone off the kitchen counter. It had a crack in the screen protector. Great. Just great. One more thing to fix. Who to call? Where had Joshua been while I was getting attacked? I half wished I hadn't told him not to follow me. I couldn't call him. It would be too weird. Maybe he could get me some pepper spray.

In my moment of weakness (or a flash of insanity), I called Sam.

"Hello."

"Sam, it's Kaitlyn."

"Well, hey." Deep and sexy. Why couldn't I just be calling to say hello? To ask him out again? But it was hard to think of something as everyday as dating when my life was in turmoil.

"Hi." I paused and took a deep breath hoping I didn't sound like a pathetic weakling. "I think I know something about the murder. I need to talk to you about it. Can I meet you somewhere?"

He paused. "I'm working tonight for another case. I guess we could meet for coffee," he said warily.

"I'd appreciate that. I mean… if you could take the time."

"Sure." He seemed hesitant. "You know the Thai restaurant over by the Shell Station on 34th?"

"Uh huh."

"It stays open late. Be there in 15."

Before I could change my mind, I threw on jeans, a sweatshirt, and sneakers. A visit to the bathroom mirror was a scary experience, but I did my best to at least look presentable. Not like a raving lunatic who never brushed her hair.

***

Sam waited at a table for four sipping from a steaming mug. He looked really good, even with tired lines on his face. I sat down across from him.

No one else was in the small restaurant at this time on a weeknight. It was quiet except for the sounds of someone moving around in the back room. Spicy aromas lingered in the warm air. Sam set his mug on the battered wooden table as I sat down.

"Like I said, I think I know something. I'm not sure what, but something." Now it sounded dumb. And his presence made me feel jittery and a little stupid. He was so commanding, so perfectly pulled together, and I was such a mess.

A waiter came by. I ordered tea and Phad Thai to-go.

"We've made some progress on this end," he said. "Dave Madden is being held for more questioning."

"But you said he had an alibi."

"Yes, but the wife... he may have covered it up. We need to know more about that relationship."

"I don't think it's the Maddens," I said.

Sam looked skeptical.

"It's... someone else on that street that I spoke to, Randall or Stanley. Or maybe it's... I don't know, but I thought if I talked it through, if you asked me more questions maybe we'd come up with something."

"Why do you think it's not Mr. Madden?"

"Just a gut feeling. He doesn't seem like the type to threaten. He was protecting his wife. If I could only..."

"Kaitlyn." His voice was soft and kind. "There is nothing for you to do. If you aren't involved in the murder, you need to stay away. We're getting a lot of pressure from the City Council and..." He didn't say anything for a moment. "Have you been messing around in this?"

"I haven't! Just closing the compliant. I thought..."

"We're working this. It'll be resolved soon. Leave it to us."

The front door chimed and a woman entered with a rush of cold air. She went to the counter. A thin Asian man, wearing a white apron, appeared from the back room carrying a to-go bag of food. He paused to point the woman to a table then brought my tea and to-go order.

"I just thought… I don't know," I said. "I guess I wanted to talk it through. Someone thinks I know something, but I don't!" I sat up straighter. I tried not to be intimidated by the cop in front of me. Or by the very good-looking guy I had hoped to impress. "I have to take charge. I can't sit back and do nothing."

"We will handle this. You don't need to…"

"Listen!" I heard the hysteria in my voice and hated it. "Someone grabbed me tonight. In the Rec Center parking lot. He told me to mind my own business. He threatened people I care about." I choked as I tried to hold back tears. I couldn't. They leaked out.

His face tightened. He looked concerned and a bit angry. "Are you okay?"

I took a breath and worked to hold my emotions in check. "I'm fine."

Tough cop face. "Not good. I'll report it."

"No, really," I said. "I'm not hurt. Just shaken up."

He shook his head and said very softly, "Kaitlyn, what have you been doing?"

"Nothing! I don't know anything. What I do know is that this isn't as simple as Dave and Rhonda Madden. Something else is going on. Maybe something at the city level." I hesitated to say anything about Newman. I had no proof, only gut feelings and he was, after all, a city councilman. Except Sam said the City Council was applying pressure, which probably meant the City Manager was involved.

"I'll send a patrol car to cruise your house. Stay in until we get this wrapped up."

I wiped my nose on a napkin and cleared my throat. "I can't just sit. It's making me crazy."

"Kaitlyn, you need to stay clear." He reached out and touched my hand. His skin was warm. "Please, stay safe."

It wasn't an order, more like a plea. Something in his eyes connected with me and sent an intense feeling into my belly. His touch lit me up in other areas too.

We left the restaurant and Sam followed me home. In my driveway, he took my hand. "Go inside and stay there. Tomorrow, go to work if you must but only work. Watch your surroundings and don't go anywhere alone after dark."

I nodded. I couldn't find my voice. I was having flashes of the last time we'd been alone in my driveway. But no kiss this time.

He looked at me with a concerned frown and went back to his car. "Someone will be cruising by your house regularly!" he called.

***

After getting home and finding a huge spider web across my front door I was done. I tried to go to bed, I really did, but I ended up just pacing. I was too wired to sleep and it was only 9:15. The conversation with Sam had perked me up and I needed someone to talk to.

Rosie had stuck by me throughout life's roller coaster. We'd stayed friends even when I was married and she wasn't. She'd supported me through the end of my marriage. I hadn't been a good friend lately. Whatever she was going through with Mac, I could be there for her. And that would keep me from thinking too much about what was happening to me and the about the murder.

I drove toward her house, carefully watching all around me, checking cars in my rearview to make sure no one was following. I stopped by 7-11 and picked up a carton of chocolate chip mint ice cream. On the way back to my car, a person started toward me. My heart raced until I realized it was just a homeless man politely asked for change. I gave him a few quarters then got in my car and locked the door.

Rosie rented a two-story duplex in North Seattle. It sat on a quiet residential street just a few blocks off Aurora Avenue. The small building looked like a dollhouse nestled between a grove of towering pines.

It was dark and had started to rain, so I ran to her front door with my hood up. I shook off the water as I waited for her to answer my knock. Nothing. Her porch light was dark, which was odd since she never went to bed before eleven.

I felt around until I found the doorbell. I heard it chime inside the house. No sound from inside, but her car was in the driveway. *Damn.* I guess I should have called first. I just figured she'd be curled up in front of the TV and would welcome a friend dropping by. My heart began to pound. Was Rosie alright? Had someone gotten to her already?

I was about call 911 when I heard footsteps inside. The door opened a few inches.

"Rosie, you're okay." I stopped. She looked like I'd gotten her out of bed. Her hair was mussed and the oversized t-shirt she wore looked like she'd picked it up off the floor. Mascara smudges lined her eyes as if she'd been crying.

"Were you sleeping? I'm sorry. I thought you'd be up."

"Hi, Kaitlyn," she said in a scratchy voice.

Her face was flushed and sheened with sweat. *Crap.* "Are you sick? I'm sorry I dropped in. I just thought you could use some company. I brought ice cream." I held up the bag. *Why hadn't I texted her first!*

She cleared her throat and said in a whisper, "Actually, I already have company."

"Huh?"

"I ran into Mac at the video store and we sort of got to talking and, well..."

"Mac is here?" Okay, I was a dork. I looked more closely and realized I had gotten her out of bed—literally. "I'm so sorry, Rosie. Here," I shoved the bag toward the door. "You take it. You might want it later..."

Rosie grinned and wiggled her eyebrows. "We might!"

I hesitated. "This is a good thing, you're sure?"

"Call me tomorrow," she whispered. "I'll fill you in on his break up with the cheerleader."

I nodded and stepped back. She smiled and shut the door. I listened to her run up the stairs, then trudged back to my car. One more thing I'd messed up. *I want my quiet life back please!* I pleaded to the heavens. Rain fell on my face and ran down the back of my collar.

***

On Friday, I called in sick, something I rarely do. Only a few days ago, I discovered all those animals and a dead body, then a note, a fire, and an attack. The first thing I did after calling the office was think about Rosie. All night I had tossed and turned and wondered how she was. And how to warn her about the threat. I almost jumped in my car and drove to her downtown office. But after last night, that seemed like a bad idea. So I called.

"Hey, Kaitlyn. What's up?" I heard her chewing.

"Hi, Rosie. How are you today?"

"I'm great. Work is slow." She munched on something crunchy.

"Can you chat for a moment?"

"Sure," she said. "You never told me about your date. Was it fab?"

"It was interesting."

"But the Detective is hot, right?" Crunch. Crunch.

"Yes, I guess he is. It got weird. Ben showed up when we got home and…"

"Ben!" She coughed, probably choking on her snack.

I tried hard not to chuckle. "Yes. Things got a little heated."

"What's wrong?" she asked.

"What makes you think anything's wrong?" I tried for fake cheer.

"Come on, girl," Rosie said. "I hear it in your voice. What happened?"

So I told her. About the attack, about my thoughts on the murder and not knowing what I rough that was so important.

"K, this is serious stuff. You need to be careful. I think you should to listen to Detective Hot Stuff, who seems to really like you by the way! More on that later. Stay home."

"How can I stay home? Someone is messing with me and my friends. I have to fix it." I paused. "And they know where I live, so I don't think my home is all that safe."

"Listen to yourself, you aren't a cop, just a control freak. There's nothing you have to do except take care of yourself." Rosie paused and munched on something. "You should get some mace. Or a taser. I've heard those are good."

"No way! I'm not going to attack anyone."

She ignored me. "Maybe Sam could get you a gun."

"A gun! Are you nuts! I'm not getting a gun. I'm not getting a taser."

"I heard you can get pepper spray at pawn shops."

"No." I said firmly.

"K, you have to protect yourself." Her voice was full of concern. "Self-defense."

I sighed. "Rosie, I'm worried about you. What if they come after you? You need to go home, or somewhere safe, and stay there."

"How would this crazy person even know who I am or where I work?"

"I don't know. Just go home and lock your doors."

"So you're going to stay home?" she asked.

I couldn't lie to Rosie. "I don't know. I need to do something. Be in control."

"Kaitlyn…"

"I'll be careful. I promise. Joshua's been following me. I'll make sure he's my shadow."

"Joshua?" she said with sarcasm.

"He is a cop."

"Well..."

"Rosie, take care of yourself. Please."

She blew out a loud breath. "You aren't listening to your own advice you know."

"I'll be okay. If I need to, I'll call Sam."

She sighed dramatically.

"Just promise me you'll take care of yourself."

"I will," she said. "Swear you'll call me every few hours and check in."

I agreed. "What about you and Mac?"

"He broke up with the cheerleader."

"So you're okay?

"Yes, K. I'm good. Real good." She paused. "You gonna call your parents?"

"No. It would just upset them. They don't live close so I don't think they're in danger."

"What about Ben, the smuck? And Kale?"

"They can take care of themselves. But I'll have to call Ben to poke him for my money."

***

We hung up and the phone immediately rang again. I automatically stabbed *Accept*.

"We're calling with a message for Kaitlyn Willis."

"Ah, that's me."

"This is Bank of America VISA. We're calling about your last payment of $167.89. The check that you sent us has been returned. Your account is now past due and with the late fee you owe $197.89. Can you take care of that today?"

Crap! Crap! Crap! Why did I answer the phone? "If I had the money, the check wouldn't have been returned, would it?"

"We can do an automatic check by phone or credit card and take care of it right now."

"My account is overdrawn so I don't think an automatic check would work."

The bored voice, obviously reading from a script, started to continue but I cut in. "I have a situation. My ex-husband didn't pay his taxes and the State has sucked my account dry. Until I straighten it out, I can't make a payment."

"It's important that we get this cleared out today so it won't affect your credit rating."

"You're not listening. I don't have the money right now, and until I get a chance to deal with that, I don't have any money!"

"We need to make some kind of arrangement. Could you cover the amount due by next Tuesday?"

"I don't know. Until I straighten this out...."

"If we don't receive the payment by the 15th, there will be another late charge and your account will..."

"I just said I don't have the money! I'm working on getting it! If you look at your records you'll see that I am a long time customer and have NEVER been late before on a payment. NEVER. So I think you can cut me some slack."

"So you'll call us by next Tuesday with a payment?"

For heaven's sake! "Sure."

"Okay. I'll make a note on your account that you will make that payment of $197.89 by next Tuesday."

I sighed. "Whatever. Bye." I hung up the phone.

I had to make time to deal with my financial mess, but when? I couldn't focus. It was Friday—Ben's deadline for paying me. If he actually came through... hah, who was I kidding?

I went to the kitchen for a Diet Sprite and then, as I had promised and as painful as it was, I called Joshua on his cell.

"Hi!" Joshua said.

"Listen. Are you planning to follow me around today?"

"Well, yes. I'm sorry, but I'm on patrol and we were told to watch your house. So I kinda have to. I know you hate it but..."

"No, it's okay. I wanted to let you know that I'm not going to work, but I will be going out later. I'll call or text when I'm leaving."

"It's okay, Ka... Kaitlyn! I'll be watching your back. You can count on me."

I hung up. Great, I thought. Just great.

I took my time getting ready, showering, fixing my hair, putting on makeup. It was gray and dreary outside, so I dug a deep blue angora cardigan out of the back of my closet. It was comfortable and provided a bit of cover from the chill. The routine of getting ready settled my nerves and gave me a sense of calm. I knew it was false.

I peeked out the front door and saw Wally in his box. I'd been in such a haze when I'd come home last night I hadn't even looked for him. "Hiya," I said.

He lifted his head and I swear the thing smiled at me. Or maybe it was me projecting my need for a smile on a silly animal. He stood, stretched, and walked over and rubbed against my leg.

Huh. Interesting. "Good morning to you too," I said.

"Meow."

Well, damn. Did people really communicate with their pets? I had always thought that was a load of crap. Or maybe he was just hungry. I went back inside leaving the door slightly open. When I returned with a bowl of food and one of water, he was still sitting on the porch.

"Good, kitty," I said feeling kind of stupid.

Wally wound around my leg one more time before moseying over to the food dish. I reached down and scratched his head the way Sam had done and heard a faint rumble from his fat belly. Was that a purr?

Then a weird feeling jolted me. If someone was out to get me, if they knew where I lived, and they thought I had a pet, did that make Wally a target? I looked down at the big lump of fur chomping away at the food bowl. I had a sudden vision of Wally being set on fire in my driveway. No way I could leave him inside if I went out. I wasn't that much of a pet person yet. But I cared enough not to put him in danger.

"You may need to come with me," I said.

Wally didn't respond. I went back inside, leaving him to his lunch.

Standing in the kitchen, munching on a PB&J, I tried to decide what to do.

CHAPTER 12

Friday, September 22, 2017

I came up with a plan. So maybe it wasn't the best plan. If I was being honest, the word plan was a bit strong. But it was something to do.

> 1. *Try and talk to GC again and get more information on Carlos*
> 2. *Call the landscaping company and get more information about Carlos*

Knowing more about the victim had to help, right?

> 3. *Somehow get all the neighbors together in one place to talk to them and get someone to confess*
> 4. *Convince Joshua to go along with this plan as my protector*

So maybe I watched too many movies. But I could talk to GC. I decided I needed more information on the victim and I had a direct line to his family. Only issue was that GC hadn't left me his number or any way to contact him. He was probably at work but worth a try.

I peeked outside making sure no lingering media vans were hanging around hoping for a new update they could air. The coast was clear.

I'd driven by GC's house thousands of times but never really looked at it closely. It was a small cinder block house with wood siding on half, fresh gray paint with white trim and gutters. The carport area had been closed in, probably as an extra bedroom. There were often several cars in the driveway and I'd seen a few small children walking to the bus stop, so I knew quite a few people lived in the tiny home.

I grabbed my purse, walked across the street, and knocked on the door. I could hear Latin music playing softly inside. It had a nice beat, very uplifting, just what I needed. I walked across the street. The air outside was cool but dry. There was no breeze, just stillness. Because it was mid-day on a weekday, the street was quiet, most of the driveways empty. I paused on the side of the street and thought about how disconnected I was from the world around me. I went along doing my own routines and not really paying any attention to anything but me. I didn't know most of my neighbors except for a hello at the summer block party or a wave here and there if I saw them in their yards. Once winter settled in, it would be dark when I left in the morning and dark at night when I got home at night. No more hellos. No connections.

If I'd been asked a week ago if I was happy, I would have said yes. I worked hard. I had friends. I hadn't dated in a long time but so what. Before WA State drained my account because of Ben, I'd been financially stable. I bought my house just after my divorce. A little savings and a city retirement account. My family was far enough away to not be a bother, but there for holiday gatherings and occasional get-togethers.

With all that had happened in the last few days, I felt disconnected. Like all I had wasn't good enough. My life wasn't enough. I'd been so insulated that I hadn't really been living. Had it truly taken a bunch of abused animals and a murder to wake me up?

A woman answered the door. She was young, maybe 25, with beautiful dark hair that hung down her back in a long braid. Her feet were bare, her toenails bright orange. She pulled on her olive t-shirt, like she was making sure it covered her post-baby tummy.

I smiled. "Hello? Is GC at home?"

"No *comprendo*. No *hablo ingles muy bien*."

Why hadn't I learned to speak Spanish? "GC. Is he at work?"

She nodded her head. "*Sí*."

I pointed across the street. "I live over there."

"*Ċeses* Kaitlyn."

"Yes! I'm Kaitlyn."

"*Sí*, yes. I know you." She stepped forward causing me to step back a bit. She whispered, "The baby, she sleeping."

"Sorry." I lowered my voice.

"Maria," she said pointing at her chest.

"I'm looking for GC. He and I spoke a few days ago and I wanted to reach him again but he didn't give me his phone number."

"GC?" She frowned. "He not here."

"Could I have his phone number?" I made the universal pantomime of talking on the phone.

She squished her face in concentration. "GC no *tiene teléfono en este momento*. He try to get a new one."

"Would you ask him to call me or come over when he comes home?" I pointed.

She bobbed her head. "*Sí.*"

I pulled a business card out of a little holder in my purse. "Here is my work number and I'll write my cell on the back. Okay?" She nodded as I wrote on the card. "Thanks so much. Tell him no big deal but I just want to chat more…"

"Carlos," she said firmly with a frown.

"Yes."

"I will tell him," she said carefully.

"What is Carlos's last name? Like Kaitlyn Willis, Carlos ..." I said hoping she'd get it.

"Hernandez?"

"Yes, thank you. And you speak English just fine."

She smiled.

"Thanks again." I walked back across the street.

Back home I procrastinated taking a next step. There must be something I could do. I pulled out the landscaping company's phone number and dialed.

"Hello. Evergreen Landscaping."

"Can I speak to Carlos?"

"Which one? We have three."

"He's on the crew working in Cedar Gove."

"Still have two in that group. And honestly, the landscaping team isn't in the office. Can someone else help you?"

"No thanks." I hung up. What had I been hoping to gain?

I had just cleaned house on Sunday but decided the bathroom could use a re-clean. I stripped down to a t-shirt, slipped on yellow rubber gloves, and jumped in. While scrubbing the heck out of the toilet, I ran through everything that had happened over the last week. I felt another twinge of guilt for not checking with Rosie enough. My friend was obviously going through something and now back with Mac? I hadn't been there for her. I'd needed to do better.

Granted, my week had been weird. My finances were in disarray. I was racking up return check charges and bank fees faster than a cheetah after an antelope. Me, the non-pet person had been adopted by the world's fattest cat! I'd met a guy with potential for something given he didn't avoid me because I had an ex-husband who was a loser/stalker or he didn't have to arrest me for murder.

The sad, neglected animals still haunted me. But to top it off, a dead body! It was starting to sink in. Carlos, whether a good guy or bad, had been a person. A father, a husband, a human being.

It was hard to accept I was involved in a murder. Someone who was angry enough to kill, in my city. That made me furious.

I moved away from the toilet and started on the ring around the bathtub.

The more I thought it through, it didn't seem like a well-planned murder. Certainly someone could have wanted to throw suspicion on the Maddens or one of the Maddens could be the killer. Rhonda was depressed and who knew what else, but I didn't think she was violent. Same for Dave. He was a gambler who allowed his wife to horde animals but being a mixed-up guy didn't make him a killer. Was I wrong about them?

I really wanted Stanley to be involved since he was a jerk. I'd feel bad for Estelle if he was, but maybe it would free her from him. Stanley had been the complainer and was taking some cues from Randall. How had Carlos threatened the certainty of raised property values? What was Carlos doing on that street? He had to have known about the animals. Was he in the Maddens' yard to take care of the animals or help Rhonda keep them locked up? Perhaps he tried to let them go after she captured them.

My shoulders and back ached from leaning over the edge of the tub. I straightened and stretched. The sink was next.

If Carlos was there to rat out the animal hording, who wanted to stop him? Animal hording wouldn't have been good for the image of the neighborhood, but who would have known until it was time to sell? Randall? Then I remembered the city newsletter. Why hadn't I followed up on that sooner! Carlos had been at the city planning meeting. He was interested in redevelopment so maybe he had a run in with Stanley or Randall there. Maybe they were working together to cleanup things so as soon as development plans were final, they could sell their homes—heck the whole block—for a nice tidy sum.

After the bathroom was sparkling clean, I washed my hands and changed my clothes. This time I put on a long-sleeved yellow t-shirt under a gray zip-up sweatshirt. Then I brought my phone to the kitchen table and sat down, prepared to dive in and solve this mystery.

I made notes on all I'd thought through while cleaning. If I figured this out, I'd get respect from my co-workers, the police, maybe even my boss and Newman. That would feel great.

My phone rang. A city number. I was supposed to be home sick, so I tried to answer in a nasally voice. "Hello?"

It was Cheryl. "I know you're home sick, but I got a message for you." Her voice was very soft.

"Okay. What is it?"

Her voice rose. "Why yes, Mrs. Crutcher. I'll take care of that." Pause.

"Cheryl?" I said, confused.

"Hold on," she whispered. "Here it is: URG BS & NEW VW K cube."

"Huh?" I tried to decipher her message by scribbling it on my pad. Urgent. Boss and Newman? VW—view K cube? Searching through my cubicle? "Cheryl, what's going on?"

She kept her voice light and soft. "Here's the rest of the message: Singer RQ CL."

"A singer wants me to call?"

"Yes. You know the one."

"Oh! Got it. I need to call Sharon."

Her voice rose again and took on a fake tone. "Thank you, ma'am. Call again anytime."

She hung up. What in the world was going on at work? I quickly dialed Sharon's cell phone. It rang five times before she picked up. From the traffic sounds, I figured she was driving and I was on speaker. "Sharon, what's going on?"

"Girl! I don't know what you've gotten yourself in to, but the shit hit the fan and it's spraying everywhere!"

"What do you mean?"

"Newman showed up all loud and arrogant. He had an argument with Richard in his office. I think Richard lost because they came out and started searching your desk."

"What are they looking for?"

"Who the hell knows? Hold on, sugar." I heard her swear then swerve onto what sounded like gravel.

"Whew!" she said. "Had to get off the road."

"Did you see them searching?" I asked. "Did it seem like they found what they were looking for?"

"I tried to listen in, but I didn't want to get too close. Maybe your files on the murder case? They sounded disappointed, so I hi-tailed it out of there lickety split. I didn't want no one asking me nothin'!"

"What do you mean?"

"They pulled Marcus into a meeting before they searched. I figured they wanted to interrogate us all so I left."

"Makes no sense." I opened a Diet Sprite and took a long swig. "What could they hope to find?"

"You don't keep no weird stuff in your desk, do ya? Drugs? Condoms?"

"No, of course not. You know city policy on desks. It's their property. Nothing personal except photos and food related items."

"I hope they search my desk. They'll find a large supply of women's feminine products—in every drawer. Always thought that would be funny to see."

"Sharon, where are you? Should we meet?"

"No can do. I'm heading to a live one." She paused. "Girl, why is Newman out to get you?"

"I wish I knew. I think you're right, they hoped to find notes on my case."

"Must be somethin' to do with that complaint on you," Sharon said.

"But we get complaints all the time."

"I don't know, but I'd cover my ass with duct tape if I were you."

"Will you tell me if you hear anything else?" My phone

beeped in my ear. "Got another call. Thanks, Sharon. Keep me posted."

"Take care, girlfriend."

I clicked over. "This is Kaitlyn," I said.

"John? It's Cheryl at the office."

I sighed. "Cheryl, it's Kaitlyn, not John."

"Yes, John. I have a message for you," she said in her best customer service voice.

I sighed. "Not more codes."

"Mr. Tolefson called. They really need you to come out now."

"Cheryl, John's been handling the Tolefsons."

"No, John. They need you to come. Meet them by the tree."

I thought it through. "Someone wants to meet me at the Tolefson's? John?"

"Yes, that's correct. Thanks, John." She hung up.

I felt utterly, totally, majorly confused. Newman was searching my desk. My co-workers knew it. But someone wanted to meet at the Tolefson's. Someone besides Sharon. John? Cheryl seemed to be on my side. She wouldn't send somewhere dangerous, would she?

I didn't know who left the message asking me to meet, but I was going. I needed info in order to make a real plan. As I headed for the door, I grabbed my keys and my Cedar Grove jacket. I texted Joshua telling him where I was going. On the porch under the eaves, Wally was splayed out on his back with his feet above his head. He rolled over and stood up when I came out.

"You doing yoga?" I asked, but he had no reply. "What do I do with you?" I said, worried about him being a target since whoever was harassing me knew where I lived. How would I get Wally to follow me? "We're going for a ride."

He tilted his head and looked at me like I was an idiot.

"Come on!" I said cheerily and hurried toward my Rav.

Wally actually followed me.

***

The day had turned damp. I started the car just as rain drizzled from a heavenly sprayer, covering everything with a slick sheen of water like the inside of a greenhouse. Except where a greenhouse was humid and warm, the air around Cedar Grove was dry and crisp. I should be at home by a fire with a cup of hot chocolate, preferably laced with something alcoholic, in front of the TV, drooling over Ryan Reynolds' movies. Instead, I wanted to solve a murder.

I drove cautiously through the streets of Cedar Grove. Dark livid clouds swirled overhead like a wire scrubber caught in a rotor. Extremely anxious about this meeting, my foot pressed too hard on the gas. I wanted to get there quickly, but I figured today was not the day to get stopped by the cops for speeding. Had Joshua gotten my message? Was my shadow behind me? Peering into my rearview mirror, I finally spotted a police cruiser a few cars back. I sighed deeply. Thank you, Joshua.

He followed me into town through the light rain. His presence provided some comfort, but did I really want him following me to this meeting? Instead of heading straight to the Tolefsons' house, I stopped at the local grocery store.

I felt antsy and frustrated. What happened to my quiet life? I wanted freedom from people threatening me. We saw some nut jobs in Code Enforcement, but nothing like this week. I'd be happy to rewind a week and have nothing more to complain about than getting stuck with the Tolefsons' call again. I needed peace of mind that the threats were neutralized or I could have my life back. Antsy, my hands moved for ten and two to eight and three and back, my left foot thumping.

I left Wally in the car with the window cracked. Inside the store, I bought a new bag of Gummi Bears and Diet Sprite, and a five-dollar bag of cat treats, then scampered back to my car. I sprinkled a few on the seat and he gobbled them up. As I pulled out, I checked my review but didn't see Joshua. Was he there?

Was the person I was meeting friendly? What would they think a cop following me was a problem? Logically I knew I was stressing about nothing.

Cedar Grove isn't that big, only four and a half square miles. It would have been impossible to lose Joshua, so I decided to let it all play out. If the meeting didn't go well, he'd be the backup. As I rounded the corner onto the Tolefson's street, I still didn't see his car. Maybe Joshua had been told to stay invisible. Or maybe he just stopped at Starbucks.

Why had someone decided I should meet them at the Tolefson's? That location only meant something to other Code Enforcement staff so it had to be John, right? "What do you think, Wally?"

The lump of fat and fur curled up on the passenger seat sleeping ignored me, as if he rode in a car every day. "Do you think it's safe?"

The lump opened one eye and glared at me. Apparently, he had no thoughts on the matter.

I wound through the wet streets toward the Tolefson's. The large pine tree that was the source of all the complaints loomed over the corner of their property. A magnificent old tree, the kind quickly cut down by developers. It dropped needles everywhere, its roots bulged in the soil around its base, and spread gnarled, fingers into nearby flower beds, bumping up through the sidewalks. But it had history. It was history, from a time when trees dominated over people.

I parked across the street and waited. The rain increased in intensity. My wipers and the sound of the defroster blocked noise from the outside. Water streamed down the side windows making them look mottled.

At first, I saw no one, the block was quiet. Then I spotted a tall figure in a navy slicker with the hood up standing near the tree. It waved at me.

I flipped up the hood of my jacket and snugged the string to pull it tight under my chin. "Sorry, buddy," I told Wally. "You have to stay here. I'll be right back."

The wind pulled at the car door when I opened it. Cool water stung my cheeks as I jogged across the street. My sneakers made slopping noise on the pavement. I slowed as I approached the hooded figure. My heartbeat rapidly and I forced myself to breathe.

The two BMWs that usually sat in the driveway were gone so I assumed the homeowners weren't there. As I got closer, I calmed down, the person waiting for me was my co-worker, John Tsai. "John!" I yelled over the sound of the rain.

Water puddled around my feet and my socks felt wet. Soon it would be time to get out my winter boots. The wind blew water sideways against my pant legs and jacket. I shoved one hand in my pocket and the second I used to hold on to my hood. Cold water dripped down my sleeve.

"Kaitlyn, you came." John sounded strained.

"Why the cryptic message?"

"It's insanity back at the office," he said. "Did you talk to Sharon?"

"Yes," I replied. "She said they were searching desks?"

"Your desk."

"Why?" I said it out loud, but I didn't really expect an answer. Marcus's I'd understand. He's always up to something, but me? I glanced at the Tolefson's house and took a few steps closer to the tree for more cover. Under the huge Alder, the rain was only a drip.

"The Tolefson's are out of town," John said. "When I was here last, they told me. Right before they said they were calling the City Manager." He looked up at the tree and shook his head. "My husband thinks I should find a new line of work."

I tried to chuckle, to feel slightly normal, but anxiety gripped my gut and squeezed. "Why did you want to meet? Do you know what's going on?"

"They were all over the office—Newman and Melinda Golden too. Richter wasn't happy, but what could he do? They suspect one of us did something. Then they demanded to see you. When they started to focus on your desk, Sharon figured we should warn you."

Frustrating! "Where are they getting their info? I don't get it. The complaint was Sharon's. I took it to be nice. I didn't plan on a dead body."

He shrugged. "You've been asking around... Kaitlyn, they think one of us leaked to the media. They also seem to think Code Enforcement is spreading bad info about the redevelopment."

"Huh? How could they think that? I never talked to the media and I don't have any info on redevelopment."

"Newman implied there was some proof. But it seems they don't know who."

"Well, it wasn't me."

He shrugged again. "I figure they're just after you for getting so involved in the murder investigation."

"Probably. But I haven't done anything."

"Sharon and I, we knew we had to get out of there. I hung around for a bit to try and hear something, but after they searched your desk they went into Richter's office and shut the door." He stuffed his hands in his pockets, jingling his loose change.

"Sharon said they were meeting with staff, did they talk to you?"

John shook his head again. "Nope, just Marcus."

I sighed. "That weasel. I wonder what he said. I bet he stoked the fire." While we stood, I felt an odd prickle at the back of my neck. I brushed it away thinking it was a wayward leaf.

John cleared his throat. "I thought maybe, if there was something you wanted to tell Richter, maybe I could bring back the message, you know. Kind of be your relay."

And there it was. John didn't want to be my buddy, my helper, he wanted to kiss up to the boss, be the one who brought in the goods. "Relay what?" I hadn't meant to but I sounded rude. "I have nothing to tell."

"Calm down. I'm on your side. I've told you, you do good work. You're more committed than the rest of us put together."

"Thank you. I just don't know what they want."

"There must be something you know or saw."

I shook my head, which flung drips of water onto my face.

John looked contemplative. "Why the complaint against you? What did you do?"

"Nothing." I leaned against the huge tree. Its bark was rough and I felt the bumps through my jacket. The dark clouds churned up the sky. Wet drops from the tree pinged on my hood. "I have some thoughts on the whole murder thing, but nothing concrete. I've done nothing that warrants a complaint."

"Maybe someone reported you for drinking or something? You don't keep anything in your desk, do you?"

I shook my head. "Are you kidding? Of course not!"

"I just thought...."

"You drug me out here in this crap for nothing." I took a breath. None of this was John's fault. "Maybe I should try and call Marcus. Maybe he'll tell me what they wanted."

"I don't know. He seemed pretty smug when he came out, strutting around the office. I think he may have ratted on you."

"For what?" I said, exasperated. "It had to be Melinda Golden who started this. We had a little chat the other day and she knew a lot."

The photos! I had never gotten a word back on them and I still wanted to try and talk to the photographer who took the redevelopment open house shots. "You wouldn't know who took the photos at the redevelopment meetings, do you?"

John shrugged.

I was losing his attention. But the odd prickle was back—like someone was watching me. For a second, my heart raced, then I remembered Joshua. He must have followed me and was now keeping his distance. A new one for him, but I was thankful.

John said, "I think the photographer was that Gregory guy from the city manager's office."

"Yeah, I've seen him around," I said. "Wasn't he taking pictures at the CPR training the other day?"

John shrugged again. "Maybe. I have two more complaints to investigate. Some of us are working." He looked up. "I wish this rain would let up."

I had been wondering why John called me here. Usually, there had to be something in it for him. I just wasn't sure what. "Haven't you ever called in sick when you just needed a day to unwind, chill out?" I said.

He shrugged.

"It's a first for me, but I needed it." I took a breath. I was doing this for GC, to give his family closure, right? But no, I was in this for me and keeping my loved ones safe.

"Watch yourself," John said. "Someone's out to get you," and he turned and walked back to his truck.

As I jogged to my car, the rain miraculously petered out. I looked up and down the street for Joshua. I didn't see him, but I felt him watching me.

***

As I cruised back toward city hall, I realized I was supposed to be sick. I couldn't just waltz into the office and say hi. Thank goodness I'd left my files and notes at home so no one would find them. I pulled over to the curb. Digging through my cluttered glove box, I found an old wrinkled copy of the Cedar Grove employee phone directory. Luckily it grouped people by department and there under City Manager's office was the name Gregory Kleinham. Had to be my guy.

I flipped open my cell phone and started dialing but stopped before I completed the call. What to say? I can't go in there but wanted to show him the newsletter picture to see if he recognized Carlos. How could I get him to come out of the building? "I guess I'll wing it," I said to Wally, who was still sleeping on the seat.

I heard five rings then Gregory's line clicked over to voice mail. Instead of leaving a message, I hit zero. The receptionist in the City Clerk's office answered. "City of Cedar Grove, how may I help you?"

I cleared my throat and tried to slightly disguise my voice without sounding like a complete dork. "I'm trying to find Gregory Kleinham but he doesn't answer his phone."

"Would you like to speak with Melinda Golden instead?" he said in a light breathy voice.

"No!"

"Ah, okay…."

I back-peddled. "I mean, I'd really like to speak to Mr. Kleinham."

"I saw him step out. He was just going for coffee. If you leave him a voice mail, I'm sure he'll call you back.

"Okay, thanks. I'll call back." I hung up, started up the car, and peeled out, hurrying the two blocks to Starbucks—the best, and nearest, place to get coffee if you were at city hall.

***

Starbucks perched in the end of an L-shaped building on a corner with glass windows and a dark green awning. Parking next to the building was full, but I found a space a few spots over in front of a dry cleaners. Trying to be as inconspicuous as possible, I peered through the windows to ascertain if any of my co-workers were inside. And, god forbid, someone like Melinda Golden.

The coast seemed clear, so I pushed open the door and stepped inside. The store was warm and the fragrant smell of coffee swirled on the air. A line, several people long, snaked in front of the glass food case. Many others stood off to the side waiting for their beverage purchases to be completed. I had officially met Gregory only once several years ago. I had probably seen him at the first aid class, but since I was out of sorts that day, I didn't pay much attention.

Two back from the front of the line, a head stuck up above the others. He was very tall and thin, like a stick of uncooked spaghetti. His dark brown hair stuck up in all directions, not like those fashionable guys who use a lot of gel, but like someone who didn't comb their hair after they got out of bed. He wore jeans and a button-up shirt with sleeves that hit mid wrist, revealing hairy arms and a Fit Bit. He looked young, almost as if he hadn't yet grown into his height. My guess was around 25 years old.

I waited for him to place his order, then sidled over while he waited for his skinny venti mocha, half-caf, double shot, double chocolate, no whip. "Hi, Gregory."

He looked at my face, confused. No recognition at all. Then he glanced down, then up quickly. "Hi."

"Kaitlyn, from code enforcement."

"Yeah, sure." He looked toward the barista with anticipation as she placed a cup on the counter.

"Tall caramel macchiato," she said.

He sighed. He had squinty dark eyes and thin brows. His thin cheeks could have used a few more pizzas. He wasn't a bad looking guy, just pointy.

"So Gregory, I've been meaning to come up and see you. I've got a question." I pulled a copy of the city newsletter out of my purse. "Nice work, by the way. The pictures are always great." I unfolded it and opened to the center page with the pictures of the redevelopment meetings. "Do you recognize this guy?" I pointed to the picture of Carlos.

Gregory looked uncomfortable, but I had him trapped. He had to wait for his drink. "Uh…."

"I know you probably take a lot more photos than get printed, so I thought you might recognize this guy." I had to crane my neck up to see his face. He must have been seven feet tall.

He shook his head. "Not really, no." His voice was a little squeaky.

"Are you sure? Maybe you chatted with him? Don't you have to get their names for the captions?"

He shifted his weight back and forth on his feet and eyed the barista again. "Usually. But we don't always get everyone. There's no caption so we probably didn't get his name."

Well, damn. I'd been hoping for what? This guy just shoots pictures. "Who decides which photos get printed?"

This time he straightened up and rolled his eyes. "Melinda."

"Of course."

"But I didn't... I mean, she's okay... she's..." He glanced around as if she would suddenly appear.

"No problem. I won't say anything. And you don't need to tell her I asked, right?"

He shook his head. "Nope. I don't tell her anything I don't have too."

"I get that," I said.

Now that we had something in common, he seemed to have relaxed.

"I guess I just hoped you'd know something about this guy. He's connected to one of my complaints," I said.

Greg paused and sipped his drink, then seemed to decide I was okay. "I remember he stayed around for a long time. He looked at the boards but also hung around on the edges of the room like he was waiting for someone. He ended up in quite a few shots."

"Did he meet anyone?"

"I honestly don't remember," Gregory said, then looked up as if thinking. "Mostly he talked with the ladies. I remember thinking he was just there for a hook up."

"That's it?"

"He might have talked with a tall guy."

"Tall like you?"

He frowned. "No. Regular tall."

Randall? "Bushy eyebrows, gray hair, and a permanent scowl?"

He shrugged. "Maybe. It was a while ago."

The barista set a cup on the counter. "Skinny Venti Mocha, half-caf, double shot and double chocolate whip."

For heaven's sake. I could never be a barista—I couldn't even get a few words strung together without tripping over my tongue. Wonder how the bikini girls did it? I guess it didn't matter if they could talk well. *Knock it off, K. That's mean.*

Gregory snatched his cup. "I gotta get back to work."

"Thanks a bunch. I appreciate it."

He hurried from the store, ducking his head as he exited.

I headed home and spent the afternoon pretending to be sick.

***

At some point late afternoon, after lounging on the couch and watching *Big Bang Theory* reruns, I looked at my cell. Since my bank fiasco and the media storming my home, I'd been ignoring my phone as much as possible. I figured if it was important, they'd leave a message. Some did and some didn't since the recent call total was double the number of voice mails. I looked at those red numbers, knowing I should listen to them, at least delete the crap ones and make sure I didn't miss something important.

I put the phone on speaker and hit play on my voicemail.

Hello, Ms. Willis. This is Rob from Channel... Delete.

Mrs. Willis, I'm calling from the Seattle Times... Delete.

Hi. This is the Everett Herald calling for Kait... Delete.

Ms. Willis, this is Puget Sound Energy calling about your account. Stop and save to listen to later after a couple glasses of wine.

On and on it went. "Leave me alone!" I screamed into the

empty house. I probably should have waited until I was calmer, but I called Ben, got his voice mail and left a scathing message. He was only responsible for half of my problems but it was one more thing I didn't need right now.

A couple more messages. I was about in tears by the time I got to the last new message.

You just don't listen, do you bitch? You are going to pay for your meddling. Get a life and get out of our business!

Now I actually felt sick. I had no energy left to deal with that threat. I ordered pizza, ate three slices, and went to bed.

CHAPTER 13

Saturday, September 23, 2017

Saturday morning I slept in and woke up feeling groggy. The weather didn't share my mood. It was sunny with only a few clouds. After a quick breakfast I went to the store for actual groceries. Distracted and out of sorts, I wandered the aisles aimlessly. I hadn't made a list or reviewed my coupons, my usual MO. I bought a few things using my emergency credit card, then headed home, sheathing all the way with bad thoughts about Ben and my bank account.

At home, as I was gathering my purchases out of the rear of my Rav, my neighbor's car pulled up in front of their house and parked on the street. GC got out. "Hey!" I yelled, setting down my bags.

He turned toward me and frowned. I jogged across the street to meet him. "I wanted to follow up with you."

"Okay, but I got stuff to do." He looked tired, his face creased, his t-shirt dirty.

He didn't sound very eager to hear what I'd learned, which wasn't much. "I've talked to the neighbors around where your cousin died. A couple are quite suspicious. I did confirm that Carlos was on the landscape crew working that street, so perhaps he got into a confrontation with the homeowner who had the animals." I felt even lamer than I sounded.

"Anything else?"

Well, wasn't he short today? What happened to the *Oh, please help me, Kaitlyn.* "I know it's not much, but I'm working with the police..."

"Police." His tone was angry. "They will do nothing. I told you that."

"But I know them, they're working on it. It just takes time."

"My cousin is dead!" he said stepping close to me. "We're having the funeral next week. What am I supposed to tell my aunt and uncle?"

Rage flowed off him like sweat. "I don't... I mean, I am doing what I can. I told you I didn't have any authority in this."

He shook his head and stepped back. "My *familia* is much upset."

I couldn't even imagine planning a funeral for a family member who had been murdered. I thought about the times my brother, Kale, got into trouble or was out of communication for a while. But Kale never ran with a rough crowd only partiers. Nothing that would end like this. "I'm sorry, GC." I'll keep looking, okay?"

He stuffed his hands in his pockets and nodded, looking dejected.

His front door opened and Maria peered out.

"I gotta go," he said.

"Okay. I'll let you know if I learn anything new."

He shot me a mean, angry look, then turned and walked to his front door.

I tried for cheery and waved at Maria. She looked tired, worn down by life. Was Carlos really who GC said he was? Why was GC so angry today? Was he more involved in this than I thought? What was I missing?

There were no answers so I walked back across the street as the sun broke through the clouds and lit up my driveway like a spotlight. I stepped into the bright circle and looked up. It was warm and beautiful, but the sky held no answers.

I spent the afternoon doing home paperwork, reviewing my finances and unhappily transferring money out of my savings to cover my checking account. Painful. I tried to stay calm about it. I was smart and capable. I would get through this. I would be okay.

***

About two o'clock, I decided I needed to get out and move. The sun was still shining and the temperature had spiked to almost 70. Good day for a walk.

I drove to CG High School and walked the track circle, headphones in with 90s Pop music playing to keep my spirits up.

I walked quickly, getting my heart rate up, working off stress. But even the music couldn't keep my mind from the murder and whatever Newman was up to. What I knew:

1. Someone leaked information about the murder to the media. I needed to look online and find out what.

2. GC asked me to help but now was acting angry, not grieving. Could he be involved? I didn't get any gut feeling about that.

3. My gut told me this mess was more about the city's redevelopment than the animal hoarding.

4. Randall, Stanley, even maybe Dave Madden, were involved. Dave gambled. He needed money. Could

Randall or Stanley have blackmailed him into killing Carlos? But why? What was Carlos' role?

As I finished my third lap, the sun was low in the sky and the air was cooling. Time to go home. Perhaps Sam would meet for coffee again and we could discuss what he knew.

***

I pulled back into my driveway and cut the engine. Something was on my porch and it wasn't Wally. His box was empty. Slowly, I climbed from the car and looked around. My street was quiet, no music coming from across the street. There a large bundle perched on the cement in front of my door. Would it suddenly explode? Somehow become a fire ball?

OMG! What if it was Wally? Should I call someone? I'd sure look stupid if it turned out to be some rolled up clothes that Rosie borrowed. But she would have texted me and let me know. Hell, she'd have brought it over when I was home.

I refused to look like an idiot in front of the police. And I refused to call on Joshua again. He couldn't be my crutch when times get tough. I would deal with this. *I am smart. I am strong. I choose confidence.* I repeated my yoga mantras as I approached the porch. *Please don't be Wally.* I should have brought him with me! Tears stung my eyes.

The bundle looked like a navy blanket or sleeping bag rolled into a ball. Weird. I went back to my car and got a golf umbrella from the back seat. Poking at the bundle elicited no response. Nothing moved, or moaned, smelled, smoked, or ticked.

Besides, no one would leave a bomb on my porch, right? I used the end of the umbrella to push the bundle until it unfurled. Inside the dirty blanket, a stuffed animal, lay on its side. *Not Wally, thank god!* I think it was a rabbit or maybe a bear, dirty and worn. Red marks splotched the belly and a short noose looped around its neck. *What the hell?*

Chills skittered through me and my pulse banged in my temple. Rolling it over, a piece of paper poked out from under the animal. I could tell there was writing on it, but I didn't want to touch it. Why hadn't I gotten out my winter gloves. Using the umbrella to secure one corner, I leaned over and unfurled the paper with my index finger. Large box letters:

BACK OFF, BITCH! KEEP YOUR NOSE OUT OF OTHER PERSONS BUSINESS OR YOU'LL NEVER WORK FOR THE CITY AGAIN! KEEP YOUR MOUTH SHUT OR YOUR CAT DIES! KEEP AWAY FROM 50TH STREET OR YOUR FRIENDS AND FAMILY ARE NEXT!

Adrenaline flooded my body and my muscles tightened. My limbs shook. Wally took off all the time—how would I know if he had been taken or killed? Could they know where Rosie lived? No way they could know about my parents in Bellingham, right?

Now I was royally pissed. Time to be done with all this. No one was going to threaten my friends, my family, my livelihood, or my sorta pet!

Using a tissue from my car, I picked up the note and dropped it in a plastic grocery bag I found behind the seat. I kicked the bundle off the porch so that it was partially hidden behind a shrub. I stomped down the driveway to my Rav. I would force the police to do their job. Sam—Detective Evans—needs to deal with this!

I drove a little too fast to the police station, swung into the parking lot, and slammed on my brakes. As I took a deep breathe, my resolve started to wane. What was I going to do? Go inside and demand to talk to Chief Dimitriadis? Joshua didn't have any real power and all he would do is tell me to stay out of it. I didn't know how to deal with Sam right now. My romantic, lust-filled feelings were out of control and got in the way every time I tried to have a serious conversation with him. Why had I

243

asked him out in the first place? Complications—I didn't need that right now.

But I knew I needed to give Sam the note. The threats were getting serious and whoever this nutjob was, he needed to be caught! Could GC be the killer? Why would he have come to me in the first place? Then Randall Wyman had to be behind this. Or was I just projecting my dislike of him? Maybe he and Stanley were in cahoots. But to what end? How did they even know Carlos and what would they have been doing in the Maddens' backyard? Why couldn't I figure this out?

I am smart. I am strong. I choose confidence.

Instead of stomping inside and demanding to see Sam, I called his cell phone, but got his voice mail. I took a breath. "It's Kaitlyn. I found... something at my house. There is a threatening note that I'd like you to see. Please call me when you have a chance." Awkward, but hopefully it would do the trick.

I pulled out of the station and headed home, putting Rosie on speaker. I got her voice mail. "And Rosie, something's happened, you need to be careful. Don't walk around alone or anything. Someone might be... well, just call me."

I should go home and look for Wally, get him inside or somewhere safe. But where to look? He could be anywhere. And then where could he and I go to be safe?

I should feel afraid, but anger overpowered my fear. No one threatens me! Some killer was out there, causing havoc in my city. I needed to act. It was up to me right now to do what needed to be done. End this once and for all. I just wish I knew how to do that.

As I pulled into my driveway, I remembered my dinner with Rosie and the overheard conversation from the couple in the next booth. It had to have been the Wymans. It hadn't sounded like Stanley or certainly it wasn't Dave and Rhonda. The negativity sounded very much like Randall Wyman.

"He thought he was a player. Probably involved in drugs."

"They're a menace to the neighborhood. If this gets them out of our hair, well, good."

Could Randall have killed Carlos thinking he was Dave Madden? Could he have written the note I found on my truck? It was during the day so wouldn't Randall have been at work? Could Mary have done it? Why? She didn't seem the type.

What was Randall hiding? Had Carlos also been sleeping with Mary so Randall killed Carlos out of jealousy? That sorta made sense. Wouldn't it be easier to just leave his wife? The two had a strange relationship for sure. I felt confident all of this had something to do with the redevelopment. Carlos was at the city redevelopment event. But would Carlos and Randall be up to something together? Carlos somehow crossed his partner, and Randall snapped? Someone needed anger management classes.

Was Mary afraid of Randall? At our first meeting she seemed worried before he came home. She'd said something about him always wanting dinner on the table. Maybe he wasn't husband of the year, but did that make him a murderer? If he was, why would he leave Carlos's body? Wouldn't he have wanted to hide it?

Or was it left in the Madden's yard to throw suspicion on Dave? No one seemed to like the Maddens and their house was the blight of the block. If Randall wanted his street to look good so it would help his property values before the redevelopment, was this just about him wanting more money for his house? Or about Carlos sleeping with his wife? Those seemed like thin motives. There had to be more to it. Too many unanswered questions. I thought of the day I'd found Mary home and half asleep. What was that about?

***

My head hurt from thinking so I made dinner. Okay, I ate leftover pizza and thought about what to do next. I needed to go back to the *Death Street* and once and for all figure out what really happened, why Carlos was killed.

From my bedroom, I heard my phone ringing elsewhere the house. Hurrying to the living room, I heard the ring coming from my purse on the entry table. I struggled to get my phone out. It had jumped out of its inner pocket and fallen to the bottom of the bag. Time to clean out the purse!

At the same time, I saw a car pull into my driveway. Immediately my heart rate intensified and I dropped the phone. Who was here? Someone I should be afraid of? Do I hide? Not open the door? Call 911?

I squatted down and snagged the phone as it went silent. I poked missed calls and saw my parents' number. *Oh, No!* Were they in danger? When I looked up again, Sam was climbing out of the car. I sighed audibly, set the phone on the table. *Be rational.* I opened my front door.

Wally was not in his box. I smashed down a swell of worry.

"Hi," he called.

Sam was here! My pulse quickened. Dressed business casual in dark jeans, black shoes, and an indigo polo shirt, he looked great. Really great. *Play it cool, K.* "Hi."

"I got your message about the item you found on your porch."

Oh, that's right. I'd called him about the bloody stuffed animal with a noose. I took a breath and sighed. *Confidence!* "Yes, it was quite disturbing so I wanted you to take a look." Should I invite him in? Stay here? *Awkward!*

Sam paused on the walkway before replying, his hands at his sides. "What have you been up to that is causing you to be threatened?"

My mouth opened to defend my actions, but I knew he knew the bundle wouldn't have shown up without a reason. He was a smart guy, he'd find out I'd been talking to people so I might as well be fess up. Besides, I'm a terrible liar. "I've talked to some of the neighbors on the block." There honest. But I felt the need to add, "I'm working to close the complaint and the

Maddens aren't around to talk to about the cleanup."

"I released the backyard." He put his hands behind him, calm, military-ish. "Animal Control did some excavation in the yard to see if there were animal carcasses to add to the animal cruelty case. I can get a message to the Maddens and perhaps provide some resources to assist them."

"Okay." Why couldn't I think of something intelligent to say? My tongue had knots and my throat was tight. "Thanks. That will help."

I'd left the bundle right where I'd thrown it, under the bushes in front of the house. I hadn't wanted to touch it but had covered it with a green tablecloth. I pointed to it. "I didn't want to mess up any evidence, but I didn't want to look at it again either."

He squatted down. "Do you have a spatula or something I can use to take a look?"

"Sure." I turned.

"And a garbage bag?"

I nodded and went into the house for the items he requested.

He used the wooden spoon I produced to move the tablecloth and peel open the bundle. "Huh." He pulled a set of gloves from his pocket and put them on.

"Kinda sick," I said making a face. "Creepy." There was that throat tightening again, but this time it was revulsion and fear. "My cat..."

He didn't say anything, very matter-of-fact this guy. He just wrapped it back up and placed the bundle in the bag.

"I'll have someone look at it, but it may take a while." Another pause. "With this and the fire... please leave the investigating to me. I'm making progress and..."

"Progress? What's new? Did you find something?"

"Not your concern."

Good one, K. Don't piss off the guy you kind of like. "I know that. But I need some personal closure too."

"And you'll get it when I arrest someone."

I knew he was right. But dang it, I was curious! I opened my mouth to speak but he continued. "Leave it alone."

A chilly breeze blew through the yard. The sky was blanketed in gray. I sighed.

"Please," he added. That one word, spoken soft and low sent happy shivers through my body.

"I understand," I said. "I'm kinda freaked by the whole thing."

"Trust us to do our jobs. Then you can finish your job."

"Okay." God, I sounded like a whiney child. No more! Time to move on and stop obsessing over this mess! Get back in control of my life!

"Thank you," he said. "You haven't had any more trouble with our ex?"

"No. He's stayed away," I said. "He hasn't paid me, but I'm still hopeful."

"Okay. I've gotta run."

I nodded.

"Take care of yourself," he said. "And watch your back."

On that happy note, he walked to his car. Watching that view was the only good thing about my day. I sent Wally positive thoughts and went back inside.

***

After the conversation with Sam, I rethought my decision to go to the *Death Street*. But I wanted answers and I thought I was pretty close to the solution. I could figure this out!

I left Rosie another message letting her know where I was going. Might as well be safe, right? Have a little girlfriend backup just in case.

Procrastinating, I went out to the front porch to check for anything suspicious and to look for Wally. He was back in his box. I reached down and patted his head awkwardly. "I'll get you some lunch, okay?"

"Meooooow."

"Right." I returned to the porch with a small dish of wet cat food that smelled like rotten fish. "Here you go."

He stood and stretched, sniffed at the food then dove in.

"How about when you are done we go for a ride?" I suggested. If I was going to leave, he was coming with me. At least I'd know he was safe.

***

In my car, Wally stretched tall in what yogis called the cat pose, which he couldn't really pull off because of bulging belly. He looked at me expectantly.

"What next? Great question. We're going for a ride."

He lay down and closed his eyes, which I took as ascent.

I pulled out my cell phone and called Joshua. Five rings then voice mail. That was odd. If he was following me, wouldn't he answer? I left a message. "Hey, it's Kaitlyn. I'm heading over to the de..." I almost said *Death Street*. "...to the neighborhood where the murder happened. I have to do a final check on the backyard cleanup." That wasn't strictly true, I knew the Maddens hadn't made progress. Still, I could check on the yard while I was there. It was Saturday, but I was making up for being sick on Friday, right?

Then guilt caused me to add, "Let's grab lunch again sometime." I hung up feeling like a dork. Was I encouraging him? Still, I felt bad he'd been assigned to watch me. I'm sure he loved it, but it was still a shit job and he'd probably get crap from the other officers.

Thinking about food made my stomach growl. The earlier pizza and a few Gummi Bears hadn't done much for me. And the fact that I was working on my fourth Diet Sprite wasn't helping my stomach. I started the car and turned on the radio. Almost every station had commercials or DJ's talking. I clicked onto a local country station and cranked up the volume on Rascal Flatts

"Bob That Head." *Rock on, dude.*

Thinking about Rosie's insistence that I protect myself, I made a stop at Joe's Pawn *Shop*. It was on the eastside of town, a bit out of the way but what the heck.

"You want two percent or five percent?" The sales guy asked.

"I dunno. Let's go with five." If I was in, I was all in.

I purchased a small can of pepper spray. The thing cost 15 dollars and was called *Wildfire*. Creative.

He gave me an enthusiastic lesson, which I only half listened to. I wasn't sure I would ever need to use it—I wasn't sure I could use it, but I'd tell Rosie I'd taken her advice. The can wasn't very big, still I couldn't figure out where to put it. If I stuffed it in my purse or the glove box it wouldn't be accessible and what would be the point? It was a bit too bulky for my jeans pocket, so I shoved it deep in the pocket of my Cedar Grove jacket and hoped it wouldn't fall out.

That errand done, I drove to the *Death Street*. Before I'd left home, I'd typed up a note and made copies on my printer: "Are you missing a cat?" An excuse to be here so I wouldn't get in trouble with Councilman Newman. Was it worth my job to find out what happened? My job was very important to me. But I had to stop the threats. I pushed the threat to my job to the back of my mind as I parked my Rav in front of the Madden's. These neighbors were not getting away with messing up my city.

Their house was dark and even more deserted-looking than last time I'd been here, the grass taller, the driveway covered in fallen leaves, branches, and pinecones. They were obviously staying somewhere else. Who could blame them? The crime scene tape was gone from the fence. I'd already gotten in trouble once for entering the yard. Would it make me look more guilty if I went there again? Sam would be pissed. Maybe I'd wait for Joshua. If he went with me, it would be all right, wouldn't it?

Wally had gone back to sleep. I put my cell phone in the opposite jacket pocket from the pepper spray and opened the car door. It was dry out at the moment, so I cracked the window.

The sky was a swirling gray mass and likely to start dumping again, but I wasn't planning to be here long.

I looked up and down the street. A quiet Saturday. A few cars here and there but nothing else to see. I checked my phone. No call from Joshua. I tried his cell. No answer. Where was he? I walked to the side of the Maddens' house. What could it hurt to take a look? See if anyone had cleaned up.

I stepped into the yard taking careful breaths, but the panic I'd felt when I'd visited with Sam didn't surface. The yard just looked bare and forlorn. The empty cages had been piled against the back side of the house. The grass was mostly brown with a few blackberry vines poked up through it. The smells, that had been so strong and lingered in my memories all week, had disappeared, washed away by the rain. That was good.

What was different? Sam had said Animal Control searched the yard for dead animals. Piles of dirt surrounded five or six large holes all around the yard. A couple of them were several feet wide and looked deep.

Looking around, I wondered what had really gone on here. I thought of the day I'd knocked on Mary Wyman's door and found her disheveled. And then I thought of the night I'd knocked on Rosie's door. At the time, I'd assumed that Mary was upset by what transpired in her neighborhood. But the more I thought about it, I think I interrupted a little afternoon delight. But with whom?

GC said Carlos was a ladies man. I'd bet he'd been fooling around with Mary and maybe even Rhonda Madden. Although she didn't seem lucid enough to carry on an affair. Perhaps something Mary said led him to the Maddens' yard. Maybe he was doing a Good Samaritan thing and trying to help Rhonda. Yet someone was angry enough to stab him. Who had taken Carlos' place in Mary's bed? I could envision a new lover pushing Randall going over the edge.

Then a random thought struck me. Marcus had been nosey about this whole affair and willing to speak to Richard and

Newman. What was his stake in it? Could he have been the one I heard with Randall at the bar? If he'd somehow took Carlos' place in Mary's bed, he would know I'd been asking questions.

A squeaky noise from the gate made me jump. Scuffling sounds. I looked around for a place to hide but there was nowhere to go. The gate on the other end of the yard had been locked before. Was it still? If I ran that way and it was locked, I was backed into a corner. I stepped closer to the side of the house near a sliding glass door. The drapes were closed, hiding whatever was inside. I reached out and tried the door but it was locked. I slipped my hand into my pocket and closed it around the can of pepper spray. A cool breeze whipped through the yard.

A figure stepped around the side of the house. I expected Randall Wyman. He was behind all of this, I felt sure of that now. He was manipulating his neighbors and hoping to cash in on the redevelopment. I could easily picture him as my harasser. And as a murderer.

Instead, Mary Wyman came into view. She wore tight black jeans and a poufy white parka. Her perfectly done hair barely moved in the wind.

"Mary, you scared me."

She jumped then recovered. "You." Her voice was deep, harsh, and familiar. From where?

"I came to do my final inspection and finish my report."

"It's Saturday." She walked toward me, her hands in her pockets. "And you're not in your city Truck."

Shoot. I hadn't thought of that. "Just wrapping things up on my day off."

"Sure you are." It came out very flat. "You have an animal in your car."

Her expression hardened as she came toward me.

"Yes. My cat likes to ride with me."

Her eyes were so flat and blank. *Oh, shit!* She wouldn't have hurt Wally, would she?

Mary moved toward me and I saw that her face, while

perfectly made up, was blotchy and pale, her eyes red. "You know what I think, I think you're here snooping. Sticking your nose in other people's business."

"Responding to complaints is my business."

"You need to stay out of things that don't concern you," she growled.

Suddenly, the voice became clear in my head. The voice that had been behind me in the parking lot after yoga. "You! You attacked me!"

"And did you listen? No. You were told to stay out of this."

I squeezed the can in my hand, then tried to relax, while moving my thumb toward the safety switch the store clerk had shown me. "Out of what? I don't even know what you're talking about or what you think I know."

"We had a nice little plan." She continued toward me. Her parka made a weird swishing sound when she moved her arms. "A way to pad our bank account and retire somewhere nice. But you had to get involved."

"I didn't kill the guy. I didn't even know who he was!"

She wasn't listening to me. She was off in her own world. "Everything was fine. Randall was going to finally take me on a cruise and buy me a new house somewhere nice. Until Carlos got so full of himself and started trying to help Rhonda." Mary laughed and I thought of the crazy killer in old horror movies— it was that kind of un-funny laugh. "He thought he could help the crazy lady. He was supposed to be focused on me. "

"You were sleeping with Carlos." As she moved closer, I inched away. But I had nowhere to go. Her back was to the gate.

"He was my friend. And yes, we had sex, so what? He was good too. He…"

I didn't need to hear about that. I interrupted, "You killed Carlos? Because he tried to help Rhonda?"

She snorted. "I didn't kill Carlos. Carlos was doing me a favor." She smiled and her face relaxed. "He was amazing. One of the best I've had. Although my new guy…"

If she kept talking about her sex life I was going to throw up. "Spare me the details."

She glared at me and then just continued as if I hadn't spoken. "I thought Carlos trusted me. And all the while he was helping Randall."

"Helping Randall do what?"

She barked a mix of a laugh and a snort. "Randall has a plan. He owns half the houses on this block. He has influence on the City Council. Made sure that this street will be included in the re-zoned area. We were set to make a nice dollar when the redevelopment started. He promised our life would change. We've already had developers coming around and asking us if we'd sell. One has a plan to buy up most of the block for an apartment complex." She grinned. "I had the developer convinced the second time he came by to chat. He stayed awhile and I can be very persuasive."

A light drizzle started to fall. So I'd been right. She hadn't been alone and grieving when I'd knocked on her door that day. "So what did Carlos have to do with it? You replaced him quick enough. Why did you kill him?"

She jerked her arm toward me, pointing a bony finger with a long red nail. "I didn't kill Carlos!"

This woman was cray-cray. Maybe more than Rhonda Madden. No doubt about it.

When I heard the squeak of the gate, I thought it was the wind and rain, but then Joshua stepped into the backyard. He wore his dark blue uniform with all the black gadgets at the waist and the shower cap covering his hat. He had never looked so good.

"Kaitlyn, I've been looking for you. I got your message. Sorry about that. I got pulled away for a while."

Relieved, I moved to step around Mary. "Don't move!" she hissed.

I took a breath. "Joshua, Mary is a little upset. She needs to be escorted home."

His face scrunched up in a slightly confused look and his tongue jutted out his cheek.

Mary whirled around toward Joshua. "She ruined everything! Why can't she just leave this alone? Couldn't she mind her own business!"

It didn't even seem that she was talking to us. She was yelling at the world.

Joshua took a step toward Mary. "Now Mrs. Wyman. Calm down. What seems to be the trouble?"

Mary pivoted toward me and suddenly there was a knife in her hand. It must have been hiding somewhere in that poufy jacket. I saw Joshua's hand moved toward his gun.

"Now Mrs. Wyman..." he said. "There's no need for that. Put down the knife."

Just then, Randall joined us in the backyard. He wore a tan Carhartt jacket and jeans. Very normal looking. For a split second, I thought we were saved. He could deal with his crazy wife. It was all her. I'd suspected him but it was her.

Then Randall swung something big and long and it hit Joshua on the head. Joshua tumbled to the ground. Instinctively, I shifted my legs and started to move, but Mary reached out and grabbed my arm. Her taloned fingernails dug into my skin. She held the knife in front of me. I had a random, weird, terrified beyond reason thought that my blood would really mess up her white jacket.

"You aren't going anywhere you nosy little bitch!" She cranked my arm behind my back just as I started to push her off.

"Shit!" A jolt of agony raced through my elbow and down toward my wrist like a hot poker had been jammed into my arm. She didn't look that strong but her grip held fast. Tears stung my eyes and pain zapped up my arm. "Let go of me! Joshua!" I screamed at his still body. He hadn't moved since Randall had decked him. He looked so still! "Joshua!"

Randall threw down a two-by-four and moved toward us. I now noticed he wore heavy work gloves. His graying hair was flat from the rain. His bushy eyebrows scrunched in concentration. "Mary, we have to go."

"Go where? You've screwed this all up, as usual."

The rain fell harder. I felt water trickle down my neck. I needed to wipe my eyes. The arm Mary had wrenched behind me throbbed, like something was torn. What were those two up to? And what would they do with me?

My other hand was still in my pocket, fingering the pepper spray. But even if I sprayed Mary, Randall still blocked my escape. Could I hit two people in a row? How close did I need to be? Would it come back on me? *Damn*! I should have paid more attention to the clerk! Did pepper spray work in the rain?

"Who killed Carlos?" I asked, mostly because I couldn't think of anything else to do and I wanted to keep their focus away from Joshua.

"Dumb ass over there," Mary said, distain in her voice. She didn't sound like someone who was looking forward to retiring with her husband.

Randall stood up straighter and stepped closer to Mary. "You slept with him!"

"So what?"

"He was the hired help I had working on our project." Randall's face turned red and through the rain I would see a vein in his neck throbbing. "And now you're sleeping with the other guy I hired. You slut!"

Mary didn't look like she even noticed it was raining. Her perfectly coifed hair held its shape, while I could feel mine going limp and hanging over my ears. Her lashes were thick with water. She said, "Everything was going fine. Another year and we'd have been able to sell to that developer. Then you could actually live up to all the promises you made me. You said we would take a cruise."

"You and that damned cruise. Why would I want to go on a cruise with you? You'd probably sleep with the entire crew!"

Mary's fingers pinched my arm.

"Ow!" I pulled away, but she just squeezed harder.

"Shut up!" Mary hissed at me.

"What do you want to do now, Your Highness?" Randall said. "I told you to stop harassing her. I told you to leave it alone and everything would work out. But you never listen to me, do you? Just once you should have listened to me!"

"Leave it alone?" Mary spat. "You killed Carlos! Everything would have been fine. This bitch wouldn't have come snooping around. But you screwed up and I had to fix it--as usual."

These two must have been in agony all week trying to play the perfect couple and now it was all coming to a head. I glanced at Joshua, but he hadn't moved. I thought about his gun and felt grateful Randall hadn't had the smarts to grab it. Maybe if he woke up while they were fighting... *Come on, Joshua. Please be okay.*

Randall stepped forward and pointed his finger at Mary. "I didn't mean to kill him!" Rage and pain radiated from him like heat off a bonfire. "I did everything for you! I tried to fulfill every nag you tossed at me. But were you grateful? No. Just more nagging."

"An accident! You stabbed him!"

Mary turned toward Randall but didn't let go of my arm. She shook with anger tightening her grip. Pain coursed through my elbow up into my shoulder.

"How was murdering Carlos supposed to help us? You brought the police in! We would have been fine—"

"Fine! We weren't fine! You were fucking everything in sight and still asking me to support you!"

"You never came through on anything," Mary screamed. "Then you took Carlos. You put him to work on Rhonda."

"To get her to cleanup her yard! He was a yard guy!"

"She didn't want him!"

These two were both crazy. They deserved the same cruel and unusual punishment. Joshua still hadn't moved. *Come on, come on. Wake up!*

While Randall and Mary argued, I glanced around the backyard looking for an escape route. If I could get away from Mary, I might be able to climb over the fence into the neighbor's yard. What about Joshua? I didn't see how I could help him unless I got away to call for help. They wouldn't really hurt a cop, would they? Mary had the knife but didn't seem like she even remembered it was there. Randall could try for Joshua's gun, but if I ran fast enough...

"You bitch!" Randall spit. "I did everything for you!"

Mary released her grip on my arm to stab the air and point at Randall. "You killed Carlos! Why did you have to kill Carlos!"

"Because he said he was going to get you to leave me!"

I took a deep yoga breath and slowly pivoted my foot and shifted my weight preparing to run.

Randall fumed. "You were going to leave me for a damned gardener! After everything I did for you!"

Mary stepped forward and slapped Randall, hard. The wet slap echoed through the air as if carried by the rain.

"I loved him!" Mary screamed, genuine raw pain in her voice.

Randall's mouth dropped open but no words came out.

I saw my opportunity and bolted toward the side fence. I turned back to see if they were following me, but I'd forgotten about the holes in the ground. I stumbled on a pile of dirt then stepped out into air and tumbled into one of the large holes. I couldn't see over the edge. The rain continued to pound creating a pool of mud at my feet. The hole was much deeper than it had looked. I clawed at the side with my good arm, but the dirt turned to mud and fell away from my hands.

If I had two good arms, I probably could have crawled out, but with one arm down for the count, I was trapped. Randall could easily get me now. Out of fear and frustration, I lifted my face to the rain and screamed—screamed as loud and long as I could. It wasn't hard since my elbow felt like it was on fire. I heard Randall and Mary yelling at each other, then a strange sound like someone being punched and a thud. Randall appeared at the side of my hole.

"Well, look at you. How convenient." He glanced around, flinging drops of water off his hair. "You can just stay there until I figure out what to do with my wife."

Randall left. He left! Sure, I didn't want him to kill me, but he left me there! What was I supposed to do? I made a few more frantic attempts at climbing out, but the walls just slid away when I grabbed hold. My arm throbbed.

Tears stung my eyes and mixed with the rain on my cheeks. Who would ever find me here? What had Randall done with Joshua? Was he dead? *Oh, God!* Why couldn't I just mind my own business?

CHAPTER 14

Saturday, September 23, 2017

I squatted down and tucked my chin to my chest attempting to keep the rain off my face. I hadn't had my hood up before, so now it was full of water. Lifting it made water run down the back of my neck. Clutching my coat tightly around my throat with my good hand, I tried to figure out what to do. Surely someone would be looking for Joshua, right? He was an on-duty cop. Could they track him, maybe through his phone or his car? But who would be looking for me? My car was too old for GPS. And why would they look in the one place I was told not to go?

"Yeooow!"

I started and fell back on my butt in the wet, muddy ground, face up toward the rain. My phone rang. I pulled it out, but it was slick it slipped onto the ground, disappearing in the mud.

A huge white blob peered over the edge of the hole. "Meow."

"Wally! What in the world? How did you get out of the car?"

My car! Surely someone would see my car! Would it be soon enough to save me? Probably not. I needed to save myself. But how?

Wally perched at the edge of the hole, leaning in, rain slicking down his fur. He didn't look as fat--just flattened.

"Cats hate water. What are you doing here?"

He cocked his head and sat down.

"I'm glad you're here," I said. But then I thought of Randall. What would he do to Wally! "You should go," I said. "You don't want to be here when he comes back."

"Yeooow!" Wally didn't move.

I guess that was an emphatic no.

It seemed like I waited for hours for something to happen, someone to come and find me. I dug my phone out of the ground but it was muddy and my wet fingers couldn't get it turned on. Zit probably was too wet to work. The rain let up—a little and my arm ached a bit less. Wally laid his head on his dirty paws and watched me.

I cried. I hate to admit it, but I did. I felt so helpless! Wally provided a bit of company and actually gave me some strength. *I can figure this out,* I chanted. *I have to save Wally and my job!* The rain petered out and blue sky peaked through the clouds. *A sign! I can do this!*

I struggled and scrambled and fought against the slippery sides of the hole. I was wet and muddy and I just didn't have enough strength to pull myself out. Standing on my tip toes I could see the 2-by-four Randall hit Joshua with laying six feet away. No way I could reach it.

I wished I could see Joshua. I tried to call to him but any sound came out of my throat was washed away on the rain. Maybe he'd escaped. Or Randall had dragged him away.

I sagged back against the side of the hole, my collar pulled up as high as I could manage. I heard a noise and Wally disappeared. I started to yell, "Help…" then Randall peered over the hole. He looked menacing, his face red, his eyes filled with hate.

I crouched down and cowered. There was so much more I wanted to do with my life! I didn't want it to end here. Then I remembered the pepper spray. I pushed myself against the side of the hole and slipped my hand into my pocket. My life was not going to end here! Not like this.

"You ruined everything!" Randall hissed at me. "You and that no good, son-of-a-bitch Carlos. Why can't people just mind their own GOD—DAMN—BUSINESS?"

He looked around, like he was trying to figure out how to get me out. He held a shovel, but it hung forgotten at his side. *Please don't bury me!*

The next time he looked back down at me, I pointed the pepper spray can straight up, pushed the trigger, squeezed my eyes shut, and prayed.

Randall screamed and stumbled back. I kept my eyes shut and my arm in front of my face, but I couldn't hold my breath forever. When I sucked in, I felt fire fill my lungs as the spray settled into the hole. I gasped. Instinctively, I opened my eyes and they were suddenly boiling! Stinging! I couldn't breathe! I coughed over and over until my abs hurt.

Above me, pandemonium broke out. There was shouting and yelling and the sound of stamping feet. "Police! Freeze! Over there! Stop him!"

Someone else, "I've got Caperelli! Call for an aid car!"

"Help!" I called, but my throat was raw and hardly any sound came out except more coughing. My eye stung and I couldn't blink or tear up enough to get rid of it.

"Kaitlyn!" Sam's voice rose above the din.

"Sam!" Only a wheeze came out. Pain burned down my throat. I coughed as loud as I could.

"Kaitlyn!" His voice was close now. I looked up and his eyes met my squinty, burning eyes. Looking at the sky made them worse. His seemed to radiate with an intense energy that made my heart pound and a tightness grip my chest. I felt ill and exhilarated at the same time. When he reached for my hand, I was afraid to move for fear I'd faint.

"Kaitlyn," his voice rumbled in my toes. "...grab my hand."

I reached up my uninjured arm. When his fingers touched mine, I felt a zap of electricity and wondered if I'd been magically transported into a trashy romance. He did have a little bit of a Fabio look. Was I going crazy? Or going into shock? I actually felt overcome like a character in a Jane Austin novel. Did pepper spray affect your mind?

"Give me your other hand and I'll pull you up," he said.

"I... I can't... my arm, something might be torn..." I said. Every word was a jagged knife as it escaped my throat.

He attempted to pull on my one good arm as I tried to get a hold with my feet on the side of the hole. It didn't work.

He lay down on the ground and stretched his arms under my armpits. I reached up with my good arm and held tight to his sleeve. He pulled as I stubbornly dug my heels into the side of the hole, struggling for a foothold. He lifted me over the edge of the hole, then sat up. I struggled up the rest of the way by rolling on my side and using my uninjured arm for leverage.

He reached out for my good hand and lifted me to my feet as if I weighed no more than a helium balloon. I felt positively giddy, then got some of my sense back and realized I probably looked like crap and might be in shock. I stumbled a bit and he slipped his arm around my waist. We were both covered with mud. I felt it soak through my jeans; even my underwear felt wet. Sam's dark jeans were streaked with grime.

I turned toward him, which made my neck hurt. I wanted to say something, say thank you, but words wouldn't come, only more coughing. My head felt slushy.

His deep green eyes bore into mine. He hesitated a moment before helping me toward the street. I became aware of a melee of people and cars. The red lights of an ambulance strobed across the gray sky. Sam headed in that direction.

The world started to come back into focus. "Joshua!" I

croaked, my throat raw and sore.

"He's all right," Sam said. "A knot on the head and a bruised ego. EMTs are checking him now."

"He thought he could save me..." I trailed off. If something had happened to Joshua because I had been stupid—well, as cliché as it was, I'd never forgive myself.

"I was stupid," I admitted coughing. "I'm sorry I messed it all up."

"Shhh, don't worry about it."

"The Wymans!"

"I know. Randall knocked out his wife and stuffed her in his trunk. We got here just as he was stumbling down his driveway ranting about pepper spray, with his eyes red and swollen like tomatoes!" Sam paused. "I told you we were working on this. We were close to an arrest."

"How did you know I was here?" I croaked.

"Your friend Rosie called the station... about twenty times insisting you asked her to check in with you and that you always answer your phone. And a neighbor, Ralph somebody, called 911 when he heard yelling over here and knew the Maddens weren't home. We were also looking for Joshua since he hadn't checked in and didn't respond to his radio."

"Ralph? The old guy?" My throat felt like I'd swallowed a wire brush.

Sam looked at me with a curious expression. We reached the ambulance and two technicians approached as Sam helped me sit down on the tailgate. "Let them look you over."

"Watch her arm," he instructed the EMT who approached, then turned away. The techs helped me onto the back and guided me to a stretcher.

I wanted to resist. I wanted to go with Sam. I needed to see Joshua and apologize. "Wally!" I pushed against the techs. "Someone needs to find Wally!"

Sam turned back. "Wally?"

"Cat. He was..." I coughed.

"It's okay. He's in your car, right where you left him."

Huh? But how… The techs urged me to lay on the stretcher. My head ached and exhaustion swept through my body as I reclined. It felt so good to close my eyes and cry.

***

I awoke in a hospital bed, an IV strapped to my arm—*Eeek!* That meant there was a needle under there! I tried to roll sideways, but the minute I moved my neck, excruciating pain knifed my head.

"Damn!" I whispered, my throat dry and scratchy. My head felt fuzzy and when I tried to move my other arm, I discovered it was wrapped in a sling.

"Kaitlyn?" a weak voice whispered.

"Hello?" I croaked back.

"Holy Cannoli, Kaitlyn!"

I tried to swivel my head. "Rosie, come closer." My friend moved into view. "What are you doing here?"

"What am I doing here? You were practically killed! I couldn't get a hold of you and you PROMISED to call every few hours. I called and called and finally phoned the police. Then they call me back and tell me that you're here—OMG! You scared the living crap out of me! You're my best friend in the whole world! What would I do without you?"

"I'm okay. I'm okay!" I jumped in as soon as she took a breath. "What's wrong with my arm?"

She brightened. "That's the good news. The doc said it isn't broken. Just strained. It'll be okay. He's a really cute doctor too."

I reached my other hand up to my throat. On the outside, it felt fine. Inside it felt raw and sore.

"I was so scared!" Rosie said. "When your mom called…"

"Mom? How did Mom know?"

"Your parents are your emergency contact so the city called them when you were hurt."

"They're here?" I wasn't sure if that was a good thing.

"No. I told them you'd be fine and I would be with you. I did promise you'd call when you felt up to it."

I closed my eyes and took a deep calming breath. "Have you seen Joshua?"

"He's was here. They sent him home."

"Alone with a head injury?"

She chuckled. "No, his dad came and got him."

"So he's okay?" I said.

"He'll be fine."

I relaxed back against the limp hospital pillows. I became aware of an odd scent in the room, a mixture of something flowery and antiseptic. Moving very slowly, I inched my head toward the window and saw three large floral arrangements.

Rosie followed my gaze. "Beautiful, huh? One's from your co-workers and one's from Ralph."

"The old guy?"

"Huh? Ralph's not old. I was here when he dropped them off. He's a software guy. And gorgeous! Cuter than the doc." She grinned. "I got his number. I think there's serious potential there—even if he does live on *that* street!"

"What about Mac?" I whispered.

"Mac is a putz. Good in bed, but a putz." She smiled. "I was so dumb. He and I are soooo over."

"What about the other one?" I gestured to the flowers.

"The big bouquet," she said. "Is from... well, the card just says "S.""

"You read the card?"

"Well, yeah." She smiled meekly.

Why had I even asked. They were from Sam. That made me smile.

***

The hospital released me Sunday morning. The sun was out when Rosie drove me home in her old battered Honda Civic.

She wore orange capri pants and flip flops as she tried to eke out the last remnant of summer. I wore yoga pants, a t-shirt and hoodie that Rosie had retrieved from my house. The jeans I had on while in the hole were stiff with caked on mud and would need some serious washing if I wanted to ever wear them again.

As we turned down my street, I saw my car in my driveway. I raised my eyebrows as we pulled in behind it. "My car?"

"Sam had it towed for you."

"What about Wally?"

"I convinced Sam Wally was an outdoor cat so he just let him out." Rosie paused, scanning the yard. "There he is!"

As I climbed gingerly from the car, Wally poked his head over the top of his box. I felt an incredible sense of relief at seeing him there to welcome me. Had he really been by my hole? I was alive. I was home. The mystery of Wally could wait.

Rosie came around the car to help me.

"I'm okay," I said, putting up a hand. "Really. I'm feeling better already." It was true. My throat was still scratchy but definitely on the mend. My arm ached, but no longer felt like it was on fire.

Rosie moved tentatively toward the house. Her red hair glowed in the late morning sun. I was very grateful to have her as a friend.

"Hey, would you grab my mail?" I asked.

"Sure," she said.

I walked to the house and fumbled for my keys as she went to the mailbox.

Wally looked up at me, his head cocked to one side. "Hi."

He just stared at me.

"Thanks," I said. "Thanks for keeping me company when I was scared." I half wondered if I had imagined him at the top of the hole. He looked no worse for wear after being stuck in my car, perhaps getting out and getting wet, and then being towed home.

Rosie returned with a pile of mail.

"Anything from Ben?" I asked when she joined me on the porch.

Rosie flipped through the stack of white envelopes, flyers, and junk. "Nope."

"That shit. How am I going to get out of this financial mess? I really hate to empty out my savings."

"It'll be okay, Kaitlyn." Rosie touched my arm. "I'd help you out if I could." She brightened. "Maybe you should buy a lottery ticket."

I sighed. "With my luck this week... probably not."

Rosie took my keys and reached to open the door.

"Hey!" A voice called from the street.

We turned to see GC jogging toward us carrying a bag.

"Hello!" The concern on his face told me he'd heard of my escapade and the arrest of Carlos' killer.

Rosie turned away from the door as he approached with a questioning look. Her body tensed, ready to protect me.

"Hi, GC," I said. "This is my friend, Rosie. Rosie, this is GC, my neighbor."

Rosie relaxed. "Hi."

"We heard what you did," GC said. "My family, they are very grateful."

I wanted to say it was nothing. That I had messed it up. But I resisted. If he felt good about it, that was okay. "I'm glad it's been resolved."

"My family feels better knowing what happened. They are very sad Carlos is gone but are happy the killer was not someone they knew. And that he was trying to do something nice for someone. They feel safe again. My wife—she's especially is grateful. She made you this." He handed me the bag. "Enchiladas."

"Yum. Thank you."

He smiled. "She took a collection at a family dinner last night. To thank you." He pulled a white envelope from the pocket of his navy hooded sweatshirt. "It is for you." He stretched his hand with the envelope toward me.

"I don't... I don't know what to say. I can't take it."

"Girl, he's trying to thank you," Rosie hissed under her breath. "Take it."

I took the envelope. It felt thick. "GC, this is really...," I was going to say not necessary, but Rosie shot me a steely look. "...nice."

"I'm glad your family has peace," Rosie said. Somehow she knew that he needed to thank me, even if I felt like I didn't deserve it.

"You let me know if I can ever help you in your yard or whatever," GC said. He nodded to Rosie. "Nice to meet you. *Adios!*" He jogged back across the street.

We watched him go inside his house. I stood there, dumbfounded at the generosity and the real caring I had felt from their gift. Wally must have felt dumbfounded too because he let out a guttural noise. Or maybe, he was just hungry.

"He does that sometimes, makes weird noises."

Rosie just nodded.

We went inside, Rosie and I, not Wally. I set the envelope on the counter in the kitchen.

Rosie cocked her head, not unlike Wally. "Aren't you going to open it?"

I shook my head. "I'm just blown away—even if it's only a few dollars. I can't take it. I don't deserve it."

"Sure you do. You kept looking for the truth even if others didn't."

"I kind of screwed up."

She shrugged. "At least you tried. Not everyone does. Most people just keep on doing their thing in their own little world."

My turn to shrug. "I guess."

"You want me to look?"

I nodded.

She took the envelope and pulled out a stack of bills. I saw some ones and fives, and at least a few twenties. As Rosie started to count it, I turned away to the fridge and retrieved two Diet Sprites. The hospital had been big on cranberry juice and black coffee. I was craving cold bubbly. I popped the top on one and took a long swig.

"Five hundred twenty-five dollars!" Rosie exclaimed.

"What!" I spit Diet Sprite on my chin. "How many people come to his family dinners?"

"That's almost what you need to get your bank account positive, right?"

I nodded again, feeling overwhelmed but thankful. "This would help my finances."

"Serendipity I'd say," Rosie said.

I nodded and felt a lump in my throat. "The city rules... I can't. Maybe I'll donate it to The Humane Society."

"You still have Ben to deal with."

"Ben owes me no matter what," I said without much conviction.

"Sure he does—and don't let him forget it."

I smiled at my friend. "Thanks for bringing me home, Rosie."

She came over and hugged me. "That's what friends are for. You'd do the same for me, hospital, bail me out of jail for stalking..."

We laughed, long and hard. It felt good.

CHAPTER 15

Monday, September 25, 2017

Monday morning dawned cool and clear. Overnight rain left its damp fingers on railings, ledges, and tree branches. The sun glistened off the water reflecting a brilliant glow, spotlight bright.

I woke feeling rested and relieved that the last week was over. Done. Final curtain. It probably didn't feel that way to Sam, but I was glad that the killer and his wife were tucked safely away in the county jail. Carlos may not have been someone I'd want to be friends with, but there was satisfaction in knowing I had helped bring his killer to justice and give his family closure.

I'd almost died myself. I'd unknowingly gotten Joshua hurt. Richard had offered to let me take an administrative day to rest, but the weekend had been enough. My arm felt much better and the thought of another day just sitting around at home sounded excruciating so I declined. He hadn't really believed all the rumors Newman had tried to start about me. He'd defended his staff at the risk of his own political clout.

As I readied for work, I thought about all the lives affected by this tragedy. The Maddens had almost taken a fall for the murder. On the good side, Rhonda's problem was exposed, which would lead her to getting some help. She and Dave would never be the same though. Sam said Dave planned to try and sell their house so they could move somewhere everyone didn't know their history. Dave loved his wife and wanted help with his gambling problem. Good luck selling that house after what went on there. But maybe with redevelopment eminent, it would be snapped up. Certainly not by Randall. Maybe by the young, and apparently gorgeous, Ralph.

I slopped peanut butter on a bagel for breakfast. My arm ached as I added raspberry jelly, but it would be fine. Mary Wyman's life was one screwed up mess. She'd unwittingly started the events that lead to the killing and she'd harassed me. But she was protecting a life she thought she wanted. Protecting a marriage while setting a plan to leave it. People were strange. She'd spend years in jail too. I felt like I should have known my harasser wasn't the killer, but at the time, I'd been too freaked out to see how simple and childish the threats were.

Stanley and Estelle survived unscathed, having no real role in the mess. But their neighborhood was in ruins, their comfortable life shattered. Who knew if the developer would keep the deal. My life felt that way. Things I'd counted on, things I believed to be true, like safety—all my security blown apart like a firecracker in a pumpkin.

I took a bowl of cat food to the front porch. Wally was in his box. He stood up and stretched his giant body, lifted a hind leg to scratch his ear, and let out a yowl.

"Good morning to you too," I said.

He padded over to the bowl, dropped his fat rear end to the ground and dug in. I accepted that I would never know where he had come from or why he chose me. There was no rational answer, but I was glad he had pushed his way into my life. I had no idea how he had gotten out of my car through the slightly open window—and back in again or if he really had. But he'd been there when I needed him.

Wally was a simple, comfortable companion who didn't ask a lot from me. Someone to talk to who didn't rationalize, analyze, or try to fix my problems. I guess this was the secret that pet owners knew.

As I drove to work, I looked around my city. The signs of redevelopment were evident. Actual signs, *Say Yes to Redevelopment!* plus smaller, less obvious changes. New paint, cleaned up walkways, and fresh landscaping went a long way. Construction sites popped up overnight in vacant lots. Change was everywhere.

Trees were quickly turning yellow and red and dropping their leaves on the ground. Seasons were changing too, hints of autumn wafting in on clouds and showing in the trees. The sun felt warm inside the car, but there was a chill in the air as I went into public works building.

Cheryl was perched behind her counter. Enormous orange leaves hung from her ears and adorned her festive autumn sweater. She wore a head set and was on the phone, so I just waved and started to stroll by.

She gestured frantically, asking me to wait. "Yes, sir, thank you, sir. Anytime."

"Kaitlyn! You were not going to just glide by, were you?" She came around the counter. I set down my cooler. Then she surprised the hell out of me when she enveloped me in a hug. When she pulled back, her headset was askew. "How are you? Are you really okay?"

"Yes. Really, I'm fine."

"We heard all about it. Grant knows a clerk over at the police station, someone named Mercury, who shared details—all hush, hush, ya know." She grinned.

"I'm just looking forward to getting back to work," I said.

"Maybe a nice quiet week." I tried to slip past her, but just then Sharon pushed through the door from the back-office area.

"Girlfriend! How are you?"

I cradled my arm in case Sharon was in a hugging mood too, but she just put one of her large hands on my shoulder. "You okay, girl? I mean really?" Then, as if she couldn't resist, Sharon enveloped me in a bear hug.

"Yes, I am. Thanks. I want to get to work."

"I want all the details about the date with the cute detective. You've been holdin' back on me," Sharon said.

"Maybe we can do lunch. It shouldn't be too busy today."

"Humph." Sharon put her hands on her wide hips and glanced at Cheryl. "She don't know?"

Cheryl shook her head, her leaf earrings swaying. "Nope."

I frowned. "Know what?" I leaned toward Sharon. "Something else happened?"

"While you was off catching murderers there was some detecting going on here in the office," Sharon said.

Cheryl's phone rang. She held up one finger, leaned over the counter and hit a button. "City of Cedar Grove, how may I help you?... of course. Hold on." She hit another button then turned back to me. "While you were off getting chased and hanging out in the hospital," she said in a conspiratorial tone. "Marcus was fired!"

"What!"

Sharon smiled. "They knew someone was taking bribes to overlook certain code enforcement issues. There had been complaints... about aggressive officers."

"And..." Cheryl jumped in. "They found out Marcus had been in cahoots with Randall Wyman."

My mouth dropped open, stunned. "Marcus?" I sputtered.

"Yep. Randall gave him money to back his complaints and ignore other things in that neighborhood."

"Marcus was the one who helped me canvas the block. He was the one who—" I was pretty sure he was Mary's new love toy, but I didn't say that. "Was he part of the murder?"

"Nope. Sounds like he was just your average jerk who thought he deserved the extra cash and didn't figure helping Randall bump up the property values in the neighborhood would hurt."

"But..." Cheryl's phone rang again and she leaned over to answer it leaving me hanging. She finally came back to our conversation. "Anyway, he was the one who called in the anonymous complaint against you. He thought you were screwing up his extra income."

"No way!" I was shocked. I hadn't really liked the guy and sort of suspected him of something but would never have guessed this.

Sharon eyed me suspiciously. "Sure you're up for work? Maybe you'd like some extra time off."

"Richard offered one whole day."

Sharon and Cheryl just looked at me like I should have taken it.

"I'm fine. Really." Sharon and Cheryl exchanged an odd glance. "What? Come on, guys. What is it?"

"She'll find out eventually," Cheryl said.

"I guess." Sharon didn't look convinced.

"Oh, for heaven's sake!" I said. "Just spit it out."

"It's just..." Sharon began.

But Cheryl couldn't stand it. "The October issue of the city newsletter!"

I shook my head. "What about it?"

"It came out today," Sharon said.

"Ah, hah. And?"

Cheryl glanced at Sharon. "Well..."

"The center feature is bad?" I said getting that sinking, heavy feeling in my gut.

Sharon and Cheryl exchanged that look again.

A shiver ran up my spine and I got goose bumps on my arms. "Me?"

Glances.

"Oh, just get it over with—show me!" How bad could it be?

"It's not so bad, not really," Cheryl said.

"No," agreed Sharon. "Not too bad."

Cheryl lifted a copy from her desk and held it close to her chest.

"Just hand it over!" I said, snatching it from her and flipping it open. There in the center page, among several smaller pictures of different city events, was a photo of the first aid class. Dummy on the ground, John kneeling next to it smiling. And me, leaning over the dummy, my ass in the air looking about the size of a small elephant.

My mouth dropped open and I felt my face flush. I took a deep breath. Sharon and Cheryl seemed to be holding theirs.

"Well," I said. "At least you can't see my boobs!"

ACKNOWLEDGMENTS

Writing a book is hard work and a long process. For this book, the process spanned almost ten years. All the while I perfected my craft and continued to write new things, but I always came back to this book and this character.

To the members, past and present, of the Mystery Writers of America Northwest Chapter board. You have always been encouraging and given me people to look up to. You have become my friends and I look forward to working with you for years to come.

To my long-time critique group. We have met together for over 20 years! Members changed here and there but we never quit. You are the reason I kept writing, my accountability partners. Steve, you are still the voice in my head when I edit! Thanks to David, Kim, and Bob, past members Jarucia and Paul, who I don't see often but still think about. Sadly, Doniella passed away in 2018. I miss her dearly. She had the strongest spirit and was never shy to say how she felt, but was always encouraging.

Thank you to Christine Dubois, my long-time friend and co-writing instructor. I always appreciate your positivity and support. I so enjoy co-leading *Write Night* with you. Thank you for helping with some copy editing. Any errors are mine, not hers.

Thank you to my family who has stood by me for all these years when I talked about writing and publishing. I finally did it!

Leslie J. Hall has wanted to be a writer for as long as she can remember. She writes mysteries and women's fiction. Dead End won first place in the mystery category in the 2015 annual contest sponsored by the Pacific Northwest Writers Association. Her non-fiction has been published by many local and regional publications. She is a member of Sisters in Crime and Mystery Writers of America and long-time MWA Northwest Chapter board member.

Leslie is a regular speaker on all-things writing, from Business Writing Basics to The Power of Writing to Beginning Fiction Writing. She teaches writing classes for the continuing education program for North Seattle College and Tacoma Community College. Visit lesliejhall.com for more details.

Leslie loves all things tropical and beachy. She lives in Washington State with her husband and cat Mia (who weighs considerably less than Wally).

Leslie is currently working on more books in the Kaitlyn Willis Road Signs series. Watch for Ice will be published June 2021 and Curves Ahead in Fall 2021.

Look for book two in the Kaitlyn Willis Road Signs mystery series on Amazon June 2021!

Made in USA - Kendallville, IN
1235271_9781638218050
02.17.2021 1137